JONES, LISA RENEE

PROVOCATIVE

LISA RENEE JONES

Book 1 of the WHITE LIES Duet

ISBN: 978-1-63576-160-3

All characters in this book are fiction and figments of the author's imagination.

www.lisareneejones.com

Provocative Playlist

"Sugar" by Maroon 5

"Ain't My Fault" by Zara Larsson

"Whisper" by Chase Rice

"i hate u, i love u" by Gnash

"World Falls Away" by Seether

"Sugar" by Maren Morris

"Make You Miss Me" by Sam Hunt

"Sex and Candy" by Marcy Playground

"Take Me Away" by Seether

"Stay" by Rihanna

"Dreams" by Fleetwood Mac

"Human" by Rag 'n' Bone Man

"Love on the Brain" by Rihanna

pro·voc·a·tive

adjective

1. causing annoyance, anger, or another strong reaction, especially deliberately.

2. arousing sexual desire or interest, especially deliberately.

Chapter One

Tiger

THERE ARE THOSE MOMENTS IN LIFE THAT ARE provocative in their very existences, that embed in our minds forever, and sometimes our very souls. They change us, mold us, maybe even save us. But some are darker, *dangerous*. If we allow them to, they control us. *Seduce us.* Quite possibly even destroy us.

The moment I stepped into the mansion that is the centerpiece of the Reid Winter Vineyards and Winery wasn't one of those moments. Nor were any of the moments I spent weaving through a crowd of suits and dresses cluttering the circle that is the grand foyer of the 1800's mansion, fancy tiles etched with vines beneath my feet. Nor the ones spent declining three different waiters offering me glasses of various wines from one of the most established vineyards in Sonoma, meant to entice me to buy their bottles and donate money to the charity hosting the gathering. Not even the instant that I spotted the stunning blonde in a snug black dress that hugged her many lush curves proved to be one of those moments, but I would call it a damn interesting one. The moment I decided the blonde silk of her long hair belonged in my hands and on my stomach was also a damn interesting one. And not because she's fuckable. There are plenty of fuckable women in my life, a number of whom understand that I enjoy demands for pleasure, which I will definitely provide, and nothing more. This woman is too prim and proper to ever agree to such an arrangement, and yet, knowing this, as she and her heart-shaped backside disappear into the congestion of bodies, I find myself pursuing her, looking for more than an interesting moment. I want that provocative one.

I follow her path formed by huddles of two, three, or more people, left and right, to clear a portion of the crowd, scanning to find my beauty standing several feet away, her back to me, with two men in blue suits in front of her. And while they might appear to blend with the rest of the suits in the room, they hold themselves like the parasites I meet too often in the courtroom, those who most often call themselves my opposing counsel. My blonde beauty folds her arms in front of her chest, her spine stiff, and if I read her right–and I read most people right–I am certain that she's found trouble. But lucky for her, trouble doesn't like me near as much as I like it.

Closing the space between me and them, I near their little triangle just in time to hear her say, "Are we really doing this here and now?"

"Yes, Ms. Winter," one of the men replies. "We are."

"Actually," I say, stepping to *Ms. Winter's* side, her floral scent almost as sweet as the challenge of conquering her opponents that are now mine, "we are *not* doing this here or now."

All attention shifts to me, Ms. Winter giving me a sharp stare that I feel rather than see, my focus remaining on the men I want to leave, not the woman I want to make come. "And you would be who?" the suit directly in front of me demands.

I size him up as barely out of his twenty-something diapers, without experience, the glint in his eye telling me he doesn't realize that flaw, which makes him about as smooth as a six-dollar glass of wine everyone in this place would spit the fuck out. A point driven home by the fact that he's wearing a three-hundred-dollar Italian silk tie, and a hundred-dollar suit, no doubt hoping the tie makes the suit look expensive, and him important. He's wrong.

"I said, who are you?" he repeats when I apparently haven't replied quickly enough, his impatience becoming my virtue as my role as cat in this game of cat and mouse is too easily established.

Unwilling to waste words on a predictable, expected question that I'd never ask, I simply reach into the pocket of my three-thousand-dollar light gray suit, which I earned by beating opponents with ten times his experience and negotiation skills, and finger the unimportant prick my card.

He snaps it from my hand, gives it a look that confirms my name and the firm I started a decade ago now, after daring to leave behind a certain partnership in a high-powered firm. "Nick Rogers?" he asks. "Is there another name on the card?" I ask, because, I'm also a fearless smartass every chance I get.

He stares at me for several beats, seeming to calculate his words, before asking, "How many Mr. Rogers sweater jokes do you get?"

I arch a brow at the misguided joke that only serves to poke the Tiger. Suit Number Two, who I age closer to my thirty-six years, pales visibly, then snatches the card from the other man's hand, giving it a quick inspection before his gaze then jerks to mine. "*The* Nick Rogers?"

"I don't remember my mother putting the word 'the' in front of my name," I reply dryly, but then again, I think, she didn't ask my father to change my last name either. She just hated him that much.

"Tiger," he says, and it's not a question, but rather a statement of "oh shit" fact.

"That's right," I say, enjoying the fruits of my labor that created the nickname, not one given to me by my friends.

"Who, or what, the fuck is *Tiger* all about?" Suit Number One asks.

"Shut up," Suit Number Two grunts, refocusing on me to ask, "You're representing Ms. Winter?"

"What I am," I say, "is standing right here by her side, telling you that it's in your best interests to leave."

"Since when do you handle small-time foreclosures?" he demands, exposing the crux of Ms. Winter's situation.

"I handle whatever the *fuck* I want to handle," I say, my tone even, my lips curving as I add, "including the process of having you both escorted off the property by security."

"That," Suit Number One dares to retort, "would garner Ms. Winter unwanted attention in the middle of a busy event. Not that Ms. Winter even has security to call."

"Fortunately, I have a phone that dials 911 and the ability

to call it without asking her."

"*If* she's your client," Suit Number One says, clearly inferring that she's not, "you're obligated to operate with her best interests in mind."

"My decisions," I reply, without missing a beat, and without claiming Ms. Winter as a client, "are always about winning. And I assure you that I can think of many ways to spin your story to the press that ensures I win, while also benefiting Ms. Winter."

"This isn't my story," Suit Number One indicates.

"It will be when I'm finished with the press," I assure him, amused at how easily I've led him down the path I want him to travel.

"This is a small community with little to talk about *but her*," he says. "She doesn't want her foreclosure to become the front-page story."

My lips quirk. "If you don't know how easily I can get the wrong attention for you here, and the right attention for Ms. Winter, you'll find out."

"We'll leave," Suit Number Two interjects quickly, and just when I think that he's smart enough to see the way trouble has turned from Ms. Winter to them, he looks at her and says, "We'll be in touch," with a not-so-subtle threat in his tone, before he elbows Suit Number One. "Let's go."

Suit Number One doesn't move, visibly fuming, his face red, a white ring thickening around his lips. I arch a brow at Suit Number Two, who adds, "*Now,* Jordan." Jordan, formerly known as Suit Number One, clenches his teeth and turns away, while Suit Number Two follows.

Ms. Winter faces me, and holy fuck, when her pale green eyes meet mine, any questions I have about this woman and the many I suspect she now has of me, are muted by an un-expected, potentially problematic, palpable electric charge between us. "Thank you," she says, her voice soft, feminine, a rasp in its depths that hints at emotion not effortlessly con-tained. "Please enjoy anything you like tonight on the house," she adds, the rasp gone now, her control returned. *Until I take it,* I think, but no sooner than I've had the thought, she is turning and walking away, the absence of further interac-tion coloring me both stunned and intrigued, two things that, for me, are ranked with about as much frequency as snow in Sonoma, which would be next to never.

Ms. Winter maneuvers into the crowd, out of my line of sight, and while I am not certain I'd label her a mouse at this point, or ever for that matter, considering what I know of her, I am most definitely on the prowl. I stride purposely forward, weaving through the crowd, seeking that next provocative moment, scanning for her left, right, in the clusters of min-gling guests, until I clear the crowd.

Now standing in front of a wide, wooden stairwell, my gaze follows its path upward to a second level, but I still find no sign of Ms. Winter. A cool breeze whips through the air, and I turn to find the source is a high arched doorway, the recently opened glass doors to what I know to be the "Winter Gardens," a focal point of the property, and a tourist draw for decades, settling back into place. Certain this represents her escape, I walk that direction, and press open the doors, step-ping onto a patio that has a stone floor and concrete bench-es framed by rose bushes. No less than four winding paths greet me as destination choices, the hunt for this woman now a provocation of its own.

I've just decided to wait where I am for Ms. Winter's

return when the wind lifts, the floral scent of many varieties of flowers for which the garden is famous touching my nostrils, with one extra scent decidedly of the female variety.

Lips curving with the certainty that my prey will soon be my prize, I follow the clue that guides my feet to the path on my right, a narrow, winding, lighted walkway, framed by neatly cut yellow flower bushes, which continues past a white wooden gazebo I have no intention of passing. Not when Ms. Winter stands inside it, her back to me, elbows resting on the wooden rail, her gaze casting across the silhouette of what would reveal itself to be a rolling mountainside in daybreak. The way I intend for her to reveal herself.

I close the distance between us, and the moment before I'm upon her, she faces me, hands on the railing behind her, her breasts thrust forward, every one of her lush curves tempting my eyes, my hands. *My mouth.* "Did those men know you?" she demands, clearly ready and waiting for this interaction. "Did you know them?"

"No and no."

"And yet they knew the nickname Tiger."

"My reputation precedes me."

"I'll take the bait," she says. "What reputation?"

"They say I'll rip my opponent's throat out if given the chance."

"Will you?" she asks, without so much as a blanch or blink.

"Yes," I reply, a simple answer, for a simple question.

"Without any concern for who you hurt," she states.

I arch a brow. "Is that a question?"

"Should it be?"

"Yes."

"It's not," she says. "You didn't get that nickname by being nice."

"Nice guys don't win."

"Then I'm warned," she says. "You aren't a nice guy."

"Is nice a quality you're looking for in a man? Because as your evening counsel, Ms. Winter, I'll advise you that nice is overrated."

She stares at me for several beats before turning away to face the mountains again, elbows on the railing, in what I could see as a silent invitation to leave. I choose to see it as an invitation to join her. I claim the spot next to her, close, but not nearly as close as I will be soon. "You didn't answer the question," I point out.

"You wrongly assume I am looking for a man, which I'm not," she says, glancing over at me. "But if I was, then no. Nice would be on my list but it would not top my list, however, nowhere on that list would be the ability, and willingness, to rip out someone's throat."

"I can assure you, Ms. Winter, that a man with a bite is as underrated as a nice guy is overrated. And I not only know how, and when, to use mine, but if I so choose to bite *you*, and I might, it'll be all about pleasure, not pain."

Her cheeks flush and she turns away. "My name is Faith." She glances over at me again. "Should I call you Nick, Tiger, or just plain arrogant?"

"Anything but Mr. Rogers," I say, enjoying our banter far more than I would have expected when I came here tonight looking for her.

She laughs now too, and it's a delicate, sweet sound, but it's awkward, as if it's not only unexpected, but unwelcome, and an instant later she's withdrawing, pushing off the railing, arms folding protectively in front of her body, before we're rotating to face each other. "I need to go check on the visitors." She attempts to move away.

I gently catch her arm, her gaze rocketing to mine, and in the process her hair flutters in a sudden breeze, a strand of blonde silk catching on the whiskers of my one-day stubble. She sucks in a breath, and when she would reach up to remedy the situation, I'm already there, catching the soft silk and stroking it behind her ear.

"Why are you touching me?" she asks, but she doesn't pull away, that charge between us minutes ago is now ten times more provocative with me touching her, thinking about all the places I might touch next.

"It's considerably better than not touching you," I say.

"My bad luck might bleed into you."

"Bleed," I repeat, that word reminding me once again of why I'm here, why I really want to fuck this woman. "That's an extreme, and rather interesting choice of words."

"Most bad luck is extreme, though not interesting to anyone but the Tigers of the world, creating it. You're still touching me."

"Everyone needs a Tiger in their corner. Maybe my good luck will bleed into you."

"Does good luck bleed?" she asks.

"Many people will do anything for good luck, even bleed."

"Yes," she says, lowering her lashes, but not before I've seen the shadows in her eyes. "I suppose they would."

"What would you do for good luck?"

Her lashes lift, her stare meeting mine again. "What have you done for good luck?"

"I came here tonight," I say.

9

She narrows her eyes on me, as if some part of her senses, the far-reaching implications of my reply that she can't possibly understand, and yet still, the inescapable heat between us radiates and burns. "You're still touching me," she points out, and this time there's a hint of reprimand.

"I'm holding onto that good luck," I say.

"It feels like you're holding onto mine."

With that observation that hits too close to the truth, I have no interest in revealing just yet, I drag my hand slowly down hers, allowing my fingers to find hers before they fall away. Her lips, lush, tempting, impossibly perfect for someone I know to be imperfect, part with the loss of my touch, and yet there is a hint of relief in her eyes that tells me she both wants me and fears me.

A most provocative moment, indeed.

"Have a drink with me," I say.

"No," she replies, her tone absolute, and while I don't like this decision, I appreciate a person who's decisive.

"Why?"

"Good luck and bad luck don't mix."

"They might just create good luck."

"Or bad," she says. "I'm not in a place where I can take the risk for more bad luck." She inclines her chin. "Enjoy the rest of your visit." She pauses and adds, "*Tiger.*"

I don't react, but for just a moment, I consider the way she used my nickname as an indicator that she knows who I am, and why I'm here. I quickly dismiss that idea. I'd have seen it in those pale green eyes, and I did not. But as she turns and walks away, and I watch her depart, tracking her steps as she disappears down the path, I wonder at her quick departure, and the fear I'd seen in her eyes. Was the root of that fear her guilt?

That idea should be enough to ice the fire in me that this woman has stirred, but it stokes it instead. Everything male in me wants to pursue her again, and not because I'm here for a reason that existed before I ever met her, when it should be that and nothing more. It *is* more. I'm aroused and I'm intrigued by this woman. She got to me when no one gets to me. Not a good place to be, considering I came here to prove she killed my father, and maybe even her own mother.

Chapter Two

Faith

I STAND AT THE LIBRARY WINDOW ON THE SECOND LEVEL of the mansion that I've called my family home, but not *my* home, my entire life. Nick Rogers exits the front door, pure sex and arrogance. He stops to talk to the doorman, both men laughing, before Nick palms the other man a tip, and then rounds his shiny black BMW that I'm fairly certain is custom designed. He begins to get in, but hesitates, scanning the grounds immediately around him, and then, to my complete and utter shock, his gaze lifts and lands on my window. Stunned, my heart begins to race all over again, the way it had when he'd touched me in that garden, but it's impossible for him to see me. I know it is, but somehow, there is no question that he knows I am here. He holds his stare in my direction for several beats, in which I cannot breathe, and then lifts two fingers, giving me a wave before he disappears into his car. Moments later, he drives away and I let out the breath I'm holding. Hugging myself, I am both hot and cold, aroused and unsettled, exactly as I had been when I was with him in the garden. Every look and word I exchanged with that man was both sexual and adversarial.

Rotating, I sit on the window seat of the grand library that was once my father's, bookshelves filled with decades of books lining the walls left and right, all with answers to questions that we might not even ever ask. Which is why I read incessantly and why I wish I knew which one to open for the right answers to why Nick Rogers felt so right and wrong at the same time, and why, so many other things are wrong in ways I'm not sure I can make right. But that would be too simple, and I am suddenly reminded of a poem I wrote long ago in school that started out with: *The apples fall from the trees. The wind blows in the trees.* I'd proudly handed it into the teacher, and quickly found myself scolded for my display of simplistic writing. I didn't understand. What was wrong with being simplistic? The words, and the concepts fit together. That is what mattered. That was what was important to me. The way the pieces fit. The way it made sense. It seemed so simple to me, when in truth, little in life is simple at all. And that's exactly why I keep that poem pinned on my bedroom wall. To remind me that nothing is simple.

Except death, I think, my throat thickening. One minute you're alive, and the next you're dead. Death is as simple as it gets. At least for the person it claims. For those of us left behind, it's complicated, haunting. Mysterious and maybe even dangerous. And death, I have learned, is never done with you until you are gone, too. My mind returns to Nick Rogers and the way he'd known that I was in the window. The way he'd stared up at me and then given me that wave, and every instinct I own tells me that Nick Rogers is a lot like death. He's not done with me either.

Chapter Three

Faith

GASPING FOR AIR, I SIT UP IN BED, MY HAND ON MY throat, my breath heaving from my chest, seconds passing eternally as I will my heart to calm. Breathe in. Breathe out. Breathe. Just breathe. Finally, I begin to calm and I scan the room, the heavy drapes that run throughout the family mansion that I grew up in casting it in shadows, while my mind casts the horror that woke me in its own form of darkness. Every image I think I can identify dodges and weaves, then fades just out of reach, like too many other things in my life right now.

Suddenly aware of the perpetual chill of the centuries-old property, a chill impossible to escape seeming to seep deep into my bones, I yank the blanket to my chin, the floral scent of the gardens that my mother loved, inescapably clinging to it, and to me. Glancing toward the heavy antique white nightstand to my right to find the clock: eight a.m., a new dawn long ago rising over the rolling mountaintops hugging this region to illuminate the miles and miles of vineyards surrounding us. It's also the dawn of my thirtieth birthday, and really, why wouldn't it start with a nightmare? I'm sleeping in my dead mother's bed.

It's an uncomfortable thought, but not an emotional one, a reality that makes me even *more* uncomfortable. When my father died just two years ago now, I'd cried until I could cry no more, and then did it again. And again. And again. But I'm not crying now. What is wrong with me? I didn't even cry at the funeral, but I'd been certain that when alone, I would. Now, eight weeks later, there are still no tears. I had my problems with my mother, but it's not like I don't grieve for her. I do, but I grieved for her in life as well, and maybe I grieved too much then to grieve now. I just don't know.

Rolling over, I flip on the light, then hit a remote that turns on the fireplace directly in front of my bed. Sitting up, I stare at the flames as it spurts and sputters to life, but I don't find the answers I seek there, or anywhere in this room, as I'd hoped when I'd moved from the identical room down the hall to this one. I'd been certain that being here, in the middle of my mother's personal space, the scent of the gardens she loved clinging to virtually everything, including me, would finally make the tears fall. But no. Days later, and I'm still not crying, I'm having nightmares. And whatever those nightmares are, they always make me wake up angry. So there it is. I *do* have a feeling I can name. Anger is one of them. I'm not quite sure what that anger is all about but right now, all I can hear is my mother shouting at me: *You're just like your father.* An insult in her book, but there was no truth in it. I was never like my father. I always saw who, and what, she was, where he only saw the woman he'd loved for thirty years, the same amount of time I've been alive.

Throwing off the covers, I rotate, my feet settling on the stepstool that is a necessity to climb down from the bedframe. My gaze lands on Nick Rogers' business card where I'd left it on the nightstand last night, after spending the minutes before sleep replaying every word, look, and touch with that man. Admitting to myself what I had not last night. He woke me up, and because of him, there is at least one other emotion I can feel: *lust.* If lust is really even considered an emotion, but whatever the case, there is no other word for what charged the air between myself and that man, for what I felt and saw in his eyes when he touched me, but *lust.* And the more I think about that meeting, the more I know that there wasn't anything romantic or sweet about our connection. It was dark and jagged. The kind of attraction that's unforgiving in its demands. The kind of attraction that's all consuming, proven by the fact that, even now, hours after our encounter, I can still feel his hand on my arm, and the sizzle that had burned a path through my body. I can still feel the hum of my body that he, and he alone, created.

And while I cannot say if that man is my friend or my enemy, I know where this kind of collision course of dark, edgy lust leads. I've lived it and it is not a place you want to go with anyone that you don't trust. I'm not sure it's a place you can even find with someone you really do trust. I think it's dark because it's born out of something dark in one or both people, maybe that they bring out in each other. Which means it's not a place anyone should travel, and yet, when you feel it, I know that you resist it. But you cannot deny it, or the person who creates it in you. It's exactly why I am certain, that despite my rejection of Nick Rogers last night, that I'll be seeing him again, which brings my mind back to one particular exchange we'd shared that keeps playing and replaying in my head.

"You're still touching me," I'd said and he'd replied with, *"I'm holding onto that good luck."*

Logically, he was inferring that meeting me was good luck. He'd already stated that coming here to the winery was good luck. It was simple flirtatious banter. So why did it bother me then, and why does it bother me now? Chance meeting or not? The timing...the men...the dark lust. It never comes from a good place. Maybe I'm wrong about him. I have plenty of darkness of my own right now. Maybe my energy fed our energy together. But it doesn't matter. He's dangerous. He's taboo.

He's not going to touch me again.

My cellphone rings, and praying it's not some crisis in the winery, I grab it and glance at the caller ID. At the sight of my attorney's number, and with the knowledge that his office just opened, my heart races, and I answer the line. "Frank? Do you have news?"

"It's Betty," I hear. Betty, being Frank's secretary. "Frank wants to know if you can be here at eleven?"

"Is there a problem?"

"He's in court. He wants to see you and he said it had to be today. That's all I know. Can you be here at eleven?"

"Can he see me sooner?" I ask, my nerves racketing up a notch at the "had to be today" comment.

"He's in court."

"Right. Eleven it is then."

My phone rings again and I glance at the unknown number, hitting decline. At least the bill collectors waited until sunrise today. Three seconds later, the ringing begins all over again, and this time it's a San Francisco number. Repeating my prior action, I hit decline and this time I have the luxury of blocking the number. I don't need to talk to the caller to know they want a piece of me that they can't have, and yet another of my exchanges with Tiger comes back to me. I'd asked, *"Does good luck bleed?"* And his reply had been, *"Many people will do anything for good luck, even bleed."*

Bleed.

Isn't that what my father did? Bleed? And bleed some more?

And why do I feel like I'm bleeding right now?

And why does that thought remind me of Tiger?

I glance down at my balled fist and open it to discover I've crumpled his card into a ball in my hand.

My phone registers five more unknown callers by the time I complete the fifteen-minute drive to my attorney's office, which is in one of my favorite places in the city. The quaint downtown area, where there are stone walkways leading to stores, restaurants and a few random businesses, some areas are even framed with ivy overhangs. I park by a curb in front of a row of side-by-side mom and pop shops, and right in front of the path leading to Frank's office, but I don't get out, nervous and with reason. The winery was everything to my father, and to save it, I did things I didn't want to do, things I regret. And the guilt I feel is overwhelming. Maybe I can't cry because it's eating away at me, like acid, that just won't stop burning away my emotions.

I straighten my funeral-black pencil skirt, that I've paired with a funeral-black sweater and black, knee high boots, the thick tights beneath it all meant to fight the chill of an October mountain day. But nothing can take the chill off death, which is my reason for choosing funeral-black attire yet again today. I don't remember the day, week, moment, that I stopped dressing this way after my father died. I guess it just happens when it feels right, and it doesn't yet. My cellphone rings again, and I grab it from my well-worn, also black, briefcase that doubles as my version of a purse. Eyeing the caller ID, the new San Francisco number has apparently called me twice now. I block it, and one other, certain from the past two weeks of hell that yet another caller will start showing up on my ID any second.

I turn my ringer off and slip my cell back in its pocket, my gaze landing on the gold Chanel logo pressed to the outside of the bag, my fingers stroking the letters. It was a gift from my father when I'd graduated from UCLA with eyes set on selling my art and buying lots of Chanel. My father declared this bag a "taste of luxury" to inspire me. And it had been, but then things had happened and-

"Damn it," I murmur, my eyes pinching shut. "Now, I'm teary-eyed? What the heck is wrong with me?"

I grab my bag and settle it on my shoulder, opening the door of my black BMW that I'd inherited from my father, while my mother's white Mercedes still sits in the garage back at the mansion. Even their cars were opposite, I think. They were opposite in all things. I stand and the card I'd balled in my hand earlier falls to the pavement. I bend down and pick it up, standing to straighten it and read: *Nick Rogers, Attorney at Law.* Mr. Rogers. Right. Well he's no sweet, sweater-vested kid's television personality, for sure.

Deciding to ask my attorney about the notorious "Tiger," I stick the card inside the pocket of my briefcase, and get moving. Exiting the vehicle, I hurry under one of those overhangs to travel past a candy store, a candle store, and then finally reach the law office I seek. Entering the office, the receptionist greets me.

"Hiya, sugar," Betty greets me, her red hair glowing maroon, when last week it had been more of an orange hue, her bold style in contrast to her boss, a true case of opposites attract. But my mind goes back to Tiger and I. I don't think we're opposites. Thus the dark energy. "Frank's on a conference call," she says, bringing me back to the here and now, rather than last night. "He should be done any moment."

"Thank you," I say, claiming one of the half dozen leather seats in the small, familiar lobby I'd often frequented with my father in my youth, hanging out here until he finished meetings, which is when we'd then grab ice cream. Usually when my mother was nowhere to be found.

My throat thickens with that memory and I'm about to set my bag down when Frank appears in the doorway, looking fit and younger than his sixty years in a well-fitted black suit, his gray hair neatly trimmed, his face lightly lined. "Come in, Faith." He backs into his office to offer me room to enter.

I'm on my feet before he finishes that statement, crossing the lobby and entering his humble office with a desk, two chairs and a window. It's simple but it's personalized with a collection of University of Texas memorabilia as well as his diploma. But he doesn't need to be fancy. He grew up in Sonoma and took over his father's trusted practice, becoming a local favorite about the time I was born.

Frank lingers behind me and shuts the door, that thud a trigger for my nerves to bounce around in my belly. So, okay. I do feel things. I'm not numb about anything but my mother's death. I claim a seat and he rounds the desk to sit down, elbows on the wooden surface, his gray eyes steady on my face. "How are you?"

"Better when I know what this meeting is about," I say. "Did the state finally approve you as executor of my mother's estate?"

"I'm afraid not," he replies. "The bank filed a formal objection based on my role as your attorney, which they claim, works against their best interests."

I scoot to the edge of my chair. "But I'm the rightful owner of the property with or without my mother's will. She inherited it from my father with the written directive that I inherit it next."

"The bank claims otherwise," he says.

"It states it in his will."

"They claim the debt allows them to supersede that directive."

"That note my father took is large, but it's not anywhere near the value of the winery. Can they even make this claim at all?"

"They can claim they own the White House," he says. "That doesn't mean they do. Your mother failing to register a will complicates this but your father's will specifically stated that she inherited the winery on the condition that you were next in line. But you do need to pay the bank debt your mother left behind. We're at six months tardy at this point."

"Five," I say, my role as acting-CEO not much different than my role the past two years, except for one thing. I still don't have access to the empty bank accounts. "I made a payment."

"Is the winery making money?"

"Yes. I've run that place and kept the books since my father died."

"Then why was she four months behind on the bank note when she died?"

"I don't know. And not just the bank note. Everything. Every vendor we use wants money. I can't catch everyone up at once. I need time. Or I need access to her personal accounts. That has to be where the money is."

"I've filed a petition with the court to appoint a neutral executor with no allegiance to the bank," he says. "But they could easily come back with names we have to reject."

"Which is what the bank wants," I assume and suddenly there is a light in the dark tunnel. Not necessarily an end quite yet, but a light. "They think time will place me so far in debt I have to surrender the property. That would be insanity and I'm not insane. It would be easier to get my hands on the money my mother pulled from the accounts, but I told you. The winery is making money. If we drag this out long enough, I'll pay off that note. Drag it out."

"You're sure?"

"Positive," I say firmly.

"Have you had any luck at all finding the money she pulled from the company?"

"None," I say. "Have you had any luck finding anything that might point me in the right direction?"

He reaches into his drawer and sets a card in front of me.

"You need a private investigator. He's good and affordable."

"I can't afford to hire a private detective."

"You can't afford not to," he counters.

"We're making money. I just need you to buy that time."

"What if you have another surprise you don't expect?" He slides the card closer. "Call him. Talk about a payment plan."

I reach for the card and stick it in my purse. "I'll call." My mind goes to my newest surprise. "Do you know Nick Rogers?"

He arches a brow. "The attorney?"

"Yes. Him."

"Why?"

"A couple of bank goons showed up last night and he was at the winery. He stepped in and scared them off."

"He's a good friend and a bad enemy."

"There's no chance that was a set-up and he's already an enemy?"

"Nick Rogers doesn't need to play the kind of games that comment suggests. He has the prowess of—"

"-a tiger."

"Yes," Frank says. "A tiger. He'll—"

"-rip your throat out if you cross him or his clients," I supply. "I know his reputation, but what I don't understand is how he, above others in his field, is so well known."

"He's one of the top five corporate attorneys in the country and he's local to our region." He narrows his eyes on me. "But back to you. Do you have any other questions about what I shared today?"

"Not now."

"Then let's get to what's important. Happy birthday, Faith."

"Thank you," I say, my voice cracking, forcing me to clear

my throat and repeat, "Thank you."

"It's a rough time to have a birthday, I know," he says. "You lost your father at about the same time of year."

"I did," I agree. "But at least every year it's all concentrated in one window of time."

"Your birthday."

"Birthdays are for kids."

"Birthdays are for celebrating life," he says. "Something you need to do. I'm glad you didn't cancel your appearance at the art show tonight in light of your mother's passing. It's time you get back to your art, to let the world see what *you* do. And a local display with a three-month long feature is a great way to get noticed again."

Again.

I don't let myself go to the place, and history, that word could take me to. Not today.

"Your agent did right by you on this," he adds.

"Josh overstepped his boundaries by accepting this placement, and had he not committed in writing before I knew, I'd have declined. He was supposed to simply manage my existing placements and related sales."

"Declined?" he asks incredulously. "This is an amazing opportunity, little girl."

"Le Sun gallery is owned by one of our competitors, a winery which infuriated my mother."

"Your mother was selfish and wrong," he says. "I know she's gone but I'm not saying anything we don't both know. And Le Sun is owned by a rock star in the art world and the godparents of said rock star artist. Every art lover who visits Sonoma wants to see Chris Merit's work at that gallery, and when they see his, they will see yours. And you've put your

27

life on hold for too long. If you decide to keep the winery—"

"I am," I say. "It's my family legacy."

"You're sure your uncle wants no part of it?"

"Yes," I confirm. "Very." And even if he did, I add silently, my father would turn over in his grave if that man even
stepped foot on the property again. "Bottom line," I add firmly. "I'm keeping the winery."

"Make the decision to keep it after you achieve some
breathing room. After your show and the chance to remember your dreams, not his." He reaches inside the drawer again
and retrieves an envelope, holding it up. "And after you read
this and give yourself some time to process it." He sets it in
front of me.

My gaze lands on my name and a birthday greeting written in my father's familiar script. I swallow hard, my stomach
flip-flopping, before my gaze jerks to his. "What is that?"

"He asked me to give it to you upon his death, if it was
after you turned thirty or on your thirtieth birthday, should
he pass before that date."

My hands go to the back of my neck, under my hair,
my throat thick and I have to turn my head away, my eyes
shutting, a wave of emotions overwhelming me. "And yet my
mother didn't even have a will," I murmur.

"People don't want to believe they're going to die," he
says. "It's quite common."

I jerk back to him, anger burning inside me at my mother, and at him for protecting her. Again. "You do what's re-
sponsible when you hold a property of this value. You just do."
I grab the envelope my father left for me. "Please just buy me
time." I stand and walk to the door and just as I'm about to
leave, he says, "Faith."

I pause but do not turn. "Yes?"

"I know you're angry at her and so am I, but it, like all things, will pass."

I want to believe him. I do. But he wouldn't be so confident, if he knew all there was to know, which I will never allow to happen. And so, I simply nod as a reply, and leave, thankful that Betty is on the phone and has a delivery driver in front of her, which allows me to pass by her without any obligatory niceties. Exiting the office, the cool air is a shock I welcome, something to focus on other than the ball of emotion the envelope in my hand seems to be stirring. Maybe I didn't want to feel again after all, and eager to be alone, I quicken my pace, entering a tunneled path beneath an ivy-covered overhang and don't stop until I'm on the other side. Clearing it, I turn left to bring my car into view where it's parked on the opposite side of the street, my lips parting, my feet planting, at the sight of *Mr. Rogers* himself leaning against it. And he isn't just leaning on it. He's leaning on the driver's side door, as if to tell me that I'm not leaving without going through him first.

Chapter Four

Faith

I NOW KNOW THE SOURCE OF THE DARK LUST AND ENERGY I'd felt with Nick Rogers wasn't just about sex. It was about betrayal. Because the fact that Mr. Rogers, no, *Tiger*, is here at *my attorney's office*, leaning arrogantly on my car, watching me with arms folded in front of his chest, ankles crossed, can mean only one thing. He's working for the bank. And he's doing it in a custom-fitted dark blue suit that I don't have to see up close to know is expensive. Because apparently ripping out someone's throat requires style. And he wears that suit well, too, it doesn't wear him. He has a way of owning everything around him that I'd actually thought attractive last night. I'd allowed myself to be drawn into a flirtation with him. And I might have embarrassment in me if I wasn't so damn furious with myself for being foolish and him for being an asshole.

I charge toward him, and he tracks my every move with those striking, navy blue eyes. I actually got lost in them last night. I also know them to be intelligent and brimming with arrogance, which I plan to use to knock him down a notch or ten. Crossing the road, I don't stop until I'm standing in front of him. "Get off my car," before adding, "*Mr. Rogers.*"

His lips, which are really too damn pretty and full for a man, but still somehow brutal, quirk with amusement. "You don't take requests well, I see, *Ms. Winter*," he says. "I told you to call me anything but Mr. Rogers."

"I can think of *many* names to call you right about now," I retort. "But Mr. Rogers was the kindest. I don't like being played with."

He arches a brow. "And… you think, I'm playing with you?"

"I know you are."

"You're wrong," he says, immediately.

"If I'm wrong, how did you know I'd be here?"

"Your staff," he replies simply.

My anger kicks up about ten notches and I can almost feel my cheeks heat. "Do you win all your cases by lying? Because my staff didn't know I was here." I turn away from him, click my locks with my keychain, and open the door despite him leaning against it. He moves without argument, but my win is short-lived as the earthy male scent of him rushes over me and I whirl around to find myself caged between a hot, hard male body and the hard steel of the car.

"Talk to my lawyer," I order, before he can speak. "Not me."

"I have no interest in talking to your lawyer," he states. "I *am not* working for, nor am I associated with, your bank." He steps closer, so close we are a lean from touching. So close that I can feel the warmth of his body and if I wanted to, I could trace the barely-there outline of a goatee. "And I don't lie," he adds, a hardness to his voice, a glint in his eyes that tells a story beyond this moment. "In fact, I hate liars, and I don't use the word 'hate' liberally."

"Wrong," I say, *hating* the way my body wants to lean toward his. "My staff—"

"-told me you had a meeting," he supplies, "and it was fairly obvious after last night that it would be with your attorney, and I'm resourceful enough to have that bring me here."

"Why would you even do that?"

"You interest me, *Faith*," he says, his voice lower now, my name intimate on his tongue, a soft rasp that still manages a rough, seductive tone, etched with a hint of something in his voice, in his eyes, I don't quite read or understand. "And unless I've developed a colorful imagination, I interest you, too."

"You don't work for the bank?" I ask, my anger easing, but not gone.

"No," he confirms. "I *do not* work for the bank, and to be clear, I do not work for anyone who has your business interests in mind. I work for me, and I have *you* in mind."

"If this is all true, then explain to me how you thought showing up here, knowing what you learned about my situation last night, was the way to get from no to yes?"

His hand settles on the window beside me, somehow shrinking my small space, somehow creating more intimacy between us. "We were red hot last night and you know it."

"That's not an answer."

"That's not a denial, but I'll answer your question. If I'd have shown up at the winery today, you would have disappeared into some corner again until I left, like you did last night. I wasn't prepared to let you run again."

"I didn't run," I say. "I simply decided you could be playing me. And I don't need more enemies than friends."

"And now?" he challenges softly. "Am I a friend or an enemy?"

"I haven't decided."

Something flickers in his eyes, gone before I can name it, before he asks, "All right then. I'll settle for either as long as you keep that old saying about enemies in mind."

"They aren't the nice guys."

"If you have an enemy who's a nice guy, it's no different than having an attorney who's a nice guy. You might as well call him a friend."

"But you're not a nice guy. You said so."

"What I am is the man who made you drop that ten-foot wall of yours when I touched you last night." His gaze lowers to my mouth, lingering there before lifting. "And I've been thinking about touching you again ever since. About tearing down that wall and keeping it down."

"That wall is to keep men like you out."

He narrows his gaze on me. "Who burned you, Faith? And what scars did he leave?"

That wall of mine slams back into place, and damn it, he did tear it down, and he did so without touching me. He's dangerous. He sees too much. Things I don't want to show anyone ever again. "I'm leaving," I say, turning back to the car, but as I do, my purse strap falls from my shoulder. I try to catch it, and only then do I realize I'm still holding the card from my father, and it tumbles to the ground. I suck in air, hating the idea of it on the ground for reasons I'll analyze later. Turning and squatting down, I intend to grab it, but Tiger is already there and it's in his hand. I wobble on the toes of my boots just enough to instinctively flatten my hand on his powerful thigh to catch myself. The impact of that connection is electric, instant, that wall he'd mentioned, falling. I can't breathe and my heart is instantly racing. I try to pull back my hand, but his covers mine.

That breath I'd sucked in moments before is lodged in my throat, and my gaze lifts to his, the impact punching me in the chest, heat waving between us, that dark lust charging the air between us. I tell myself to stand up, but I don't. I tell myself to jerk my hand back from where it rests against him. But he smells so good, a cocoon of earthy masculinity that seduces me to stay right where I am, lost in those deep, blue eyes of his, and he smells so good.

"Touching you again," he says, his voice as earthy and warm as his scent, "or rather you touching me this time, is better than the first time." He offers me the card. "Happy Birthday, Faith."

I don't ask how he knows it's my birthday. It's on the card. It's also on documents that he, no doubt, studied before he came here today. I reach for the envelope, but he doesn't let it go. He holds onto it and me, and it hits me that the two things in life that I've learned you cannot explain nor can you control, have now collided: *Death and lust*. And I have never needed control more in my life than now.

Tiger reaches up and strokes the hair from my eyes, his hands settling on my cheek, a stranger that somehow feels better than anything has in a very long time. And just as I feared, I'm reminded of how good an escape that dark lust can be, how addictive. He's right. I *am* afraid. I'm afraid of losing what little control I have right now.

I stand up and go on the attack. "You researched me like a client or someone you're prosecuting," I charge, knowing it's a ridiculous reason to be mad. I would have researched him too had I gotten in earlier last night, but I don't like it right now. I don't like how he's taken my life by storm. "You knew it was my birthday before you came here."

"I researched you like a woman I want to know. And I *do* want to know you, Faith."

His tongue strokes my name again, soft yet rough edged, which somehow screams sex to me. HE screams sex to me. "Stop saying my name like that."

"Like what?" he asks, and in that moment, with his long hair tied at his nape, and his deep voice, roughened up, he is lethal for no logical reason.

"Like we're intimate," I say. "Like you know me, because the internet doesn't determine who or what I am."

"Then you show me who you are."

"Why?" I challenge. "You already read me like a book. I need to get to work." I turn and climb into my car, as I should have before now.

He kneels beside me, and I brace myself for the touch that I am both relieved and disappointed doesn't follow, but I can feel him compelling me to look at him. "This is what I do," he says, undeterred when I do not. "I push and I push some more to get what I want."

I look at him before I can stop myself. "You officially pushed too hard."

"If you're still running, I haven't pushed hard enough."

"This doesn't work for me."

"Good. It doesn't for me either."

I blink, confused by a reply that conflicts with his pursuit. "What does that even mean?"

"Our shared state of mind simplifies the attraction between us and even explains it. Bottom line: We both just need to fuck a whole lot of everything out of our systems, including each other."

"Who even says something like that to someone they don't know?"

"Me, Faith. I might not always show my hand, but as I said, I don't like lies. When I say something, it's honest. It's real."

"You don't think not showing your hand is a lie?"

"Do you?" he counters.

"Good dodge and weave there, counselor," I say. "There's more to you than meets the eye, Nick Rogers."

"I could say the same of you, now couldn't I, Faith Winter?"

"Yes," I dare, because most likely he already knows this as fact, and anything else would challenge him to prove otherwise. "You could."

He arches a brow. "I expected denial."

"Seems you didn't learn everything about me on the internet that you thought you learned."

His eyes glint with something I can't name. "The internet was never going to give me what I want from you anyway."

I tell myself not to take the bait, but there is more to him than meets the eye. More that I don't just want to understand. More than I almost feel I need to understand. And so, I do it. I dare to ask, exactly what he wants me to ask.

"Which is what?"

"You. Not the you that you show the world. The one be-hind the wall that intrigued me last night and now. The real you, Faith, stripped bare and not just exposed. *Willingly* ex-posed." He stands up, backs away, and shuts the car door.

Chapter Five

Faith

I LEAVE DOWNTOWN WITH NICK, OR TIGER, OR WHATEVER I decide to call the man, on my mind, and he stays on my mind. Five minutes after my encounter with him, much to my dismay, I can still feel that man's touch, and the warmth of his body next to mine. Ten minutes later, the same. Fifteen. The same. This, of course, was his intent when he suggested we fuck and then left without so much as another word. He wanted me to crave his touch. He wanted me to be ready for next time, which we both know will come. And it worked.

I hit the twenty-minute mark with Tiger haunting my thoughts, but I finally have the blessed distraction from him as I pull onto the long, winding path leading to the place I call home. The white country-style house I'd bought with my inheritance six months after my father's death. I'd finally accepted that my mother would run the winery into the ground if I didn't leave my life in L.A. behind. I'd had this crazy idea back then that I could merge my world with that of the winery. I'd been wrong, but today it's my birthday, and I'm giving myself the gift of a weekend with my art, including a brush in my hand.

I park in the driveway rather than the garage, and quickly grab my bag, hurrying up the wooden steps to the porch that hugs the entire front of the house. Once I'm inside, I clear the foyer and hurry across the dark wood of the floors of the open living area to my bedroom. I enter the room I haven't slept in for a month, everything about the space artsy and clean, done in cream and caramel tones. A cream leather-framed bed and fluffy cream area rug. Caramel-colored nightstands. A cream chair with a caramel ottoman. My painting, a Sonoma landscape, is the centerpiece above the headboard, because hey, I can't afford a Chris Merit, though Josh loves to tell me I could be the *next* Chris Merit. I'd be happy to just be the next me, and actually know what that meant, which reminds me of the card from my father. I set my bag on the bed, and pull out the card, staring at my father's script. I run my fingers over it, missing him so badly it hurts, but I remember that he saw my art as a hobby, and the winery as my future. I've accepted that destiny. I'm protecting our family history and his blood and sweat. But I can't open a card tonight and risk gutting myself before a night I've already committed to surviving. I set the card down and whisper, "I love you, and I'm going to make you proud."

My eyes burn and the guilt I have over the tears I haven't shed for my mother has me rushing to the closet off the bathroom to change. I need to paint. I need to get lost with a brush in my hand. I turn away from the bed and enter the bathroom, done in the same shades as the bedroom, including the checked tiles, with an egg-shaped sunken tub, and continue to my walk-in closet. Once there, I change into jeans and a t-shirt, as well as sneakers.

A few minutes later, I'm on the second level of the house, which I had converted to my studio, with a smock over my clothes, a blank canvas in front of me. A brush in my hand for the first time in months, and my phone on the table beside me. And impossibly, somehow, Nick Rogers is still on my mind. I don't like arrogance. I don't like men with long hair. I don't like men like Nick Rogers. And yet, that man is haunting me. I go to work, determined to paint him off my mind, long strokes, heavy strokes. Soon my creation begins to come to life, a work that is like no other I have ever created, and I am driven, obsessed even, to finish it.

Time passes, an hour I think, maybe more, when my phone rings. I set down the brush, wipe my hands on the smock before picking it up. "Hi Josh," I say, after noting my agent's number on caller ID.

"I'm finally here," he breathes out, sounding decidedly grumpy.

"Finally? What time is it?"

"Five," he says. "And why the hell do you not know that, Faith? This is a big night for you. Chris Merit won't be there, but he donated a never-before-seen painting for the charity auction. The event's been sold out for months. And this is your event, too."

"It's his event. I'm showing my work."

"It's your event, too, and I will spank your pretty little ass if you say otherwise, again."

"You do not need to say things like that to me."

"Because I scandalize you? We both know that's no more true than Cinderella. Besides A) You'd bust my balls if I ever tried anything with you, which I would not because B) I like submissive types. You are so far from that it's laughable. If you were, I'd already have you past this nonsense that you can't paint and run your family business."

I grimace. "Where are you going with this exactly?"

"You should be at a spa getting a facial or whatever you women do before fancy black tie affairs that would never cross our male minds."

"Actually," I say, blowing out a breath. "I was—" I stop myself, not wanting to give him the wrong idea about where this is going, "—about to take a shower."

"Please tell me that sentence was supposed to finish with the word 'painting' because that's the only answer acceptable in my mind."

I inspect the project I've been working on for hours, my inspiration coming from an unexpected place.

"Faith?" he presses.

"Yes. I've been painting."

"Thank you Lord," he says, his voice exaggerated relief. "I have to see whatever it is before I leave Sunday."

"No," I say quickly. "This is nothing like the black and white landscapes I'm known for. This is just for me."

"Now I'm really intrigued. And after tonight, you'll be a hot mama in the art circuit. Maybe this new project is the one where we make big money together."

"You know that doesn't matter to me," I say. "I just needed to pay my outrageous L.A. rent and selling my work helped."

"You mean you downplayed your dream of quitting the art museum and painting full-time every chance you got. I've told you before many times. There is *nothing* wrong with dreaming big and getting paid big for your work. I need new work to keep that dream alive. You've given me nothing in a year."

"I don't have anything to give you," I say despite the dozen covered easels around the room that say otherwise.

"Liar," he accuses. "We both know you can't live without that brush in your hand. I want to see what you did before I leave."

"No," I say. "No, this one is for me."

He's silent a beat. "Do you know how long I've waited to hear you say you were painting for you again?"

I inhale and release a shaky breath. "Josh—"

"Don't tell me the reasons why you can't paint, because I know it's in your blood. It's like breathing to you and I also know that you've been secretly painting. But tonight isn't about me pressuring you to paint. It's about celebrating the success of the work that you've already given me, and the art lovers of the world. This night is my birthday gift to you. So. Happy birthday, Faith."

"Thank you," I say, always amazed at how he remembers this day when others who should have often forgot. "How are you so bad with women and so good with your clients?"

"Being single is not about failure. It's about choice. I want what I want, and I won't settle, something we both know you understand."

The man knows far more about me than most of the people who I called friends back in LA, but then, he lives in the art world, as I once did. "I walked right into that one," I say,

"Yes, you did. Meet me at my hotel at six-thirty. I'll see you soon, sweetheart." He hangs up and my lashes lower, a hotspot in my chest and belly where emotions I don't want to feel have formed. Emotions I swore I *wanted* to feel when I moved into my mother's bedroom. I was wrong. Emotions weaken me. They make me feel instead of think. They change my judgment calls. Yes. I was definitely wrong about welcoming them back into my world. Just like I was wrong two years ago when I bought this place, thinking I could paint and help at the winery, and give up nothing. I can't do both, and when I dip a toe back into the art world, that's what I want to do full-time. I wish tonight wasn't happening. I wish I had said no. And yet, I need to go change and dress.

Still holding my phone to my ear, I shake myself out of my reverie, and stick my cell inside my jeans pocket. I have to shower and get dressed. Tearing away the smock, I toss it on the wooden stool beside the table. Exiting the studio, I rush down the stairs and back to my bedroom, and finally reach my closet. Flipping on the light, I walk into the giant box-shaped space and stop at the far wall where my party dresses hang. I remove two choices, both still with tags, both splurges meant for shows I was to attend just before my father's death. One is a deep royal blue, made of lace with a V-neck and gorgeous sheer long sleeves. I love those sleeves but my favorite part of the dress is that it's ankle length with a classic front slit. I like classic. I like the way it makes me feel like the woman I forgot I was until I met Nick Rogers. I'm not sure why he woke me up. I'm pretty sure I will wish he didn't later, but tonight, I need to feel like me, like Faith Winter, not an employee of the winery.

I refocus on the second dress, which is… well, it's a black

dress. That's the problem. No matter what it asserts otherwise, its color is my deterrent, that says death to me, a reminder of all loss. Of the people I love. Of hope. Of dreams. Of so many things. I don't know if I can survive this night, while being reminded of all those reasons I can't allow my past to be my present. But tonight is about that past, and about my art, though I really don't know what that means to me anymore. It's a hobby and nothing more. It can't be. It's...wait. My spine straightens. Josh said tonight could set me up for a good payday, and I already know a second mortgage on a new mortgage won't do for me. But do I dare believe, my art, my past, could help me get out of this hole that I'm in with the winery? Or at least buy me some time to find the money my mother has to have somewhere? I hope.

I set the blue dress on the bench in the middle of the room and turn around, then sprint from the closet, through the bathroom and bedroom. Running back to the stairs to my studio, I start pulling sheets off easels, staring at each of the dozen pieces I've completed, one by one. Looking for the ones that Josh might think are worthy of his representation. And the truth is, I never think any of my work is worthy of representation, so why am I even trying to figure this out? But I've sold work for up to seven thousand dollars. Okay, only a couple of pieces and they took time to sell, but if I could sell just some of these, I could buy that time I need. And if I wasn't so damn confused about how my two worlds fit together, I might have already thought about this. I'll just show them all to Josh. I rush to the office in the corner, ignoring the glass desk in the center and walk to a closet, where I remove a camera.

Returning to the studio, I snap photos of my work. I'm

about to head back downstairs, but somehow I end up standing in front of the freshly painted easel. A portrait. I never paint portraits, and not because I don't enjoy them, or have no skills in that area, but rather because of the way the brush exposes secrets a person might not want exposed, and I value privacy. I value my secrets staying my secrets and I assume others feel the same. But I want to know Nick Rogers' secrets, and I know he has secrets. Which is why I haven't gone to the internet for answers, where I will discover only sterile data. Instead, I found myself painting him, and the hard, handsome lines of his face are defined, but it's his navy blue eyes that I've fretted over. Eyes, that along with what I've sensed and spoken of with him, tell a story I don't quite understand, but I will. I have the weekend off from the winery as my gift to myself, and I plan to finish the painting. I plan to know that man more and figure him out before I see him again. Doing so feels important, for reasons I can't quite say right now. Maybe he's my enemy or maybe he just enjoys the dynamics of playing that game. Perhaps I'm just trying to feed myself a façade of control by trying to figure out the unknown that I simply won't and don't have with that man. I wonder if he knows he doesn't have it either.

Whatever the case, it won't matter tonight. As Josh said. The event has been sold out for months. No one, not even Tiger and his arrogance, can snag a ticket. And since I'm not going back to the winery until Sunday night, I suspect he'll be gone back to wherever he practices by then. In fact, maybe I'm wrong about seeing him again. If he gets back to work, and gets busy, he might even forget whatever challenge I represent. My painting might actually be the last I see of the man. This should be a relief. It's not.

By the time I email the photos to Josh, I have an hour to shower and dress. By the time I fret over underwear and thigh highs as if Tiger might show up and rip them off of me, then move on to change from the blue dress to the black dress twice, I'm running late. Finally, though, I return to the blue dress, and rush through fussing with my makeup and curling my hair that I usually leave straight. Even choosing shoes becomes an ordeal, but I settle on strappy black heels, and a small black purse, with a little sparkle, which is also Chanel, and purchased by someone I'd rather not think about.

I'm in the car, starting the engine, ten minutes before I'm supposed to meet Josh and it's a thirty-minute drive. He calls me at fifteen, "Where are you?"

"The traffic was bad."

"There is no traffic. Faith—"

"I sent you photos of the work I have done." All except one particular portrait.

"Did you now?" he asks. "I'll take a look now and you're forgiven."

"You don't have time now. I know that."

"I'll make time. Meet me at the gallery instead of the hotel. Go to the back door. Expect security." He hangs up.

I let out a breath I didn't know I was holding. He's looking at them now. I suck another breath in. What if he hates them? What if dabbling at my craft has made me forget what my craft is all about? "What was I thinking?" I pull up to a stoplight and I know exactly how to make myself feel good about this decision again. I grab my phone and tab to my voice mail, and hit the button to play all messages. One after another, harsh messages play from the bank, or a vendor that is past due. Each a brutal reminder of why I chose to send those photos to my agent. I have to get everyone caught up, and one by one, I've been working to do just that.

It's right at seven when I turn into the Chateau Cellar Winery that is home to the gallery. It's literally a stone castle, covered in ivy with a dungeon-style front door. Just the sight of it has my nerves jolting into action, fluttering in my chest and belly, and not just because I'm late. I've never been featured in a show this high profile. And while I tell myself this night is one last hurrah, as I turn into the parking lot, I see every space is filled, and all I can think is that this is my dream. This is still my dream. I pull on around to the back of the building and find the lot equally full, those nerves expanding but I dare to allow myself some excitement as well. How amazing would it be if my dream saved my father's?

I park and I've just killed the engine when there is a knock on my window. I roll it down to find Josh in view, his dark hair trimmed neatly as always, his handsome face clean shaven. "They're waiting on you to make announcements."

"Oh no. Oh God. I shouldn't have taken the photos tonight." I click the locks and he immediately opens the door, offering me his hand. I snag my purse and flatten my palm in his, struck by how good-looking he is in his tuxedo, and how unaffected I am by his touch, even before I'm standing and under the full impact of his dark brown eyes giving me a once over. "You are stunning, Faith Winter." He releases me and waves a hand in the air. "I see it now. You in a bathtub on the cover of a magazine with a headline: sexy, successful and talented." He doesn't give me time to reply. He shuts my car door and snags my arm. "Let's go."

I double step to keep up. "I'm never going to be naked on a magazine."

"Not if you keep smashing grapes instead of painting."

My heart sinks. "You hated the photos. You think I lost my touch."

He stops walking and settles his hands on my arms. "They're magnificent like you are. Go in there and be a painter because I don't represent wine makers."

The door opens and a woman steps outside. "Josh. Now."

"Let's do this," Josh says, taking my hand and leading me into chaos. There are greetings and handshakes and before I know it, I'm sitting in a chair on a spotlighted stage with two other artists I don't know but admire on either side of me, the gallery around us in darkness, the crowd standing around us.

"Welcome all," the announcer says, from the podium in front of us. "As you know, we have three new artists to introduce you to tonight, but because I know you are all anxious to see the Chris Merit release, I want to explain how this works. We'll unveil the painting in exactly one hour. Highest bidder wins and all proceeds, one hundred percent, are donated to the Children's Hospital. In the meantime, we have our three featured artists here tonight. They will be donating twenty percent of all sales tonight as well to the Children's Hospital. Please visit them in the crowd tonight. Please visit their displays and our many others." He has each of us stand and after a few more words the lights come up. I stand and look left to find Josh waiting for me at the steps, but something intense, something familiar compels me to look right, and I suck in air. Nick Rogers is standing there, looking like dirty, sexy, delicious lust in a tuxedo.

Chapter Six

Tiger

I DON'T LIE. I MEANT THAT WHEN I SAID IT TO FAITH earlier today.

She *does* intrigue me and the reasons are many. For starters, I like a challenge and she is that, both in character and physical perfection. She doesn't look like a killer, but rather a beautiful woman, who is somehow delicate and strong at the same time. She doesn't smell like a killer, but rather like the garden where I'd first touched her. She doesn't even read like a killer on paper, but then I knew that when I sought her out. And right now, standing on the stage, staring at me, stunningly beautiful in a blue dress, I vow to know her body as well as her mind, vowing to feel every curve that dress hugs, of which she has many next to me before this night is over. Right after I find out if she tastes like the killer, and enemy, I still, regretfully, suspect her to be.

I watch now as she recovers from the surprise of my appearance, the shell-shocked look on her heart-shaped face fading, her composure sliding back into place, remarkably fast. She walks toward me, grace in her steps, those long legs of hers peeking out from the slit in her dress, teasing the fuck out of my cock in the process. Legs I want wrapped around my hips, but not before I've licked every last inch of them and her. She stops at the edge of the stage, at the top of the stairs while I'm at the bottom, those full, lush lips of hers painted a pale pink, subtle and yet beautiful, the way she uses a brush on a canvas. She's talented, gifted as few are, and capable of making a living on her own, without involvement in blackmailing my father or killing him.

"You look beautiful," I say, and I allow my desire for this woman to radiate in the deep rasp of my voice. "You *are* beautiful."

To my surprise, her cheeks flush red, shyness in the lowering of her lashes, as she says, "Thank you," and once again proves she's a contradiction, a beautiful, complicated fucking contradiction that I have to understand. But I'm adding another level of complication of my own that I *want* to understand.

I take the bottom step, leaving only two between us and offer her my hand. She looks at it and then me, and when those green eyes lock on mine, the connection delivering a punch in my chest. I'd revel in how alive this woman makes me feel, in how much I want to fuck her, if I didn't think there was a ninety percent chance that she's a blackmailer and a killer, but the facts are clear. Her chin lifts defiantly, but she offers me submission, settling her palm on mine, her eyes flickering with the contact. My cock twitching with the contact. Her hand slides against mine, delicate and small, and I close mine around hers.

"Free will," I say. "Exactly what I wanted from you."

"I didn't want to make a scene," she counters, allowing me to walk her down the stairs to stand at the side of the stage.

"That's a coy response," I accuse, daring to settle my hand on her slender waist, pleased when *her* hand settles on my arm, rather than pushing me away. "It's beneath you," I accuse.

"You're right," she surprises me by saying. "It was coy and I don't do coy. You're touching me because I let you."

"That's true," I say. "You are letting me. Why?"

"Because you touching me is better than you not touching me."

Heat courses through my veins, perhaps because I'm playing a dangerous game with a beautiful woman who might just kill me, too. Or perhaps simply because I want Faith Winter in a way I don't remember wanting anyone in a very long time.

"How are you even here?" she asks. "The tickets were sold out."

"I know Chris Merit."

"Of course you do."

I arch a brow. "What does that mean?"

"You seem to know everyone or they know you."

"Why is that a problem?"

"It's not."

And yet, I can almost hear that wall of hers slam down between us. I step closer to her, my free hand settling on her waist as well. "What just happened?"

"Nothing that matters."

"And if I think it does?"

"Then I'll rephrase. Nothing that I plan on explaining."

"I don't like secrets."

"It's not a secret just because someone doesn't choose to share it with you," she says. "It's simply that person's right to privacy. Besides. You want me naked. That doesn't require deep conversation."

"I didn't say I wanted you naked," I counter. "I said I want you stripped bare and not just exposed. *Willingly* exposed. The two are vastly different."

"And what exactly do you expect to expose?" she replies.

I lower my head, my cheek near hers but not touching, "All of you," I say, lingering there, letting my breath trickle warmly on her cheek and ear.

"We'll see," she says, her hands settling on my chest as if she means to push me away, or pull me close, but before she can do either, we hear a male voice say, "Faith."

At the sound of her name from behind and to the right, my jaw clenches and Faith jolts, her hands falling away from me. In unison, Faith and I rotate to face our intruder, my hand settling possessively at her lower back, reminding her, and anyone else that might hope otherwise, that I'm here to stay tonight.

"Josh," Faith says, greeting the tall, dark haired man I recognized from my research as her agent, Josh Miller. Age thirty-eight, bank account status – not as rich as me, but rich enough to declare his success.

"You did wonderfully during your introduction," he says, glancing at me and back at her, before he adds, "but you need to mingle with the masses."

"This is Nick Rogers," she says, as if he's nudged for an introduction I suspect he'd rather not have at all. "He owns a law firm in San Francisco."

"I know that name well," he says, looking at me. "You represented our top football player when he sued us to get out of his contract with our sports division."

"Who was that?" Faith asks.

"Connor Givens," I say. "Damn good quarterback."

"And what happened?" Faith asks.

"He left the agency," I say. "We won."

"And we lost," Josh says, flicking a look between Faith and myself. "I'm not sure how I feel about that."

"It's business," I say. "Like Faith is to you." There's a message in those words. I know he wants to fuck her or he wouldn't have had his hands all over her when they entered the gallery tonight.

Josh narrows his eyes on me. "Business I take seriously," he says, an obvious warning in those words that he'd have been better off not delivering. He'll discover that soon, but now, now he dares to give me a two-second stare, before cutting his gaze to Faith. "Let's mingle."

"Yes, of course," she says, looking at me, her body angled in my direction, a silent question in that action. I take her hand and draw it to my mouth. "I'll be close," I promise, kissing her knuckles, and I don't miss the tiny tremble of her hand in mine.

She nods, and I release her, and the way she hesitates in her departure tells me that I've taken her "no" to a "yes," and done so faster and easier than expected. But then, there is a reality here neither of us can deny: We really are red hot together. She departs, and Josh latches onto her arm, touching her yet again, but she never touches him. She doesn't seem to know that he not only wants to fuck her, and perhaps is even in love with her, which considering how intelligent she is, amazes me. But then, women who don't return a man's feelings often don't see what is there to be seen. I, however, have made my intentions clear. Her naked. Me naked. Lots of sweaty, hot, dirty fucking.

I watch her chatting with one guest, and then another, remembering my conversation with the star artist of the night, who I'd met while representing a mutual friend.

"Chris Merit, artist and superstar," I'd said. *"I need a ticket to the event at Le Sun Gallery tonight."*

"I didn't know you were into art."

"I have a Chris Merit on my wall."

"Really? You never said a word. But, hey man. I'm always honored to hear someone chose my work over someone else's."

"You're humble as fuck man."

"You sure as fuck are not."

I laugh and so does he, but he's not laughing when I add, *"How about a ticket in exchange for a fifty-thousand-dollar donation to your charity?"*

He whistles. "I'll give you a ticket, man."

"Happy to donate. It's not a problem or I wouldn't have offered."

"All right then. That's generous as hell. I'll call my godmother and arrange a ticket. Or do you need two?"

"Just one."

"Got it. It's business then."

"I wouldn't call her business. What do you know about Faith Winter?"

"Not much personally, but my wife and I are the reason she's in that display. I saw her work in L.A. and had a flashback to her visiting me at Le Sun a good several times a decade ago

and with big dreams in her eyes. She's talented and it's clear from looking at her work that she took some inspiration from mine, which I find flattering. She executed her work, not only well, but with her own style."

"Most people wouldn't like that inspiration."

"Most people are insecure." He'd laughed then. "Funny side note about Faith. She'd felt like she was betraying her family by visiting me at Katie and Mike's vineyard. I told her that Katie and Mike not only knew her father well, they knew that I don't give a damn about wine. She told me she didn't either."

"She didn't what?" I'd asked.

"She didn't give a damn about wine and yet I hear she's now running her family vineyard, and that, my friend, could be where her dream dies, if she lets it. My wife reminded me how easily that could have happened to me when I inherited my mother's cosmetic business."

"Thus why you made sure Faith was on the ticket tonight."

"Exactly."

"Does she know that?"

"No and keep it that way. I offered her an opportunity. It's up to her to decide what to do with it."

I return to the present, watching Josh's damn hand settle on Faith's back as they stand talking with two older, distinguished men. Possessiveness rises in me and I clamp down on the urge to go break his damn arm, reminding myself that I want to fuck Faith, and then fuck her over, not marry her. Irritated at myself, I turn away from her, walking to the Chris Merit displays, admiring his skill, these particular pieces all San Francisco skylines in black and white, that of course even a damn near blind eye to art would call brilliant. Interested in Chris's reference to Faith's inspiration, I cross the white tiled floor of the gallery to a corridor that has Faith's name on it, two high, glass-blocked walls, creating her walkway.

Entering her display, I find ten or so guests viewing random paintings, and decide to continue on past them to the farthest corner, to view from the end of the display forward. At the far corner, I find myself standing alone and studying a painting of the Reid Winter Mansion, rolling hills behind it that most would craft with the brilliant colors of Sonoma's many grapes, flowers, and trees, while Faith does not. Instead, this work is black and white, a technique Chris also favors, but there are differences between the two. Chris sticks to various shades of gray and whites, but as with this painting, Faith always adds a splash of red. In this case, a blood red moon.

"I'm afraid to ask what you think."

At the sound of Faith's voice, I turn to find her a few feet away, her blonde hair brushed behind her shoulders, her neck as creamy white and delicate as the rest of her. "You know you're talented," I say.

"No actually," she says, a flicker of something in her eyes. "I don't. I never..." She lifts a hand and gives a wave. "I just don't."

I close the space between us, stopping toe-to-toe without touching her. "Well, you are."

Her face flushes a pretty pink like her lips. "Thank you."

There are footsteps to our left before we hear, "Ms. Winter."

At the sound of her name, Faith turns to the several guests now beside us, who in turn rave about her work. She signs autographs for them and they declare their intent to buy one of her paintings. They depart on that note, but another couple steps forward. This continues in a rotation of guests for a good half hour or more.

"You don't take compliments well," I say, when an announcement about the Chris Merit auction approaching clears the hallway, leaving Faith and I alone again.

"Everyone can't be as arrogant as you," she says, an obvious teasing note to her voice.

"Confidence isn't arrogance," I say.

"Is that what you are?"

"No. You're right. I'm arrogant, but it works for me and against my opposition."

"You'd make a bad enemy," she says. "My attorney says so."

I close the space that distractions have placed between us, my hand settling at her hip, and I do not miss the slight tremble of her body in response. "And what do you think, Faith?" I ask.

"That there are a million reasons in my head right now that say you're a bad idea."

"Then why am I touching you right now?"

"Because you touching me still feels better than you not touching me," she says, surprising me with her quick, direct answer. "And because tonight, I'm allowing myself the freedom to be someone and something I cannot be tomorrow. That's my hard limit. No tomorrow."

"Hard limit," I say, the term inferring knowledge of a world I know well, but did not expect her to know at all.

"I know that this is mine," she says, neither denying nor confirming her understanding a broader, kinkier meaning.

"Negative," I say. "I do not accept that limit."

"It's my *hard limit*."

"I *don't accept* that limit," I repeat.

"Then we end before we begin," she says, backing away and leaving me two choices: Let my hand fall away from her hip or pull her close.

"It began the minute we met," I say, letting my hand fall away from her, rather than pulling her close. Seeking that free will I've told her I both want and will have. "And if we're really done," I say, "why are you still standing a step from my reach, instead of walking away? And why are we both thinking about how fucking good fucking each other will be?"

"One night," she breathes out.

I close the step she's put between us, but I don't touch her, my voice low, for her ears only. "I could spend one night with just my tongue on your body and never get inside you. In fact, if I had my way, your dress would be up, and I'd be finding out how sweet you are right now."

"That was—" she begins.

"Dirty?" I supply. "Yes. It was. And I am. And so are you, or you wouldn't know what a hard limit is." I lower my head, my lips near her ear, breath intentionally warm on her neck. "You have no idea how dirty I can be," I say, "but you will. And soon."

"You think—" she begins, only to be cut off as we both hear, "Faith," spoken from behind us.

My jaw clenches at the sound of Josh's voice, which denies me the end of that sentence, my head lifting, as Faith faces Josh and I step to her side. "They're unveiling the Merit piece in less than twenty minutes," he says, focused on Faith. "It would look good for you to be there." He glances over at me. "Are you going to bid?"

"Depends on what it looks like," I say.

His expression sours. "It's a Chris Merit one of a kind."

"And if it fits well with the one already on my wall," I say. "I'll buy it."

"You already own one?"

"He knows Chris," Faith supplies. "I'm pretty sure he can get a painting when he wants one."

Josh arches a brow. "Is that right?" he asks, looking at her, but I watch his eyes narrow, the sly intent they register before he looks at me and adds, "You know. Since you're obviously trying to win over Faith, supporting her work would go a long way. If you can afford that Chris Merit painting, why not buy her entire collection?"

Faith gasps. "No," she says firmly. "No, he will not." She looks at me. "I don't want you to do this. Please don't."

Her reaction, far from that of a blatant, money-grubbing killer in a financial bind, pleases me, but I need to know it's not a coy show. "I think me buying your work is an excellent idea."

"No," she snaps, looking between myself and Josh. "No. This is not an excellent idea." She rotates to face me, giving Josh her back. "I *do not* want you to do this."

"A portion of the sale does go to charity," I point out.

"You donated to the charity to get your ticket," she argues. "And I'm going to tell the gallery not to sell to you."

"That's like telling them to deny a donation."

"No," she repeats. "You *will not* do this." Her jaw sets and her eyes narrow on me. "I don't understand where you're going with this, but I *am not* for sale." She turns and starts marching away. And since that conclusion really is shoving a square peg in a round hole, considering she's already agreed to fuck me, I've obviously hit a nerve.

And judging from the smirk Josh casts my way, he knows

it, and planned it. "I guess you had better bid on the Merit auction," he suggests, before pursuing Faith, and no doubt doing so with the certainty that he's now gotten rid of me, but I am not dissuaded from what I want, ever. And I want Faith Winter. And in truth, Josh has given me a gift, a couple actually. He's allowed me a glimpse into what makes Faith tick, and at her core, there seems to be pride, not greed. That doesn't make her innocent of the crimes I suspect her of, and in fact, it might simply make her a perfect criminal, able to hide behind a perfect façade of innocence. But that second gift Josh gave me was the realization that at some point, maybe even from that very first provocative moment when I first made eye contact with Faith, my original agenda has changed. I stopped looking for ways to prove her guilt, and started looking for ways to prove her innocence. That might seem as if it works for her, but the truth is, it doesn't. Because when I want to believe in someone and they let me down, they betray me, my wrath is vicious.

I start walking, pursuing Faith myself, not about to let her get away. When I reach the end of the hallway, I find the immediate area a ghost town, the main gallery area cleared. An announcement sounds over an intercom: *The Chris Merit auction begins in twenty minutes in Room 4C. The painting is available for viewing in ten minutes.* In other words, the guests are now piling into room 4C, and so likely, is Faith. I'm about to hunt it, and her down, when I spy Faith crossing the corridor toward the "staff only" door, clearly trying to use the twenty-minute gap before the auction to escape and compose herself. I decide to lend her a hand.

With long strides, I pursue her and manage to arrive at the door she's exited, only sixty seconds after she disappears on the other side. Following her, I open it and enter the next room, shutting it behind me to find myself at a crossroads. Forward is the exit, and I'm about to step in that direction, when a sound catches my attention, and I look right to find Faith hurrying down a narrow hallway. Again, I follow, and as I pick up my pace, she gives a quick glance over her shoulder at me, but doesn't stop walking. Just before I catch up with her, she turns and enters a doorway.

I give the "Women" sign an inconsequential look, and as I know she knows I will, I push open the door and enter.

Chapter Seven

Tiger

I STEP INSIDE THE TWO-STALL BATHROOM ONLY TO HAVE Faith whirl on me and attack, obviously waiting for this moment. "I meant it," she declares, her eyes flashing with anger. "I can't be bought. And why would you even try? I can't figure it out. I said I'd fuck you and yet you still do that? Is it a power play? A way to stroke your ego?"

I lock the door, and step toward her, expecting her to back away, but she fearlessly stands her ground, and I swear this woman gets more interesting by the moment. She's also made it easier for me to shackle her wrist and pull her flush against me, her hands settling on my chest. "How people handle other people's money tells a story of who they are."

Her fingers close around my lapels. "I gave you *no reason*

to believe I was that kind of person."

"I don't know you, sweetheart," I say. "And you don't know me. But I do know that I've seen many a thief in virgin clothing."

"You mean you got burned. Well, I'm not her, whoever she was, and why does this even matter? You just want to fuck me out of your system."

"Because I do the fucking. I don't get fucked," I say. "A motto I live by, and I don't intend to change that for you or anyone else."

"Sounds to me like you have trust issues, that aren't my problem," she accuses.

"A bit like you thinking I was trying to buy you when you already agreed to fuck me," I say, tangling fingers into her hair and not-so-gently tugging her gaze to mine. "I'm not him," I add, "whoever he was, but as you said. Why does it matter? You just want to fuck me out of your system."

"*Why* do I want you?" she breathes out. "You're such an arrogant bastard."

"The arrogant bastard who's going to fuck you better than you've ever been fucked, sweetheart," I promise, my mouth closing down over hers, and I can feel her breathe out in reaction, as if my kiss is what she's been waiting for, and it turns me on. Fuck. She turns me on. Too fucking much considering I sought her out to destroy her.

Angry with myself for losing focus, and at her for being that damn distracting, I tear my mouth from hers, my hands settling at her hips. Staring down at her swollen lips, her lipstick untouched, but she will not be, in every possible sense, when I am done with her. "You want one night?" I ask. "That's your hard limit?"

"Yes," she confirms, grabbing my lapels again and tilting her chin up to add, "That's my hard limit. Take it or leave it."

"Then here's my hard limit," I say. "We agree that I'm going to change your mind about *your* hard limit."

"No," she says in instant rejection. "That essentially makes my limit obsolete."

"Your limit stands," I say. "But I'm telling you up front. I'm going to change your mind. Starting now."

"Are you asking for my agreement or demanding it?"

"Stating a fact and sparing us time considering we have about ten more minutes before that auction starts and you're missed."

"Fine," she says. "I'll save you lost energy while you spare us lost time. You can't change my mind."

I react to the absoluteness in her tone, lifting her from the wall and turning her to face the sink, her hands settling on the counter, my big body caging hers from behind. Her reaction is a lift of her chin, her gaze meeting mine in the mirror with defiance in the depths of her stare. "One night," she repeats, adding a smooth, "Tiger" to the end of the sentence, as if she wants to poke the very tiger she's just called me.

"Do you know how much I enjoy a challenge?" I demand, tugging her lace dress up to her hips, her nearly naked ass now under my palms.

"Too much," she replies, not even sounding breathless. "In fact some might say that indicates you're insecure at your core."

Amused, *challenged,* I give her backside a teasing smack that earns me a yelp, before I turn her to face me. "Tell me if it's too much and I'll stop."

I pick her up and set her on the counter, spreading her

legs, my hips settling between her knees, hands on the lace bands of her thigh highs. "Then again," I say, my fingers sliding up her naked thigh, to rest just at the edge of her silk panties, "since I'm such a bastard, if you tell me it's *not* enough, I might not care. But I'll try to be polite about it all."

"Polite?" she asks, giving a choked laugh, her hands covering mine on her thigh. "You?"

"I'm so fucking polite," I say, "I deserve an award for proper manners." I stroke the silk between her legs, her spine arching as I do. "I'll carry your bag for you," I continue. "I'll hold the door for you." I lean in and press my cheek to hers, mouth at her ear. "I'll make you wet," I say, shoving aside her panties and stroking the slick heat of her body, my reward in the soft moan that slides from her lips. "I'll let you come when I'm ready for you to come. I'll even warn you right before I rip your panties off." I grip the silk in my hand and yank it away, shoving them in my pocket before settling on one knee in front of her. "And now I'm going to lick you in the very spot you want me to lick you but I'm not going to let you come." I lean in, and run my tongue along the exposed skin just above the lace of her hose, then caress a path to her sex, where I pull back just enough to allow my breath to trickle over her, my cock so fucking hard it hurts.

She makes a sexy, desperate little sound, her hips arching ever so slightly, urging my mouth closer, and I give her nub a tiny lick. She moans, and I swear I feel that sound like a stroke of her tongue on my cock. Restraint is my friend and her satisfaction, and for that reason, I suckle her gently, then tease her with a long swirl of my tongue. And damn I do want more, I want everything right here and now, but waiting for the sweet taste of her orgasm, and that perfect moment that

I bury myself deep inside her, is all about anticipation, about submission. *Her* submission.

I pull back, my fingers flexing into her legs. Her eyes go wide, a pained moment in her eyes when she realizes I'm really not going to let her come. "You're evil," she says, as I stand and set her on the ground.

"But polite," I remind her. "I warned you in advance." I pull down her dress. "I even put your clothes back on."

Her eyes flash and she reaches into my pocket and grabs her panties. "You don't get to keep these," she declares, scooting past me to walk to the trashcan where she tosses them.

I shackle her arm and pull her to me, her hands on my chest, my hand at the back of her head. "I didn't want the panties," I say. "I wanted this." I slant my mouth over hers, my tongue licking long and deep into her mouth, and I don't give her time to object or submit. "Now we both will taste like you for the rest of this event," I say. "Until we both taste like you at the end of the night."

"Like I said," she whispers. "You're evil."

"Your torture is mine," I promise. "I'm hard as fuck and want to be inside you, but without limits. And this bathroom is one big limit." As if proving my point, knocking erupts at the door. "Faith! Are you in there?"

At the sound of Josh's voice, Faith's eyes go wide, her fingers curling on my lapels again. My hands come down on her shoulders and I lean in close to her ear. "Easy, sweetheart. Answer him." I lean back and she takes a deep breath, giving me a nod.

"I'm here," she calls out.

"Did you fall in or what?" he demands. "The auction's about to start."

"I'm coming," she says, her voice a bit louder now and when I smile, she glowers at me, and adds. "I'll be right there."

I barely contain a laugh, and she must think I won't, because she pushes to her toes and presses two fingers to my lips. The flare of heat between us is instant, and I take her hand, leaning in to brush my lips over hers before my lips finger her ear. "This is our secret. Go. I'll follow." I lean back and she nods, but when I would move away, she grabs my sleeve and gives me a confused look that turns to gratitude, before whispering, "Thank you."

And once again, she is nothing I expect, and it seems everything I want. I give her an incline of my chin, and step around the corner and into one of the stalls. I can hear her moving around, fixing herself before the click of the lock sounds, and she opens the door. "What the hell, Faith?" Josh demands. "You need—"

The door shuts, but I still hear her reply, "You embarrassed me," and the way her voice trembles with accusation with those words. "Why would you ask him to buy my work?"

I don't hear his reply, their voices moving further down the hallway, but I heard what was important. She's embarrassed. But is she really, or is it an act? "Fuck," I murmur. I want it to be real. I want to prove she's innocent, but the facts are inescapable. There were checks equaling damn near a million dollars written to her mother by my father, and notes that lead me to suspect blackmail. And my father and her mother died of unexpected heart attacks and my father died after her mother. That points to Faith double-crossing her mother, but if she did it for the money, where's the damn money?

I push off the wall and press fingers to my temples. Maybe her mother had another partner who took the money.

Or maybe Faith is in bed with that partner, who's hiding the money. I unbutton my jacket, my hands settling on my hips. I don't do stupid and I'm not going to start now. My father ran through women, including my mother. He didn't write them checks and he damn sure wouldn't write nearly a million dollars to one woman. And no one proves guilt while trying to prove innocence. I cannot lose my focus. I have to kiss Faith to taste the murderess beneath the woman and I have to tear down that wall of hers to ensure she can't hide behind it. I'm not here to save her. I'm here to expose her, even destroy her. And I have to make sure that every moan I get from her is one step closer to one, or both, of those goals.

I walk to the door and yank it open, stepping into the hallway, my stride measured, with purpose. Find Faith. Get her out of here and alone. Fuck her. Expose her. *Own her*. With this intention, driving my every step, I find my way to room 4C where the mostly seated crowd encircle another stage, the easel on display there still covered. Scanning the chairs middle, left and right, as well as the rows of people standing behind each, I locate Faith, standing behind the chairs in the center row, Josh by her side, and I watch as he pats her shoulder, and then leaves his hand there. And she lets him.

I inhale on yet another rush of possessiveness over this woman that could easily lead me to Faith's side, pulling her to me. But I am not a man to act rashly, or without calculated action. My mentor back in LA, the smart, hard-ass bastard that he was, used to say that if you have a bird and it flies away, if it doesn't come back you never had it in the first place. He was talking about clients and reliable witnesses, but I've found that premise to have broad reach. I've pursued Faith. It's time for her to come to me. It's in that moment of decision that an elegant woman I estimate to be in her late fifties to early sixties takes the stage, her dress floral, her hair long and gray.

"Hello everyone," she says. "I'm Katie Wickerman, Chris Merit's godmother, and I am so very proud to share his newest release. This one is special to him and while I believe you will find it rather different for him, as well, I believe it's his most brilliant work to date. But I won't talk your ear off. Without further ado..." She reaches for the sheet. "I give you Rebecca."

My spine straightens at the name of the painting, and when the sheet slides away, gasps and murmurs fill the room, while the familiar scene the work depicts punches me in the chest. It's a beachfront, on a pitch-dark night, and yet you can make out the hundreds of people gathered there with lights in their hands. Honoring a woman named Rebecca, who, after months of being missing, was declared dead.

"And now I'll hand the stage over to Kenneth Davis, our auctioneer," Katie says, while a short man with a Santa Claus beard joins her.

"We'll open the bidding at fifty thousand dollars," he announces, but right now, I'm not in this room. I'm back on that beach, reliving that night that was less than one year ago now. The cold wind. The heavy emotions. The profound way one woman brought together a city and touched so many hearts and lives. She certainly did mine.

"One hundred thousand," the auctioneer calls out, snapping me back to the present, my gaze pulling left to find Faith still standing with Josh, and delivering way more satisfaction than it should, his hand is no longer on her shoulder. I inhale and glance at the painting again, and I am suddenly far more connected to the many dark secrets of Rebecca's life, death, and murder than ever before. I want this painting.

Decision made, I walk to the table positioned by the door, and register to bid. Faith appears by my side, my beautiful bird returning to me at the same time "three hundred thousand dollars" is shouted out from the stage. "You're going to bid?" she asks.

"I'm going to win," I tell her, accepting my paddle, as I hear "Four hundred thousand dollars," shouted out. Not about to allow the auction to close before I win, I give Faith a nod and start walking, looking for a spot near the stage. A moment later, Faith catches up to me, pursuing me now, and then and only then, do I snag her fingers with mine, guiding us to the right side of the stage, close enough for the auctioneer to see and hear me. "Five hundred thousand dollars," he calls out. "No," he amends quickly with another raised paddle. "Make that six hundred thousand."

I release Faith's hand and she murmurs, "My God," at the dollar figure and links her arm with mine. Touching me by choice, that free will she is showing motivating me to win my auction sooner rather than later, and get her out of here. I hold up my paddle and call out, "One million dollars."

The room seems to let out a collective gasp, but the auctioneer is not fazed. "We have one million dollars," he says. "Do we have a million one?"

"A million fifty thousand," a woman call outs.

I scan the crowd, a forty-something woman in a red dress is directly across from me giving me a wave, a smug look on her gaunt, overly made up face that says she thinks she's won.

"A million one," I say loudly, lifting my paddle.

The woman scowls and the room fills with murmurs before the auctioneer says, "Do I have a million two?"

My competition purses her pre-puckered lips and lowers

her paddle, then sits. The auctioneer delivers final warnings and it's done. I've won my painting. Faith steps in front of me, gripping my lapels as she had in the bathroom. "You just bid a million dollars on one painting."

A million one, I think, but I don't point that out. "It's a charitable donation," I say instead.

Josh appears beside us and goes on the attack. "How the hell does an attorney have the money to pay that kind of bid?"

"Josh," Faith snaps. "Stop."

"I've invested well and inherited well," I tell him. "Not that it's any of your business."

"I want to invest where you invest," he snaps.

"I'll give you my guy's name," I say dryly, "but I have to warn you. I make most of my own picks."

"Of course you do," he says, repeating the exact words Faith had used about me knowing Chris Merit earlier. I arch a brow and he smirks. "Bottom line. You have money to throw around, and you thought you'd use it to impress Faith."

He's trying to take us back to our bathroom argument and I'd shut him down, but Faith steps in first. "Josh," Faith chides, and looks at me. "I'm sorry."

"Don't apologize, sweetheart," I say. "I do want to impress you, but not with my money." I glance at Josh. "Because what your agent here fails to understand is that smart people do not surround themselves with those chasing their money, or with any misplaced agendas."

His eyes sharpen with hate before he spouts back with, "My agenda is to protect and support Faith."

"I wasn't aware we were talking about your agenda at all," I say, making his misstep obvious.

It's in that moment that Katie chooses to join us, smiling

at us all, her greeting first directed at Josh and Faith, before she focuses fully on me. "Nick Rogers," she says, offering me her hand. "Thank you for being so very generous."

"It's a special painting," I say, shaking her hand. "It took me off guard, but in a good way. I had to have it."

"Chris told me when he called about your ticket that you'd understand the painting in ways others would not."

"Rebecca not only means something to me," I say in confirmation. "But I was on the beach the night that painting depicts."

"You knew the woman who inspired the painting?" Faith asks.

"I knew her," I say, thinking of the many times I saw Rebecca with my client, in what is now my sex club. She was his. He just didn't know how much he wanted her to be his. But that isn't information for Faith or anyone else. "I was involved in the investigation into her disappearance and represented someone close to her."

Josh jumps on that. "Someone suspected of murdering her?"

"Rebecca was killed by a woman who was jealous of my client's love for her," I say.

"Thrown in the sea," Katie supplies, "Chris's wife found her journals and ultimately she was a key to solving the crime."

"Really?" Faith says. "That's...incredible. How must she feel being a part of such a tragedy?"

"She feels like she knows her," Katie says. "Chris did know Rebecca and it guts them both that she's gone. Though I admit, I keep hoping she'll show up one day, and we'll find out she's been on some island somewhere, living life well."

"We all do," I agree, "including everyone on that beach

that night who didn't know her, but knew her story."

"Indeed," Katie agrees. "Indeed." She inhales. "On to brighter topics." She turns to Faith while Josh slips away, hopefully shamed into staying away. "Faith," Katie says, taking her hand and patting it. "You are so very talented. We're honored to have your work here."

"Thank you," Faith says. "I'm honored to have it here."

"Your father would be proud," she says. "Reid *was* proud of you."

I watch Faith's delicate little brow furrow. "You knew my father?"

"I did," she says. "And your mother. Our neighbors are like family. We loved hearing your father tell stories about the many Reid Winter's before him. We actually used to get together with them when you were a young girl."

I watch confusion slide over Faith's face. "But I thought you were competitors. My mother said—"

"We were competitors? I mean, technically yes, but variety is the spice of life. It's not us or you."

"I'm very confused right now. My father—"

"Loved your mother very much and we had a falling out with your mother before you even hit your teen years. But Reid and Mike spoke quite frequently. And just so you know, my husband wanted to be here tonight, but we had a private party at the winery that got a little rowdy. Perhaps you can come by for dinner one night." She glances at me. "With you of course."

A woman in a suit dress, clearly not here for the party, appears beside us, her attention on Katie. "Sorry, Katie, but I have a situation."

"What is it Laura?"

"The bidder who lost the auction insists that Mr. Rogers cash out before she leaves."

Katie flushes with obvious embarrassment. "That's inappropriate."

"It's perfectly fine," I say. "I'll cash out now."

"It's not necessary," Katie assures me.

"It's really not a problem," I say, looking at Laura. "Where's the cashier?"

"I can help you," she says.

I glance at Katie. "I'll calm the beast in red for you." I refocus on Faith. "I'll be right back."

She nods and I motion to Laura, who leads me out of the room and through the gallery to an office, where a college-aged male clerk attends to my paperwork. I fill out a promissory note, with my banking information and connect him with my personal banker. "One last form," the man says, shoving his heavy-rimmed glasses up his nose. "This indicates delivery location and instructions."

My mind goes to Faith and I fill out my information, but put a huge note at the bottom: *Hold for guest viewing until Faith Winter's display is discontinued.* I hand the man the form and he glances at me. "Are you sure about this?"

"Completely. Let your customers enjoy it." Impatient to get back to Faith, I enter the gallery, the crowd thinned to almost nothing, and end up walking toward Katie.

"Paperwork signed," I say. "Let me know if you need anything else."

"Of course," she says. "I'm sorry again."

"It's really fine."

Her lips curve. "But you just want to get back to Faith. I know that energy you're putting off. She's in the Chris Merit display area." She pats my arm and steps around me, but my feet stay planted.

A muscle in my jaw starts ticking. What the hell kind of energy am I putting off? Damn it, this woman is *way* too far under my skin if I'm reading like a man who has a woman under his skin. I really do need to fuck her out of my system, and there is no better time than tonight.

I start walking, crossing the gallery, and find an entire room dedicated to Chris, but the only person left inside is Faith. She's standing in front of a painting I recognize as the Paris skyline, but if she senses I'm here, she doesn't turn. I close the space between us and step to her side, my hand settling at her back, and touching this woman fires me up in ways something so simple should not fire me up.

She glances over at me. "The lady in red didn't attack you, did she?"

I laugh. "No. The lady in red did not attack me."

"It's an incredible painting," she says. "Obviously special. Rebecca's story touched me and I barely know it."

"It's not an easy story to know," I admit.

She studies me a moment. "Not a nice guy, but he has a heart."

My lips curve. "I'm human despite my best efforts not to be."

"Don't worry," she says. "Your secret's safe with me." Her lashes shut as if her words have hit a nerve, and she quickly turns away, changing the subject. "He's incredible. I really can't blame the lady in red for wanting the painting. And he has such supportive godparents."

"Spoken wistfully," I observe, certain she's still thinking of that conversation with Katie, and looking for revelations, I add, "People have secrets, Faith. It's part of being human."

"My mother sure did."

I turn her to face me. "What kind of secrets, Faith?"

"Her kind of secrets. Like you have secrets. *Tiger.*"

"My enemies call me Tiger. You call me Nick."

"Why do I keep feeling like you're the enemy?"

"Why are you looking for an enemy?"

"Why are we standing here talking when we agreed this was about sex and then goodbye? Because this, whatever it is, still doesn't work for me."

"All right then," I say. "Let's go fuck." I take her hand in mine and start walking, aware that she's using sex as a distraction, another version of her emotional wall. Certain that her "hard limit" understanding means that she's played the kind of sex games that makes sex an escape, not a commitment. One might say I'm perfect for this woman. Except that I'm not, because the naked truth awaits. I just have to reveal it.

Chapter Eight

Faith

NICK.
Not Tiger.
Friend.
Not an enemy.

I still don't know if "not an enemy" is true, and actually, he didn't clarify our status outside of a name. Tiger is for his enemies. Nick is for me. Technically, that makes me a friend. But as we walk toward the main hall of the gallery, having already determined we're both parked out back, him holding me close, with his arm at my waist, my bet is on me being neither friend nor enemy. I am simply a challenge to Nick Rogers. And he has proclaimed how much he enjoys a challenge. Once I move from challenge to conquest, he'll be back in San Francisco where he lives and works, and I suspect I'll be forgotten. And that works for me. It's the reason I stopped pushing him away. I get my one night with him, lost in the fierce masculinity of a man who is so big, bold, and demanding, and he's already proven that he will leave no room for anything else. No guilt, anger, or thought of the new revelations about my parents that just keep adding up every single day.

Just Nick.

Just passion.

Just escape.

Nick and I cross through the center of the gallery, thankfully without delay, the crowd no longer a crowd, using the back employee exit I've been granted access to, and other than a few people milling around with no interest in us, we are undeterred. We exit to the dimly lit parking lot, a cool breeze lifting my hair and then traveling straight up my dress. I shiver, and squeeze my thighs together, reminded not just that my wrap is in the car, but that Nick ripped away a crucial piece of my clothing.

"Apparently, panties serve a purpose outside of looking pretty," I murmur, hugging myself.

He laughs, a deep, sexy sound, and suddenly that cold spot between my legs is hot. "It's not funny," I chide, shivering again, deeper this time.

He halts our progress, and surprises me as he shrugs out of his tuxedo jacket. "This should help," he says, wrapping it around me, but he doesn't move away, his hands gripping the lapels as I had earlier, his big, broad, wonderful body crowding mine. The chilly air around us is suddenly as warm as that spot between my thighs. "Better?" he asks, his voice gravelly, sexy, the overhead light catching the warm heat in his blue eyes.

"Yes," I say, the intimacy of me wearing his jacket doing funny things to my stomach. I swallow hard. "Thank you. But I thought you weren't a nice guy?"

"I'm not a nice guy," he says, his voice that hard steel I've already come to know from him. "But," he adds his eyes lighting with what I would almost dare call mischief. "I *am* a very polite guy. Remember?"

"Your *bad* manners are why my panties are in the trash and not in your pocket," I say, finding his teasing rather charming, despite the way he tormented me in that bathroom.

His full mouth, that I now know feels really good on my mouth and other parts of my body, curves. "As long as the panties are off, I'm a happy man." He slides his arm around my shoulder, and turns us toward the cluster of ten or so random cars.

"I'm on the right far row," I say, and we quickly walk in that direction, while I dig my keys from my purse and unlock my car. Proving he's polite all over again, he opens my door, which has me biting back curiosity about his mother, but if I ask questions, he'll ask questions that I don't want to answer.

I step into the alcove created by the car and door, and when I turn to face Nick to determine our plan for travel, once again I'm trapped between this hot, hard man, and hard steel. But unlike last time, I don't want to escape. I want to get lost in the way he smells, and the way he feels and… "Where are we going, Faith?" he asks.

I wet my lips, jolted out of a fantasy that was headed toward him naked, and me enjoying the fact that he was naked. I'm now back to a hard reality: the decision between inviting him to my private space and personal sanctuary or daring to go to his hotel, which isn't much of a decision at all. "Small towns have wagging tongues," I say. "And I really don't need that right now, with all I have—I don't need that."

"I'm in a private rental house," he says, seeming to read my thoughts. "We can go there if you're worried about your staff."

A private rental house should be a safe zone, but in that moment, I know I need the known of my home, to balance the unknowns, and the powerful force that is this man. "I own a house also close to the winery and I'm staying there this weekend. We can go there."

He considers me for several beats, a keen look in his eyes telling me he's read my need for control, and I wait for him to insist he retain it all. Maybe he'll push me too hard. Maybe this is a bad idea, but that isn't what he does. Instead, he does the exact opposite. He arches a brow. "Interesting. I thought you'd pick my rental."

"Why is that?"

"It fit your hard limit of one night."

"My space. My control."

His hand slides to my hip and he pulls me to him, his hips aligned with mine, my hand settling over his heart, and I am surprised to find it thundering beneath my palm. "Sweetheart," he says. "I'm going to demand control, because that's who I am and what I need. I can read you on this, just like you do me."

He's right. I do. Because I'm drawn to men with his type of appetites. Because apparently, that's who I am. "I do know that about you. But ultimately, I have control. I say yes or no."

"As it should be," he says. "But I'm going to make sure you don't want to say no and that you never forget me for all the right reasons. That's a promise." He covers my hand where it rests on his chest and lifts my wrist to his lips, caressing the delicate skin before pressing my hand to his face, as if he's getting me used to touching him. But he leans into the touch as if he craves it, and then he kisses my palm, and I swear, it affects me. It's tender, and sensual, and probably the sexiest thing anyone has ever done to me, and I am not without experience, but he affects me. Intensely, deeply.

With obvious reluctance, he releases me and takes a step backward, his hand on my door. "I'm two rows over I'll pull around to follow you. I'm in a—"

"—black custom BMW," I supply, letting him know that yes, I *was* watching him at the window before I slip back inside the car, fully intending to, for once, leave him with a revelation as he did me today. But I should have known Nick Rogers would not leave his curiosity piqued without resolution.

He squats down next to me. "You *were* at the window."

"Yes," I confirm, turning to look at him. "How did you know I was there?"

"I felt you watching me." He lowers his voice to a deep rasp. "Like I can feel you now, Faith, and I'm not even touching you." And once again, like this morning, with a bombshell statement, he is gone, doing to me what I failed to do to him moments before. He's already standing, the door shutting, and without question, as he's intended, I am left in a sea of simple words that are not simple at all. And this time I do not have hours and a paintbrush to try to make sense of the way this man so easily affects me, the way my heart is thundering in my chest at this very moment.

He can feel me without touching me. I can feel him without touching him. I think back to my past, to the relationship that gave me the hard limits, and a turbulent, addictive, completely wrong for me relationship. Was it like this and I just can't remember? I don't think so, and yet it *was* passionate. It *was* intense. But it wasn't this. And yet this isn't romance. It's sex. I mean, my God, we almost had sex in the bathroom. So, what makes Nick Rogers, different? And I still can't get by that sense of something darker than just our passion between us, that battle of friend vs enemy that should have scared me away. Earlier today, it would have.

Headlights now burn behind me, telling me that I am out of time, with no answers, and accepting this is how it must be, unless I plan to go panty-less and unsatisfied, which I don't. I quickly turn on my car. Or I try. The engine clicks but doesn't come to life. I try again. "No," I whisper. "No. No. No." The lights flickered when I unlocked the door. The battery isn't dead. I try again with the same result. The headlights behind me shift, and Nick pulls in beside me. I try the ignition again, but the car doesn't start. There's a knock on my window and I sigh, caving to my enviable circumstances.

I open my door and Nick rounds it, once again, squatting beside me. "Has this ever happened before?"

"No," I say, "but I hate to admit this because it's completely irresponsible, which is not who *I am*, but I can't remember the last time I took it in for maintenance. And it's a BMW. They're high maintenance."

"Yes, they are," he says, and to my surprise he doesn't make me feel more stupid than I already feel. "But they handle the San Francisco hills and the Sonoma cuts and curves like no other car. We'll get it towed and fixed in the morning. Let's take my car."

In the morning.

The inference being that he's not planning on leaving

tonight, but that rattles me far less than him feeling me without touching me. But right now, I need to deal with my car. "Yes," I say. "That works." I rotate to get out of the car, and he snags my fingers, and then my waist, to help me stand, and suddenly I'm flush against him, his hands at my waist.

And while moments before he'd held me captive with words, with the idea of touching him, now it's the way he feels when he touches me. The way I can't breathe unless he's breathing with me when we're this close. "I'm going to go inside and tell them we're leaving your car," he says, warmth in his voice.

"There you go being polite again," I accuse.

"I guess my mother raised me right after all," he says, stroking a wayward strand of hair from my forehead, and not only do I barely contain a shiver, I barely contain my desire to ask a question about his mother, which he doesn't give me time to ask anyway. "Come," he says, or rather orders, which is, I've decided, as natural to him as is that need for control we just talked about, and I don't mind. It's actually sexy when done at the right time and place by a man who knows that time and place, which is preferably while naked. And we're both already mentally undressed.

In a few steps, and moments, I'm sliding inside his BMW, its soft cream-colored leather encasing me while that earthy scent of the man himself surrounds me. "I'll be right back," Nick says, shutting the door, and I inhale that alluring scent of him again, and pull my seatbelt into place, the sound of soft music stirring curiosity in me. Turning up the volume, I find it's classical music, which I know well. Somehow it fits Nick.

The driver's door opens and he joins me, and I swear the man has this energy that consumes the very air around him.

And me. He consumes me. Suddenly, the car is smaller, more intimate and I am warmer, my heart is beating faster. "That was fast," I say.

"A guard just showed up and made that easy on me," he explains. "He's letting Katie know the situation." He reaches for the gearshift, but pauses, seeming to listen or think, before casting me a sideways look. "You found my music, I hear."

"I did," I say. "*Symphony No. 5*. I know it well. It suits you."

"Don't let that fool you," he says, starting the engine and backing out of the parking spot before placing us in gear. "I'd just as easily have Kid Rock or Keith Urban on the radio. It depends on my mood and where my head is at the time."

"And tonight it was classical, why?" I ask, casting him a curious look.

"It's a work state of mind," he says. "When I'm prepping for court, opening and closing statements in particular, words distract me, but music helps me set the tone in my mind."

"Are you working on opening or closing statements now?"

"Actually, in this case," he says, driving us through the narrow path connecting the gallery to the winery, "it's deposition prep for next week. If you do them right, and I do, you convince the enemy that you're going to win in court, and they make a deal out of court."

"There is that word again," I say, my gaze scanning the Wickerman's castle as we turn toward the exit.

"What word?" Nick asks, pulling us onto the highway.

"Enemy," I say. "I don't like it, but I guess for you, that's not a word, but a rule of life. You always have a new enemy, right?"

"In most cases," he says. "I have opponents."

"You said enemy."

"In this case, enemy applies. I used to work with the opposing counsel back in LA. We co-chaired an insider trader case for one of the biggest clients in the firm."

"And what happened to make him an enemy?"

"I like to win," he says, "but I do it the right way. With my brains. He likes to win as well. By playing dirty."

"And you never play dirty? They do say you'll rip someone's throat out if they cross you."

"If someone hires me to do a job, my job is to win. Not to feel sorry for the person coming after my client, or even the person aligned with the person coming after my client. My client needs to know that if he or she is with me, he or she is protected."

"And what if the witness is pulled into the case without wanting to be pulled into the case?" I ask. "Are you still that cold-hearted to that witness?"

"Yes," he says with zero hesitation, even doubling down. "Absolutely. Because I didn't pull that person into the case. The person attacking my client did, and my client has the right to protect themselves. And believe me, if you were the one needing that protection, you'd be glad I was the one on your side."

"That sounds vicious."

"It is vicious and I'm unapologetic about it. But there's a difference between being a cold-hearted asshole, and breaking the law. And the man I call an enemy broke laws to obtain evidence which could have gotten us both disbarred."

"What did you do?"

"I was forced to throw out what would have been good evidence if obtained legally and find another way to win."

"And the enemy of yours, he agreed to throw it out?"

"No. I threatened to go to the board at the firm and he

read my willingness to do it accurately."

"And you won the case?"

"Yes. I won."

I rotate to my side to face him. "Can you tell me about it?"

He glances over at me. "You want to hear about the actual case?"

"I want to hear about how you won it under those circumstances, yes."

"Why?"

Because I need to hear about someone else overcoming another person's crimes, and winning, I think. But I say, "Because you intrigue me," and it's true. He does.

He laughs at my play on his earlier words, the passing lights illuminating his handsome face. "Aren't you the witty one, Ms. Winter?"

"Actually, not many people call me witty."

"You sure about that? Because that comeback in the bathroom where you called me insecure was pretty witty."

"That was snarky."

"So, you're known for your snark?"

"No," I say, "but I am known for excellent pancakes and an incredible knack for sprucing up a box of Kraft macaroni and cheese like nobody's business."

"You're known for your paint brush," he amends.

"I'm *almost* known," I correct, before I can stop myself, but I've said it so I just wade on into it. "Which is like almost winning a case to you, I suspect."

"You downplay your achievement," he says. "Chris Merit wanted you in his show. That's pretty damn powerful in the art world."

"Our families share a connection," I say. "Apparently

more so than I realized." I change the subject that I wish I hadn't breeched. "Tell me about winning that case."

"I'd rather hear about you. Tell me about your art."

"You teased me with part of a story," I press. "I really want to hear about how you won the case."

His phone rings and he hands it to me. "Tell me who's calling so I don't drive us into a cliff."

Stunned by something that feels rather private, I nevertheless take the phone and glance at the caller ID. "It's says North and why don't you use Bluetooth?"

He grabs an earpiece from the visor and attaches it to his ear. "Hackers love Bluetooth and I deal with confidential information for powerful people. And I need to take that call, sweetheart. It's my associate working on the depositions with me."

"Of course," I say, the endearment doing funny things to my belly all over again.

"Punch the button for me, will you, before he hangs up?" he says, battling his headset.

"Yes," I say, turning down the radio for him, "but take the next right and it's going to be about five miles before we turn again."

"Got it," he says, and I hit the button to answer the call, and then face forward, sinking into my seat. I feel as if I'm intruding on his world now, when really, I haven't even searched him on the internet or otherwise, as he has me. It's a thought that does not sit well. I really don't want him in my world, just in my bed. I don't want anyone in this hell with me right now. I inhale and shut my eyes, listening to him speak, and I don't remember ever being so attracted to a man's voice. But there is something about his deep, masculine voice that is almost musical to me, and judging from the warm heaviness in my body, a song that plays all the right notes for me.

"No," Nick says to the person he's labeled as "North" in his phone. "Don't ask him that. He'll walk right around the topic and you'll alert him to what comes next," he pauses to listen. "No. Explain your reasoning and you're going to need a miracle to get me to agree to this."

As his conversation continues, I'm struck by how certain Nick is about everything he says and does, wondering how long it's been since that was me. And it was. There was a time when I was young and thought I could rule the world with a paintbrush, back when I was as confident as he is today. When I'd thought big dreams and hard work would get me to the level of success Nick is at now. But I wasn't Nick. I wasn't hard enough. Life chipped away at me, and right now, that makes me feel more of that anger I've been feeling. Only I realize it's not really my mother's fault at all. She did what she did but she didn't make my choices for me. I did. I chose how I let me handle me.

"And I'm off," Nick announces.

"And all is well?" I ask.

"All is well when I finish a deposition with a settlement." His brow lifts and he surprises me by turning the radio back up and testing my musical knowledge. "Do you know this one?"

"*Dawn* from *Also sprach Zarathustra*, Richard Strauss. Did you know that this is the opening to the movie *2001: A Space Odyssey*?"

"Did *you know* that Elvis used it for his entrance to concerts?"

"I did," I say. "Mostly because I had an art teacher who

not only thought painting to classical music gave the work depth, but she was also insanely in love with Elvis. Painting to Elvis gave the work sexiness."

He laughs, a deep rumble that feels real to me when not much else has lately. Maybe that's why I need this man so much. That lust we share, can't be faked. It's real. "Is that art teacher the reason you know classical music?" he asks, pulling me back to the present.

"Oh yes," I say. "That's how I know classical music and every word to every Elvis song ever recorded. Doesn't everyone know the words to every Elvis song ever recorded?" I laugh, his lighter mood lightening mine as well. That is until he asks, "Do you still paint to classical music and Elvis?"

I am instantly thrust back in time, to the excitement I once woke up to every day to just hold a brush. "Sometimes I'd just turn on the music and let it run through songs until one inspired me." Except today, I think. He was my inspiration.

"Why was that statement past tense?"

"It's complicated."

"I think I've made it pretty obvious that I'm good at complicated," he counters.

"I'm not. And take the next right. You'll go down about a half a mile and then turn at the white gate. That leads to my property. You can park in the driveway. I left the garage door opener in my car and the door sticks half the time anyway."

"Back to complicated," he pushes.

My phone buzzes with a text and I lift his jacket, searching for my purse under the sea of cloth. By the time I have it in my hand, my phone buzzes again, and I unzip my purse, digging it out to glance at a text from Josh: *Where are you? Your car's still here but I can't find you.*

"Oh no," I murmur. "I didn't say goodbye to Josh." I turn to Nick. "What was I thinking? He's my agent and I said nothing to him."

"Text him, sweetheart, or we'll never get to those morning-after pancakes."

"Who says you'll be around for pancakes?"

"Me."

"You know, I don't like arrogant men."

"Since we both know I make a living being arrogant, what's my appeal? My money. My good looks." His lips curve. "I'm just so damn polite that you can't help but lose your panties?"

"You're bad."

"Dirty. And bad. So, is that the appeal?"

"It's definitely not your money," I say, while he pulls us onto the driveway by my house, dim lights casting us in a glow.

"Most women like the money," he says, killing the engine.

"Which means you can't ever know if a woman wants you for you or for your money. There's a reason you're what, thirty-five or thirty-six, judging by your career, and either divorced or never married."

"Thirty-six," he says, turning to me. "Never married and never plan to be married. I don't believe in marriage."

"Then I guess we are perfect for each other," I say.

"Are we now?"

"For tonight," I confirm and when his lips quirk, eyes lighting, I quickly add, "That's not a challenge."

"Of course, not," he says, and there is the distinct vibe radiating off him that he knows something I don't know.

"What does that mean?"

"Whatever I make it mean," he says, giving a low chuckle before he adds, "I'll come around and get you," and he's already exiting the car, clicking the locks before he departs. I turn to my door, and try to open it but it won't budge. Frowning, I try again, and still it won't move. Nick grabs the door and opens it, and I twist around to get out, and to go right along with the rest of my day, my skirt catches on my heel. Much to my distress, as I rotate to face him, the slit down the middle of my dress tears straight to my bare-naked crotch.

I gasp, and as much as I want to cover myself, my heel and my skirt are still not where they should be. But when embarrassment would kick in, Nick is suddenly squatting in front of me, his hand on my knees, his gaze sliding to my sex, lingering and then lifting to mine, the connection stealing my breath.

"If you're trying to seduce me," he says, his expression all hard lines, and passion, before he adds, "it's working."

It's cold outside, and I am warm all over. "I…that wasn't the idea."

He leans in and kisses my leg just above my thigh high, and then, to my shock, he leans in and licks my clit, and then he's doing this slow teasing swirly thing with his tongue, and now I really can't breathe. I brace myself on the dash and just when I think I might melt right here in this car, Nick pulls back and stands, taking me with him.

I pant with the impact. "You can't keep doing that to me," I whisper. "Seriously. That is—"

He leans in and kisses me, hand at the back of my head, his tongue now doing that same slow, sexy tease he'd just done in much more intimate places, before he speaks, "I won't stop next time. That's a promise."

Chapter Nine

Faith

NICK LACES HIS FINGERS WITH MINE AND GUIDES ME away from the car, shutting the door. Somehow though, instead of walking forward, we're standing toe-to-toe again, and when our eyes meet, there is this flutter in my chest that somehow turns into heat radiating across my chest and down my arm to where our fingers touch. To where he holds my hand, and with all I have dared sexually, with good and bad outcomes, with all I know he will dare of me, this is still what affects me.

"You hold onto me like you think I'm going to run," I murmur. "You wouldn't be here if that were my plan."

"I hold onto you like a man who doesn't want to stop touching you." He reaches up and caresses my cheek, the touch tender, my body reacting, my breasts heavy, my nipples puckered under the lace of my bra. That flutter in my chest repeating. "Let's go inside where I don't have to," he adds.

"Yes," I say. "Please."

His lips curve. "Please."

"I'm polite too," I say, but I don't add anything about my mother teaching me right, because she did not. My father did.

"I wonder if you'll be so polite when I finally get you naked."

"Don't count on it," I say, and it's meant to be playful but there is this pulse of adrenaline in me that makes it more raspy and needy.

He knows it too. I see it in the darkening of his eyes. "Come," he says, draping his arm around my shoulders, and turning us toward the door, leaving my hands free to tug his jacket around all my gaping, naked places, while I'm thinking about being truly naked with this man. And with each step we take, I am aware of how our legs move together, hips aligned. How he holds me close, touching me just as he said: Like he doesn't want to stop touching me.

We've just reached the eight steps leading to the dimly lit porch when my cellphone rings in his jacket pocket I'm still wearing and I stop dead in my tracks. "Oh no," I say, digging in the pocket. "I didn't send Josh that text. It's going to be him and where is my phone? I can't find it but I hear it."

Nick moves to the step in front of me, and reaches in the opposite pocket from the one I'm struggling with, retrieving my phone, which has stopped ringing. "Thank you," I say, reaching for it, and I have no idea how this man handing me my cell, has turned into something sexual, but he's holding it and my hand.

"I still don't have you inside the house," he murmurs softly, walking backward to lead me to the porch, only steps away from the door. "I still don't have you naked."

And that's when my phone starts to ring again.

Nick sighs. "I'm starting to feel like this is a threesome." He releases me. "Talk to the man so I can have you to myself."

"Sorry."

"Don't be sorry. Just be done."

I nod, and answer the call, "Josh." And then I say that word again, "Sorry. I just saw your text."

Nick walks to the door and leans on it, and while I intend to walk to the security panel to key in my code, I instead find myself standing just above the steps, embracing my first opportunity to fully appreciate Nick without a suit or tuxedo jacket on. His white shirt stretching across an impressive broad chest, his arms, also impressive from what I can tell, folded in front of said impressive chest.

He notices my attention, of course, because how can he not when I'm boldly watching him, he arches a brow, the look on his face, a wicked invitation. Josh says something about the parking lot followed by "And I texted and tried to call you," while I have no idea what else he's said.

Cutting my gaze from the distraction that is Nick, I reply with, "It didn't ring," and cross to the keypad, on the wall, right next to the spot Nick leans on.

"And you didn't think about finding me before leaving?" Josh demands.

"I had car problems I was dealing with." I key in my code to have it beep in rejection.

"Which means you were leaving without finding me," he accuses.

Giving up on the code to the door, wishing now that I didn't let the security company convince me to use this keypad system, I rotate and rest against the wall, next to Nick. Focusing now, on surviving this conversation with Josh. "You disappeared along with the crowd."

"Where are you now?" he asks. "Do you need help with your car?"

"I got a ride home."

"A ride with Nick Rogers," Josh says, disapproval in his voice.

"Josh—"

"That's a yes," he says. "He's an arrogant bastard, that will fuck you and leave you. You know that, right?"

A fizzle of unease slides through me at the harsh words, that do not fit Josh, but then again, he's still close to a past that I've left behind. A man that I've left behind and I'm not going to go there with him with Nick standing here, or ever, if I have my way. "Thank you for the advice," I say, trying to recreate the professional barrier between us that seems to have fallen. "And for everything tonight. I'm excited that you liked my new work. I can't wait to see what happens with it," I can feel Nick's eyes on me, heavy, interested.

"In other words," Josh says, "he's with you, and you don't want to talk."

"Now's not a good time," I confirm.

"Right." He's silent several beats. "Just be careful."

"I always am."

"We'll talk before I head back to LA." He hangs up and I stuff my phone back in the jacket pocket. "Well, that went well," I say, glancing over at Nick. "And I have to call the security company. I don't have a key. I use the keypad."

Nick pushes off the wall and steps in front of me. Big and overwhelmingly male, but he really makes overwhelming delicious. "What's the code?" he asks.

"8891 but I tried it twice. It won't work."

He keys in the code and the front door clicks. "Of course, it opens for you," I murmur.

"You were focused on Josh," he says, and instead of making a move for the door, he presses one hand on the wall above my head, those blue eyes of his, too intelligent, too probing as he repeats Josh's words. "*An arrogant bastard who will fuck you and leave you,*" he says.

"You heard. Obviously."

"I heard. And *obviously*, he doesn't know that the description 'arrogant bastard who will use you and leave you' makes me perfect for you. Why is that, I wonder?"

"I could ask you the same."

"You could," he agrees, "but right now. We're talking about you. Should I guess your reasons you like your men here and gone?"

"Should I guess the reasons you like your women here and gone?"

"Go for it, sweetheart," he says, and the challenge is clear. If I make my guess, he can make his, without my rightful objection. But I do object, deny, and reject, the idea of this man, who sees too much as it is, seeing anything more than my body. The rest is off limits.

"No," I say. "I don't want to know. Who you have in your bed, or in your life, aside from a wife you've said you don't have, is none of my business. And we've already filled this night with too many words. Tonight isn't about conversation."

I dart away from him to the door, opening it, but I also

know that I do not have to rush. He won't rush after me. He's a man of control. A dominant, that will follow at his pace, pursue in his way. And he'll catch me but it won't be for conversation, which is exactly why I'm making him pursue me. Entering the house, it hits me that the light is on, when I don't remember it being on, but then, it was daylight, and I was in a rush. Dismissing the concern as nothing, I walk down the hallway, and I'm almost to the living room, when I hear Nick's steps in the foyer, the door shutting behind him, locks turning. Adrenaline rushes through me, no longer a slight bump in energy, but a fierce surge, but really, how can it not? Nick Rogers, is nothing, if not an injection of adrenaline. And while I call him a dominant, that isn't just a personality trait. He is a sexual dominant, and as I expected when I threw out the term "hard limit," experience in a world where that word has heightened meaning. That knowledge should have been enough for me to decline this encounter, and yet, it wasn't. I don't know what that says about who I am, or what I want or need, and I haven't for two years now. Maybe before, but maybe that's the gift Nick will give me. I'll figure it out through him.

Entering the living room, I turn the dial on the wall that brings the lights to a soft glow, a chill clinging to the room. Nick's footsteps grow closer, and I move deeper into the room, walking past the kitchen to my right and around the overstuffed chocolate brown couch and chairs, my destination the fireplace directly in front of them. Once I'm there, I flip the switch on to heat the room, and I can feel the moment Nick joins me, feel his energy, his dominance. It crackles and snaps, the way the gas fire does not, charging my skin, and suddenly, I am hyper aware of the tear in my dress that goes nearly to my belly button.

Inhaling, I turn to face him, and I don't use his jacket to cover myself. I let it gape open, my lower body exposed. He's leaning one broad shoulder on the wall just inside the archway that encases the hall, and directly in front of me. "I thought you weren't running from me, Faith?"

"I told you. I'm not running from you, or you wouldn't be here."

"Then why am I over here and you're over there?"

"That's your choice not mine."

"Is it?"

"Yes," I say, shrugging out of his jacket, and tossing it on a brown stool in front of the fireplace, a fluffy cream-colored rug beneath it. Exposed now for Nick's viewing, I straighten, a silent command from me to him, that he look at me, but he does exactly what I expect, what any true dominant would do, and that's not what I've bid. His gaze is fixed unwaveringly on my face. His way of telling me that he is in control, that he looks and touches, at his own inclination, as will I. It's simply his way, a part of who he is, and even a huge portion of what turns me on about him. But my mind flashes back to a time when another dominant was in my life. When I was naked and exposed, tied up. Submitted and it was pleasure, and then it wasn't anymore. And that has nothing to do with Nick and everything to do with my choices and my own self-discovery. I am not a submissive but I want this man, who will want that of me and I do not understand it, or myself, right now.

Certain Nick is going to read my trepidation, if that is even what I'd call it, I need something to fill the room other than him and my hyped up crazy energy. Ruling out the television behind me above the fireplace, I decide on music, and quickly walk to the artsy, built in, entertainment center in the corner. Once I'm there, facing a portion of the dozen shelves, that gradually get shorter and smaller as they climb the wall, I can feel Nick move again. God. I can feel him just like he said he could me. Even when he's not touching me, which is exactly why he is nothing like my past. Nothing made me feel this then. No one made me feel this.

I reach for the CD player and hit "power" and then "play" knowing that I have a CD inside that is downloaded, random music, that is about as eccentric as the taste he described in the car. Music fills the air, an Ed Sheeran song, and with another deep breath, I rotate, finding Nick sitting on the ottoman to one of the chairs, angled toward me. And while sitting might seem a submissive position, it's not. It's him watching me. It's him on the throne of power, while I stand in front of him. Which is exactly why I sit down on another stool I keep by the shelf, meant to reach the books on the bottom row now behind me. And I do so with my knees primly pressed together, aware that while my lower belly, legs, and thigh highs are exposed I've denied him a view of what's in between.

Our eyes lock and hold across the small space of several feet, separating us, a challenge in the air that I've created by choice this time. Can he make me submit? But it's not a real question. We both know he can. And I don't have to fear that is all there will be between us, that he will think he can bend my will every moment he's with me. There is only this moment, this night.

The song skips and just when I fear I'll have to break this spell with Nick and change it, it changes on its own, to an old 90's hit: Marcy Playground, *Sex and Candy* and that's exactly the lyrics that fill the air: *I smell sex and candy here. Who's that lounging in my chair.*

Nick arches a brow at the rather appropriate words and says, "Sex and candy?"

My hands press to the cushion on either side of me. "Sometimes, you just need sex and candy."

"Indeed, you do," he agrees, leaning forward, his forearms on his knees, his sleeves rolled up to expose several tattoos I cannot make out, and I don't try. Not when his piercing gaze lingers on my face, and the song continues with: *And then there she was, like double cherry pie, yeah there she was.*

"And there she was," he says, his blue eyes burning with that dark lust we share. "Like double cherry pie," he adds, followed by the command of, "Open your legs, Faith."

My breath hitches, and I don't know what happens. I want to do it. I plan to do it, but nerves erupt in me like I'm some inexperienced school-girl. I'm not a school-girl, nor am I suppressed or reserved sexually. I didn't get raped. I don't fear or dislike sex. And yet I haven't had it in a very long time. And my heart is racing again, or maybe it never stopped, my mouth is dry. So very dry. Somehow, I'm standing without consciously making that decision and I'm darting toward the connecting kitchen. I enter the archway, open the stainless-steel fridge and grab a bottle of water, open it and I start guzzling.

Nick is suddenly in front of me, reaching for the bottle and taking a drink, his hand on my hip, leg aligned with mine. "Water?" he asks, looking at the bottle. "I thought you were going for liquid courage but I didn't think it would be water."

"I don't like to dull my mind with booze," I say. "My mouth gets dry when I get nervous, but this was really not smart because nothing like a girl needing to pee to ruin the mood and I—"

He kisses me, and the lick of his tongue is cold from the water, and fresh, and I have no idea why, but it calms me. Him touching me, not watching me, calms me but the kiss is too short, and his question too fast. When he pulls back to look at me, he takes the water, setting it in the refrigerator. "Why are you nervous?" he asks.

"I don't know."

"Hard limit," he says. "That phrase comes with experience." He rotates us slightly and kicks the door shut. "You've been a part of a world that doesn't match your nerves."

He's right. It does. "It's been a long time."

"How long?"

"Two years."

"Since you were in that world or since-?"

"Nothing for two years."

"It's just like riding a bike," his voice lowers, "only you'll be riding me." He rotates me and presses me against the island, his body lifting from mine, hands pressed on the dark wood of the counter behind me. "Were you someone's submissive?"

"No. I'm not a submissive."

"But you were with someone who wanted you to be."

"Yes."

"I don't want you to be."

"But you're dominant."

"I don't take submissives and you have to sense that or you wouldn't be with me."

"You think I could *sense* that?"

"I think we're remarkably in tune with each other to be virtual strangers. Which is why we're both here right now. I like control. You like making me have to earn it. But as we've established, I like a challenge. And you, Faith, are that and so

106

much more. Which means I'm okay with earning control, and you get the control you want, because you decide when I get mine."

And there it is. The many reasons I want this man. His power. His control. The challenge I enjoy delivering and he enjoys conquering. But there is more there, too. There is the reason, a few moments ago, that nerves controlled me instead of our game, and him. And it had nothing to do with who tried to control me in the past, at least, not sexually. He sees too much. He knows too much when he should know nothing. It's illogical, but he's right. I did know him without knowing him and he knows me without knowing me. And that makes him, and this, dangerous. But now that I know what is happening, and why I should run, I have less desire to do so than ever.

I want him. And as if his mind is in the same place, he says, "I want you, Faith," and then reaches down and rips my dress all the way open. I gasp, shocked, aroused, more aroused. His hands end up at my knees where the final tear allows my dress to fall open, away from my body, but they do not stay there. They glide from my knees, my thighs, and over my hips to the front clasp of my bra that he manages to unhook. It falls away like my dress, replaced by his hands. "I want you, Faith," he repeats. His thumbs stroke my nipples, his cheek pressing to mine, "Like I don't remember ever wanting in my life."

I might reject these words, but there is this raw, and almost tormented quality to his voice, that tells me he doesn't want to feel this whatever it is that is happening, any more than I do. It tells me that he has a past as do I. It echoes with every spiraling emotion inside me, right now, and deep inside every night that I cannot sleep. He pulls back, his eyes meeting mine, and while his expression is impassive, there are shadows in his eyes he doesn't hide, that he lets me see, and I think…I think this is to let me know, that I am not alone. But I am alone, and the fact that I've had this thought is confusing, and yet, somehow I'm not with this man, not this one night, that we dare be whoever it is we are together.

He lifts me, setting me on the counter, his hands on my knees that are now pressed together, my dress hanging from my body.

"Now open for me," he orders softly, but he doesn't press them open himself. He waits for me to open them, giving me the control and taking it at the same time. The look on his face, the warmth in his touch on my legs, promising me salacious wonderful rewards, and a deep throb radiates in my sex. I open my legs, and my dress hangs from my body. His hands settle on my shoulders, branding my skin, under the silk and lace of both the dress and my bra. His gaze lowering, sliding over my breasts, a heavy caress that is not a caress at all, but my nipples pucker, my sex clenches.

Slowly, he inches the material down, over my back and when it falls to the counter behind me, I slip my hands away from it. "I loved this dress," I say.

"I'll buy you a new one," he says.

"No," I say immediately, my hands going to his hands where they rest on my thighs. "No. I do not want you to buy me a dress. I don't want your money, and don't make this about that."

"Make this what?"

"I don't need anything from you but an orgasm. Or two or three, *if* you're up to it."

The blue of his eyes burn, hot coals and simmering heat. "A challenge we can both accept."

"But I still think you need to pay for my dress."

His eyes narrow. "You said—"

"That I don't want money but I want an even playing field." I reach in the drawer beside me, and grab a knife, removing it.

I don't even get it beyond the counter, before Nick grabs my hand, pulling it and the blade, between us, his jaw steel, his voice tight. "What are you doing. Faith?"

Chapter Ten

Tiger

MY FINGERS WRAP FAITH'S SLENDER WRIST, THAT knife between us, but as I look at her, I think that if she intends malice, she's far better an actress than any opponent I've ever faced. I see no intention in her face, nor do I sense any in her energy, see any in her eyes. But this moment damn sure reminds me that I'm not here because this woman rocks my world like no other, despite the fact that she does. I'm here because my father and her mother are dead. Because she is the only logical place murder leads, even if it now feels illogical to me.

"Trust issues much, Nick?" she challenges. "Who was she? Because clearly she fucked with your head."

"You're the one who plays with knives, sweetheart."

"I don't play with knives," she says. "You inspired me."

"Forgive me if I'm not flattered."

"Do you have any particular fondness for that shirt?"

"Actually, I do. It's one of my favorites."

"Good. I felt the same about my dress. You owe me my revenge."

"Revenge is not a word a man wants to hear from a woman with a knife in her hand."

"Trust me and let go of me. I know that's hard for a dominant like yourself, but fear isn't a good shade for you, Tiger. And if it makes you feel any better, if I was going to kill you, I'd get that orgasm you've denied me not once, but twice, first."

"The name is Nick," I say, my gaze sweeping over the knife that just happens to be right in front of her beautiful breasts, before I refocus on her face and add, "unless you attempt to stab me. Then you meet Tiger." And I think I'm losing my fucking mind, because I've decided that letting her have the knife is a good character test. I release her and press my hands on the island on either side of her.

"Now what?" I challenge, the current in the air electric, the push and pull of control between us damn near explosive.

Her eyes narrow, mischief in their depths, but again, I find no malice. More seduction, and playful sexiness that I rarely partake in. I like sex. I like fucking. I don't like games that I don't dictate and my games are not playful. But this woman, she is not like the others, she does not affect me like anyone before her, and the jury is out on whether that is good or bad.

She grabs my shirt and pulls it from my pants, and then takes the knife to the last button. It pops and flies into the air, hitting the ground with a magnified sound. Her gaze lifts to mine, and she says, "Still scared?"

"Don't poke the tiger, sweetheart. You won't like the results."

"I'm not scared," she promises, popping another button, then another, her free hand on my stomach, and if she wasn't holding a knife, I'd move that hand to the damn throbbing in my cock. Instead, she just makes that throb worse, that hand following the path of the knife higher, and farther away from where I want it and her. I endure the torture of not touching her, and patiently at that, until she is finally at my tie, a little too close to my neck for comfort. I grab her wrist again, taking the knife this time, and tangling fingers in her hair. "Are you going to buy me a new shirt?"

"You can buy your own," she says, her fingers tangling in the hair on my chest and not gently, that bite of pain, adrenaline in my veins, her determination to challenge me proving relentless. "And we both know you wouldn't have it any other way," she adds.

I toss the knife into the sink to my left, and before it's even landed, I'm kissing her, drinking her in and this time, and unlike the kiss by the refrigerator, I don't hold back and neither does she. Our tongues connect, stroke, battle…but it is one I *will* win. I will demand everything she has to give me. I want her free will. I want her as exposed as I vowed to make her, and it's not to prove she's a killer. It's for me. For the man in me who not only wants to own this woman, I will. And when she tries to resist, when I sense her trying to withhold even a piece of herself, my hand covers one of her breasts. My fingers stroke her nipple with delicate, sensual touches that become rougher and rougher.

She pants into my mouth, and satisfied that wall she just tried to put up has fallen, I nip her lips, lapping at the offended area before I pull back, fingers still tangled in her hair. I yank at my tie and unbutton the last two buttons still intact, but I don't move away. Not yet. I kiss her again, hard and fast, and while the resistance is gone, the taste of challenge remains on her lips, but it will soon be submission. She just doesn't know it yet.

My hands go to her hips and I lift her off the counter and pull her to me, molding every soft perfect female part of her to my harder body, one hand cupping her sweet little ass. My lips linger just above hers, and damn it, there is this deep ache in me for this woman that is unfamiliar, unwelcomed. The lies I've told her are a fist in my chest that I reject. I have to know the truth and it's not a truth someone just tells.

I squeeze her ass and then draw back and smack it, testing her, feeling out the depth of those nerves she showed me, her comfort level with where I might take her. Making a judgment on where I think she wants me to lead her. She doesn't jolt with the impact. She doesn't act shocked or angry. She leans into me, her body already submitting to me even if her mind has not, her hand covering my hand where it covers her breast. Her message is clear: She wants the kind of escape I've just offered. She wants me to push her to go to places that consume, to leave room for nothing else but the here and now. No fears. No nerves. No emotion, of which I hope like hell does not include guilt.

Whatever particular sins she wishes to escape—and to me emotions that control us are sins—she doesn't just want someone to fuck. She wants that invisible something that she believes I can give her. After two years of trusting no one, she's chosen to gamble on a man who's here to expose more than her passion. If she is guilty of murder or blackmail, or both,

I'm a master in every sense of the word. If she's innocent, I'm a bastard in every sense of the word. I kiss her again, and this time there is anger on my tongue, accusation, my own lies, and maybe hers.

And when I pull back, my anger, my own torment over my actions, her trust, her possible sins and mine, have shifted the mood between us. Intensity that wasn't there moments before pulses between us, a living thing, a band wrapping us, pulling us closer but in a dark, volatile way. Her hands grip my arms, fingers flexing into my skin. Our breathing is ragged, heavy. I scoop her up, aware of how naked she is but for her thigh highs and her high heels, aware she is mine to own now, and mine to destroy if I so please. And she doesn't know it. There is something powerful and arousing about this idea that I'm pretty sure makes me a sick fuck, and I'm accusing her of being no better, she just doesn't know it. But I reject the guilt that pierces a tiny part of my black, steel heart for her and her alone. I'll make being owned feel so good for her.

I carry her to the living room, but I don't take her to the couch. I take her to the rug in front of the fireplace and lower her to her feet in front of me. She reaches for me, and damn, as much as I crave those hands on my skin, I resist and catch her wrists.

"You touch me when I say you can touch me from this point forward."

Her eyes flash with defiance. "And if I don't agree?"

"Then I don't touch you." I walk her to me, her elbows bending, arms resting between us. "We both know what you want from me."

"Which is what?" she demands, a hint of vulnerability in her voice that I find sexy as hell.

"An adrenaline rush. The kind that pushes your limits but comes with a burn for more tomorrow, not with the regret your nerves fear I'll give you. But your hard limit pushes for just that. It says, all or nothing tonight. It says, go there now or there is no chance to go there later. I won't go there now just to live up to your hard limit."

"I didn't set sexual limits. I set a time limit."

"If you didn't have a sexual limit, you wouldn't have gotten spooked earlier and you wouldn't have gone untouched for two years."

"That two years has nothing to do with us tonight."

"It does to me. You have limits. Someone broke them."

"I don't have limits tonight."

"Except one night. And that creates a limit for me. I won't take you too far and find out it's too far, too late, to turn back time. Consider that my new hard limit, added to my promise to make you want more than tonight. Because I do."

"If you plan to treat me like a delicate flower, this ends now."

"I don't do delicate flowers, sweetheart. Cowering females don't get me off. But you aren't that, and you do. You get me off, Faith. But submission isn't weak. It's fearless. It's pleasure. But it's also trust. You have to trust me like I did you with the knife. Trust for trust."

"That's why you let me use that knife."

"I gave you what I give no one. My submission."

She laughs. "That wasn't submission."

"As close as you'll ever get from me. But that's not what you want from me anyway, now is it?"

"No," she whispers. "It isn't."

116

"And I want your trust, but I'm not demanding it. I'm asking you to let me earn it."

"You're asking?"

"Yes. I'm asking. Do what I say, but tell me to stop at any time. Just say stop. Or no. Or whatever language you want to use. I'm not the man who'll tell you no means yes. Understand?"

"I understand that you are not what I expected."

"Is that good or bad?"

"I haven't decided."

"That's a good answer. Because you shouldn't, and if you did, you wouldn't be the woman that has me this fucking hard." I lean in and brush my lips over hers, licking into her mouth, before I add, "You taste like temptation and I am never tempted." I inhale. "And you smell like amber and vanilla, not flowers tonight. This suits you better than the flowers."

She breathes out with those words, her face lowering as if I've punched her in the chest. I release her wrist and cup her face. "What was that?"

"You talk too much and ask questions I don't invite. Fuck me or leave."

Her tone is defensive, but I've observed and pushed enough people in depositions and in the courtroom to know torment when I see it. And I don't like where torment leads us. I don't want to be there with her right now. "You're right. Too many words." I rotate her and press my hands to her shoulders, stepping into her, lowering my head. "Trust for trust. On your knees, Faith."

She inhales deeply, but she does as I order, kneeling in front of me, and her spine is straight, her hands on her knees. A submissive position, and more and more, I am curious about her past, her sexual coming of age that she then denied until tonight. I squat behind her, stroking her hair away from her neck, my hand on her naked shoulder, my lips at her ear. "I own your pleasure for the rest of the night." I brush my lips over her ear lobe. "And we're going to start by getting you out of your own head." My lips trail down her neck to her shoulder, where my teeth scrape before my tongue soothes that bite. "A nice guy doesn't bite."

"And you're not a nice guy," she whispers.

"Nice guys are boring," I say, caressing down her arm and back up again, my fingers stroking the edge of her breast in both directions, "but you already know that, now don't you?"

"But safe. They're safe."

"Like I said," I gently tease her nipple, "you didn't want a nice guy." I cup her breast and meld it to my palm, two fingers tugging at her nipple. She reaches up to cup my hand, something I've noticed she does often, and I lean into her. "You don't touch me unless I tell you to touch me."

"I want to touch you, Nick."

"And I want you to touch me, sweetheart. But not yet. Now, you let me take you where you want to go. Put your hands on the stool."

She pants out a breath and does as I command, her palms flattening in front of her, and I notice her nails, a simple gloss, not manicured and fake. I don't think she's fake. Just guarded. I cup her face and lean around her. "Don't move," I murmur against her lips, kissing her, a slow lick of tongue against tongue before I release her, standing and removing a condom from my wallet. I tear it open, making sure she hears it, that she knows she doesn't have to think. I'm protecting her. I shove the package back into my pocket and unzip my pants, rolling the condom over my painfully thick erection, but I leave my pants on, removing the ease of slipping inside her, that is tempting, but now is not that time.

I go down on a knee beside her, my hand on her lower back and slender belly. "Elbows on the stool," I order, and the moment she complies, I lift her hips, placing her on all fours, my hand on her lower back, my lips pressing between her shoulder blades. She arches forward, and I reach under her, teasing one of her nipples, my hand sliding to her backside. "Do you know what I'm going to do to you?"

"Spank me," she whispers.

"Yes," I say, squeezing her backside. "I'm going to spank you, but I won't hurt you."

"What fun is that?"

There is that challenge again, and I caress her shoulder blades with one hand, while the other pinches her nipple, tugging it roughly. She arches forward while her backside lifts into the air just as I expect. I immediately give her nipple another tug, moving my other hand down to her backside and over it, stopping right above her sex. I give her a slight smack there, not meant to cause any pain, just pleasure. I earn a gasp and can hear her breathing now.

"What's your tolerance level, Faith?"

"I don't know."

But she does know. No one plays in this world, and leaves it, without knowing her limits. She just doesn't want to give them to me. That answer, the knife, the lack of sexual limits. They fit a pattern that says hard limit. One night. I get nothing else, not even all of her tonight, but there is another layer to this. The layer that screams abuse. I lift her and move her to the stool, placing her hands on my knees.

"Tolerance level, Faith. I'm not—"

"I don't know," she hisses. "Don't you get it? I don't know, Nick. That's an honest answer. I don't know what worked for me. I don't know what felt like too much because of who I was with and what was too much because it hit the wrong buttons for me. All I know is that I wanted this tonight. And I want you to put me back on my knees and finish what you started for once."

There she goes. Pushing me. Challenging me, but I don't let anyone push me. I study her, search her face, and she says, "That is as honest as I have been with anyone in a very long time, Nick. I need—"

I pull her to my lap, straddling me, my hand at her face. "I know what you need," I say, kissing her, tasting that need, tasting what I've wanted to taste on her lips every time I've kissed her. Honesty. Hunger. Need. But it's real now. She's real, at least one part of her wall has crumbled. "And I'm going to give it to you."

I stand up with her, carrying her to the couch where I sit down next to the arm, with her still on top of me, those gorgeous legs of hers spread across me. Her hands press to my shoulders, and I fill my hands with her breasts, my thumbs stroking her nipples, my head lowering, tongue lapping at one stiff peak and then another. "Please tell me why you still have clothes on," she whispers, sounding desperate, breathless, and I like her breathless.

"I'd be inside you already otherwise," I say.

"What's wrong with you being inside me?"

My hands settle at her waist. "It's not time," I say, my

gaze raking over her body, her long blonde hair draping her shoulders, touching the tops of her high, full breasts. Her plump, tight nipples are rosy red. "On your knees beside me and then lay across my lap, Faith."

Chapter Eleven

Faith

I WANT HIM TO SPANK ME. I WANT TO FEEL HIS HAND ON my backside. I want that sting and shock that leaves no room for anything else. No worry. No loss. No death. No guilt. And no room for the way Nick makes me feel too much. The way Nick sees too much. The way he seems to peel back layers I don't want peeled back. The way he exposes me emotionally. I just want him to fuck me. I just want this to be what it was supposed to be. Nameless, empty sex.

I move to bend over his lap, but he catches my hips, his gaze probing mine, penetrating, and I want to look away, but I have learned that will only make him look harder, dig deeper. So I meet his stare, and I mask my emotions that I can't even name. His eyes narrow on me, a flicker of something I also cannot name in their depths. His hands fall away from me, a silent offer of freedom and that free will he vowed to pull from me. And he has it. I want this and him. Of that, I cannot even begin to deny, nor did I intend to when I invited him here.

And so, I take that free will and settle my knees on the couch facing his legs. But nothing with Nick is just fucking, which is what I know, what I understand. He wraps his arm around my waist, tangling fingers in my hair, leading my mouth to his, and then kissing me until I think I might shatter. "I'll warn you before I spank you," he says. "Understand?"

"Yes," I whisper, and just hearing him say "spank you" has my sex aching, and my nipples tingling. As if he realizes this, as if he can read my mind, or perhaps just my body, he leans over and licks one of the stiff peaks, swirling it with his tongue, and then sucking it deep, teeth scraping ever so slightly, the pull on my nipple like a pull on my sex.

His hands move to my hips, mouth trailing lower, and lower, and suddenly, I don't want that spanking as much as I want his mouth on the most intimate part of me. But he stops short, pressing his mouth to my belly and lingering there, his tongue flicking, licking, before he looks at me, and says, "Not yet, Faith. I want you across my lap, on your elbows, backside up." There is a command to his voice that I have always resisted from others, resented even, but for reasons I cannot explain with this man, I'm aroused, vulnerable in just how much he affects me. But most striking is the moment I dare to submit, to spread my body across his, his hand on my belly and lower back. There are nerves tingling and fluttering through me, but no dread, no fear. Things I know as preludes to pain that lead to oblivion, things that perhaps, I wanted tonight, because I feel like I deserve them. But just aren't here now and I do not know why. I don't know this man. I can't trust this man, but my body appears to disagree.

"Ah, Faith," he murmurs, running a hand up my spine. "How did you manage to go untouched for two years? You are too beautiful to be left untouched." His voice is low, gravelly.

I was too damaged to be touched, I think. I needed a break. I needed something that I couldn't have. I need something that felt as right as this man's hands on my body. His teeth scrape my hip, his tongue following, and I'm really starting to like that combination. That tongue that I know is wicked magic, but always denies me the reward of that magic. He caresses a path to my backside, and at the same time, his other hand finds my sex, cupping it. And then he is stroking my bottom at the same time as he is stroking my clit, teasing me, touching me until I am so wet and aroused that the ache in my sex is as fierce as the ache I know will come from his palm.

"Faith," he breathes out, and I don't know why, but it feels like a question. Am I ready? Am I okay? Am I sure?

"Yes," I say. "Yes. And yes."

His reply is not in words. He begins to pat my backside, just above my sex, while deft fingers slide through the wet heat of my body, an attack on my senses from all directions. And we are never going to get to the spanking because I'm going to come. Or maybe that's the idea. He wants me to come. He wants the sting to be lost in the pleasure. But I don't want that. I want the sting. I want—"Nick," I pant out again, so close, I am about to tumble over.

His hands still, and he replies with, "That's what I wanted, sweetheart," seeming to understand exactly what I was telling him. "You on the edge, but not there yet. I'm going to spank you now, Faith. Seven times. The first two will be the hardest, but they will get softer from there. Count them out. Repeat that."

"Count," I say, adrenaline setting my heart into a gallop. "Harder then softer."

"And then I'm going to fuck you, Faith. I'm going to turn you around, and you're going to ride me. Understand?"

"Yes. Please stop talking or my heart is going to explode from my chest."

"Deep breath, sweetheart. This isn't new to you, but I am. And I'm not going to hurt you."

I have no flippant remark this time. His hand is caressing my cheeks, warming them, as it should be, but too often, I have known a hard palm with no preparation. But he doesn't rush. One second. Two. Three. Four. "Nick," I plead.

"Now, sweetheart," he says, and I barely have time to realize the impact of that endearment before his palm is on my backside, a hard sting that arches my back and oh God. It's back. "Count," he orders.

"Two," I breathe out.

And another. "Three." I can't breathe, and fingers are stroking my sex. I forget to count but he does it for me. "Four," he says, and then another palm, softer now, just as he promised.

"Five," I breathe out.

"Six," he says, that gravelly tone to his voice is back now, the force of his palm on my skin following.

"Seven," I breathe out, and it's done. He smacks my backside and then to my shock, his mouth is on it, kissing it, a strange tenderness to that act that I swear has me as breathless as the spanking. And then he is turning me to face him, cradling my body against his, his mouth coming down on mine, and it too is tender, a slide of tongue, but I can feel his passion, his need that he controls, as he has me.

"Tell me you're okay," he demands.

"I am," I say, shocked that he's asked, that I believe he cares.

"You're sure?"

"Yes," I promise, my hand on his face. "I liked it. I like it so much that it's…"

He is kissing me again then, and this kiss is different. This kiss is hungry, greedy even, and fierce. Addictive. Seductive. And it unlocks those things in me. I am kissing him back, and kissing him and kissing him. And he is touching me and I am touching him, hard, sinewy muscle beneath my palms. And I can't get enough and that is what I feel from him. It's not enough but we try to find that place where it is, where it will be. And some part of me knows that he's given me what I want. There is nothing but this man, and yet, this experience is nothing as I expected. It's good now.

I am so lost in Nick that I barely remember him pulling me around to straddle him or how his pants got down. But they are, and his thick shaft is between us. I reach down and stroke it, and I revel in the low groan that slides from his lips. "I feel like I've needed this since before I ever fucking met you." His hands go to my waist and he lifts me while I guide his cock to my sex, and press him inside me. He's so hard, so big, stretching me, filling me, and it's been so long, and I can barely catch my breath. I breathe out as I take all of him, and finally, we've reached the place where we are here, wherever here really is.

But we don't move. We're staring at each other, and there is this magnetic pull between us that has nothing to do with sex. Or maybe it does. I just don't know. But I feel this man inside and out. I feel him and see him as he does me and it's not what I wanted, and yet, I am hypnotized by this moment, by him. A charge seems to spark suddenly between us, and we snap. He moves first, or maybe we move together, but he's cupping my head, and my breast, and as our lips collide, I reach around him to the band at his hair and pull it free, sinking fingers in the long strands that surely must touch his shoulders. I tug on them, using them as an outlet for all the crazy sensations pulsing through my body.

Nick deepens the kiss, and then we are moving, swaying, *fucking*. Slow. Fast. Slow again. Our mouths lingering a breath apart before we erupt into wildness again. And I don't want this to end. I don't want to go back to reality. I want to stay lost in this man. And I fight to make that happen, to stay right here with him, but the build of pleasure is fierce, the passion on his tongue, in his touch, consumes me, and I have been so on edge for so long. And when he pulls me hard against him, thrusting into me as he does, I am there, in that sweet place that tenses my body.

The next moment, I'm tumbling over, my body spasming around him, my head buried in his shoulder. He wraps his arm around my waist, and thrusts again, a guttural sound sliding from his lips as he shudders beneath me. Time spirals and sways until we collapse into each other, and for long moments, neither of us move. We just lay there, breathing together, heavy, then slower and softer. And still we linger. It's Nick that breaks this silence. "Faith, sweetheart," he says softly, cupping my face. "As much as I want to hold you like this the rest of the night, and I will again, I had better take care of this condom before we make baby Tigers."

We won't, I think. We can't, but I don't say that to him.

"Yes. Of course." I start to move away, but he shifts us and rolls me to my back, pulling out before he says, "Always trying to run."

My brow furrows. "How was that running?"

"It was in your eyes."

"It wasn't in my eyes."

"No?"

"No."

I wrap his hair in my hand. "Why does an attorney of your stature get away with long hair?"

"I am nothing anyone expects. And that works for me. Does it work for *you*, Faith?"

I release his hair, and my fingers curl on what I now know to be perpetual stubble on his jaw. "It pisses me off," I say, honestly, because I still don't want to want this man, and I am so far from fucking him out of my system, as he'd suggested, that it's almost laughable.

His eyes darken. "I'll take that for now." He covers my hand with his and brings it to his mouth, kissing it. "Where's the bathroom, sweetheart?"

"My bedroom is the closest one," I say. "The door right behind you." He kisses me and grabs a blanket from the back of the couch, to cover me. "I'll keep you warm when I get back." He stands and adjusts his pants.

I sit up. "You didn't even get undressed."

"The night is young," he says, giving me a wink that sets that flutter in my belly to life again, before he heads to the bedroom.

I watch him cross the room, the muscles of his back flexing, confidence in his every step. He's gorgeous and unexpected in every way. *I'm* unexpected with him. I've been tied up, flogged, paddled, displayed, clamped and more, and as time went on, to extremes that didn't arouse me or make me cower. They made me angry. They made me withdraw, but not out of fear. Out of self-respect, something the past few months made me lose, I realize now. And so I went with Nick, telling myself he would take me back to that punishing place, but he was right. On some level, I knew that wasn't true.

He is the unexpected.

Different than what I've known. And I'm different with him. He didn't spank me hard, he didn't push me to uncomfortable places, and yet he pushed me. I felt exposed and vulnerable with him in ways that I have never felt before. I don't want to be exposed, and I glance at the bedroom, and in light of these thoughts, I wonder why I've sent him to my most private space alone. I stand up, and the straps at my ankles cut into my skin, reminding me I still have my heels on. I sit back down and quickly unclip them and kick them off, then wrap the barely there throw around my shoulders, and hurry across the living area. Entering the bedroom, I hear Nick talking on the phone. "It's nearly midnight, kid. I give you an A for dedication but an F for strategy. You still aren't going at this the right way."

Relief washes over me as I realize his delay isn't about nosing around my room, like a man like Nick would care about my personal items. He's talking to his associate again.

"Okay," Nick says. "Let's try this another way. How do you think he perceives himself? That's what you need to find out in questioning him, then use that to finish the questioning." He's silent a moment before he says, "Because how he perceives himself reveals strength and weakness, and we need to know what both of those things are."

My brow furrows with Nick's comment. How do I perceive myself? I think about this. And I think some more and I don't have an answer. I don't know me anymore. Maybe that's why I don't know the woman who Nick just brought to her knees in so many ways. Who Nick seemed to know when I did not. My gaze catches on the card on the bed and I walk to it. I stare down at my father's script, a knot in my belly. I pick it up and sit down, the low pedestal allowing my feet to easily touch the ground, and when the blanket begins to fall from my shoulders, I don't even try to catch it. I just stare at the card, trying to convince myself to open it but what's the point? It won't surprise me the way Nick has. I know what it says. I know what he thinks of me and what he expects. Those thoughts and expectations have driven every moment of my life for two years. I just don't want the reinforcement of him saying it again from his grave on this particular day.

"Faith."

I look up to find Nick standing in front of me, and I never even heard him approach. He goes down on one knee, draping my pink silk robe around my shoulders. "I thought you might want this."

There is a protective quality to his actions, again unexpected, and unfamiliar in every way. No one protects me, and I don't know what to do, how to react. It scares me how good it feels to have someone actually care, what I feel or need, and I know that I cannot allow myself to want or need. But it's a moment in time, one night, and I cannot wish it, or him, away, any more than I could the chance to experience that art display tonight.

I stuff an arm into the robe, and shift the card to my opposite hand, then do the same on the other side. Nick reaches down and grips the silk, his gaze raking over my breasts, a touch that is not a touch, my nipples and sex aching all over again. But he doesn't touch me. He doesn't turn this into sex. He pulls the robe closed and ties it for me, our eyes locking and holding as he does. And it is then that I see the shadows in the depths of his stare, and for the first time since meeting him, I see beyond the arrogance and sexuality of the man. I see his own torment. I see a man as damaged as me, and I think, maybe, just maybe that's why our connection is so very intense. That something I felt when we were naked and lost in each other, moves between us again, a living, breathing thing that bands around us. "Is it from him?"

I don't play naive. He means the card and he knows there was someone in my life. "No," I say, and I shouldn't say more, but yet, I do. "I don't talk to him."

"Ever?"

"Ever."

"For how long?"

"Most of that two years I mentioned."

"But the card—"

"It's from my father. He died two years ago, but apparently left it with Frank for me on my thirtieth birthday."

Nick glances at his Rolex but I am looking at the craftsmanship of the black and orange tiger tattoo covering his entire right forearm. "You still have fifteen minutes to read it on your birthday."

I give a humorless laugh and set the card on the bed. "If I read that, I might need you to spank me again but harder and longer this time."

"Then you should read it before I have to go back to San Francisco Sunday night."

I don't miss the inference he's going to stay with me until then, but any right or wrong I might feel from that is muted by the fact that he'll be gone. This will be over.

He sits down next to me and as his hand settles on my knee, allowing me to catch another glimpse of his tattoo, the black and orange ink evident now. Curious, I reach for his arm and turn it over to study the detail of the beautifully detailed blue-eyed tiger etched into his skin. "It has your eyes," I say, glancing up at him. "*Tiger.*"

"That was the artist's idea."

"Who did it?"

"I had it done six months ago by someone Chris knows in Paris, actually. A guy named Tristan."

"He's incredible. I'd be terrified to ink someone's skin."

"Your ink would be as incredible as your art, Faith."

I look up at him. "You don't have to keep complimenting me."

"I'm no sweet talker, Faith. Surely you know that by now. You're talented, and like my tattoo, your art is a part of you, Faith."

Rejecting the many places those words could take me right now, I quickly grab his other arm and study the ink there. Just words that read: *An eye for an eye.*

"That one I got in college," he says, but I barely hear him speak, the phrase replaying in my mind: An eye for an eye, clawing at me, to the point that I feel like I'm bleeding inside. I can feel the rise of emotions, when only yesterday I was afraid because I could feel nothing. I jump to my feet, and try to escape Nick, but he grabs my arm and turns me to face him.

"What just happened, Faith?"

133

"I don't know if I should admire you or fear you, Nick Rogers. *Tiger.*"

His eyes narrow, his energy sharpening and he pulls me between his legs, hands on my hips. "Why would you fear me, Faith?"

Chapter Twelve

Tiger

I STARE AT FAITH, WAITING FOR HER REPLY, AND WHILE I DO not share my father's name, I cannot dismiss the possibility that her reaction to my tattoo is about her knowing who I am. That she always knew and she's a damn good actress. That she knows that the words "*an eye for an eye*" etched in my arm motivated me to come for her and she's trying to manipulate me as I suspect her mother did my father. And the idea that he and I, men who do not get manipulated, could be by a mother and daughter, grinds along my nerve endings. Or maybe my tattoo, and the words it spells out, simply stir guilt in Faith over the sins I suspect her of, which isn't much better. Or it could be something else entirely, and considering the way she's rocked my world, I hope like hell it is.

My fingers flex at her hips where I've pulled her between my legs, I repeat my question. "*Why* would you *fear me,* Faith?"

"I said admire or fear." Her hands close down on mine. "Why are you honing in on the fear?"

"It's a strange thing to say, sweetheart."

"Don't call me sweetheart with that condescending tone. And you're shocked about the word fear? Really? This from a man who admitted to me in the gallery bathroom that people fear you?"

"But not you. You said not you."

"I don't fear the Nick Rogers with me now. But the words 'an eye for an eye' infer that you might love hard, but you hate harder. That's who you are, right? You'll tear my throat out if I ever cross you? Which, I guess makes it a good thing that I have that hard limit. We fuck. You leave. *Now,* if you want."

Relief washes over me, and the intensity of it, my desire for her innocence, shakes me to the core. I do not get personally involved, but then, I don't fuck my friends or enemies, either. I fuck for release. For pleasure. And she's personal. In more ways than I expected. "I don't want to leave and until you saw my tattoo, you didn't want me to leave."

"I don't want your kind of viciousness in my life."

"You knew I was Tiger before you ever invited me here. But let's clear up who Tiger is. Who *Nick Rogers* is. I don't hate. It's a dangerous emotion that feeds irrational actions. And as for 'an eye for an eye'… I began my career in criminal law, and in fact, did a two-year stint in the DA's office that started when I was a law student. I got my tattoo after putting a man on death row for brutally raping and killing a fifteen-year-old girl. So, fuck yeah. An eye for an eye. Only, he's not dead yet, but you can bet I'll be in the front row when he does."

She breathes out. "Oh."

"Yes. Oh." I fist my hand and show her my forearm again. "Those words," I say. "They do matter to me. I read them often when I'm protecting someone who's been done wrong. I deliver justice."

She stares at my arm for long seconds before she reaches down and covers the tattoo with her hand, her eyes meeting mine. "I'm sorry. I'm afraid I reacted prematurely and convicted you for someone else's sins."

"Him," I say, referring to the man in her past that I have a good idea is the artist she lived with in LA.

"You keep going back to *him*."

"Because he's in the room now and he was with us when we were fucking, Faith."

"This is one night," she argues.

"This is whatever it turns out to be," I amend. "And for the record, I don't stay the night with women or have them stay with me, but I'm not leaving without a fight and at least three more orgasms. Yours. Not mine. And as for *him*, I keep going back to him because he's the reason you might try to insist that I leave. He's the reason you just tried to push me away over my tattoo. And if I'm right, he's the reason you keep everyone at arm's length."

"You don't know me well enough to make a statement like that."

I've studied her for three weeks, obsessed over the details of her life like I do every case I take on, because I win. I always win. I know her better than she thinks. But I settle for, "I know enough."

She studies me for several long beats, her expression

tight, her voice tighter as she says, "Macom Maloy. That's his name and 'an eye for an eye' was his justification for doing something I consider unforgiveable."

"Unforgiveable," I repeat. "That sounds personal." And, I silently add, perhaps like murder and blackmail.

"I'm not going to talk about this or him," she says firmly, her gaze meeting mine, no coyness. No cowering, no lowered lashes and turned head. Just straight up. No more conversation. She's not having it.

"I'll let it go," I concede, clear on the fact that if I push, she'll push back and I'll end up at the door. "But I'm not him." I fist my hand and show her the tattoo again. "I do believe in these words. I do live by 'an eye for an eye,' but I apply that in a controlled fashion, and I fight for those I protect."

She covers the tattoo with her hand again, but she searches my face, studying me, looking for the truth in my words before she says, "I believe you, but sometimes the need to punish—*an eye for an eye*—gets out of control, Nick. Maybe it hasn't for you. Maybe it has. But be careful. It could."

I cover her hand with mine where it rests on my arm, my eyes never leaving hers. "That's a sign of weakness and I am not weak."

"Until you are."

"Not gonna happen, sweetheart. I have a spine of steel."

"There's that arrogance again."

"Yes. There it is. Like I said. It works for me." My jaw clenches with my need to ask her more questions that I just promised not to ask. "How about those pancakes, sweetheart? I haven't eaten since about three today."

"That's it?" she asks, sounding dumbfounded. "You aren't going to press me for more? I'm used to you pushing too much and too hard."

"I told you I wouldn't." I stand up and cup her face. "I pushed to get you to say yes to me, Faith. I pushed to get here. I'm not going to push to get kicked out the door. And free will, sweetheart, does not just apply to sex. So," I pause, and ask again, "how about those pancakes?"

She blinks at me, seemingly stunned by me actually doing what I said I'd do, which tells me more about Macom. I might be a bastard, but not his kind of bastard. "I can't make you pancakes, Nick," she says firmly.

"I pissed you off that bad, did I? You're going to starve me?"

She smiles and damn she's pretty when she smiles. "I actually don't have eggs or milk in the house. I'm not here often."

"I see. What do you have?"

"Cereal."

"But no milk."

"Right. And boxes of macaroni and cheese but—"

"No milk."

"Right." Her eyes light. "But I do have lots of ice cream. This is my cheat place. I eat junk here."

"Ice cream it is then."

She points to the bathroom. "But I'm going in there first. I'll be right back."

"I'm going to the car to get a t-shirt."

"You have a t-shirt in your car?"

"I always keep an extra suit, jeans, and a t-shirt, in the car." I give her a wink. "You never know when someone might slice off all your buttons." I pull her to me, kiss her, and head for the door as her laughter follows. I pause under the archway and she does the same at the bathroom entrance.

She laughs again. "You should have seen your face when I pulled that knife, Nick. I mean, I get it. I should have known it would freak you out. I'm a stranger and all, but you looked like you'd just realized you gone home with Chucky's Bride." She turns earnest. "But don't worry. I'm not as easily provoked as she is." She laughs again and disappears into the bathroom, leaving me to scrub my jaw and run a hand through my hair. *Holy fuck.* She's joking about being a killer and the ways that could fuck with my mind right now, if I let it, are too many.

Exiting into the living room, I head down the hallway, and when I reach the foyer I stop dead in my tracks as darkness greets me. The light was on when we came into the house. Suspecting a bad bulb, and feeling rather protective of this woman I ironically came here to prove is a killer and who ironically just joked about being one, I walk to the switch and flip it on. Frowning, I decide it must be on a timer the security company has installed. I unlock the door, and exit to the porch, and make my way to my car, where I open my trunk, and when I would grab my overnight bag, I am instead drawn to the identical one next to it. I unzip it and pull out the two death certificates on top, both with the same cause of death: heart attack. Two months apart. Also in the bag is every detail of Faith's life, and her family's, heavily focused on her mother, none of it leading me to a clear answer. But I've looked in the eyes of more than one killer and I'd bet my practice that Faith isn't a killer, but not my life. Not quite yet. Not when I'm smart enough to know that I want this woman beyond reason. But if I'm right, and she's innocent, where that conclusion leads me, I don't know. But the woman. She leads me right back in the door, to her.

I grab my overnight, open it and pull on a white t-shirt,

slipping it over my head, and then pull the zipper, and settle the bag on my shoulder. Shutting the trunk, I waste no time crossing the lawn and re-entering the house. I lock up and flip off the light, having no intention of going anywhere tonight but Faith's bed. Traveling the hallway, I find Faith in the kitchen, standing at a pantry with her back to me, my lips curving at the sight of her bra hanging on the door handle. Her dress is laying on top of the trashcan and I make a mental note to find that dress and buy her another one, pretty damn certain good ol' Macom is behind her dislike of other people's money. Which sure doesn't lend to the premise of Faith being involved in blackmail.

Walking to Faith's bedroom, I'm presumptive enough to drop my bag inside the door, and then return to the kitchen. She obviously hears me this time, glancing over her shoulder from the pantry she's still studying. "I have cherry Pop Tarts," she says, facing me. "Cool Ranch Doritos, protein bars, and microwave popcorn."

"The protein bars and popcorn don't fit the cheating while you're here theme."

"Sometimes I feel guilty after all the Doritos and ice cream, and force myself to eat protein bars and popcorn."

"Ah," I say. "Makes sense." And it makes her all the more adorable and she doesn't seem to know it. "Not to dismiss the delicacy of cherry Pop Tarts, Doritos, protein bars, and popcorn," I continue, "but what happened to the ice cream?"

"My favorite choice is well stocked," she says, opening the bottom drawer freezer and waving a hand across it. "I have Haagen-Dazs only because it's my favorite. My top choice: pralines and cream which is so very, *very* incredible."

"Two verys. That sounds serious."

"It is. It's addictive."

Like her, I think, when normally it's simply fucking a beautiful woman I find addictive, until it's over.

"I also have rum raisin," Faith continues, "and I promise you. You can't go wrong with rum raisin."

"I've heard that," I say, my tone serious. "You can never go wrong with rum raisin."

She smiles. "Don't joke. I take rum raisin very seriously."

"Only one 'very,'" I point out. "I predict you choose the praline."

"I'm still deciding," she says. "And so are you, because I also have two pints of coconut pineapple which sounds simple, but it's creamy and sweet and addictive." Her hands go to her hips. "And each of these pints contain my entire day's calorie intake, but I haven't eaten all day so I don't care."

"Nerves over the show?"

"Yes. Nerves and the birthday thing. You know. You self-analyze and do all those things the big birthdays make you do. But it's over. No more of that." She points at the freezer, but not before I see the flicker of emotion in her eyes I can't quite name. "What's your sin?" she asks, glancing back at me, her expression checked now.

You, I think, but I say, "I'll take the coconut pineapple," and reach down, grabbing a pint before adding, "because sweet and addictive is exactly what I want right now." I watch her cheeks flush over that comment, when in contrast, her bold order for me to spank her had not. Beautiful, sinful in bed, and sweet when she's not. I might be fucking in love. "What about you?" I ask. "What's your sin, Faith?"

"I'm pretty sure it's you," she dares to say. "But as for the ice cream. Praline." She grabs her pick, shuts the freezer and

142

then walks to a drawer to grab two spoons, which she holds up. "No knives, I promise." She clunks her pint on the counter. "Though I think I might need to cut this, it's so solid."

I motion to the living room. "The fireplace will soften it up."

"And warm me up," she says, shivering. "The freezer gave me chills." She darts past me, my gaze following her to note her bare legs and pink fluffy slippers. Adorable all right, and I'm so fucking hard all over again, she might as well be wearing leather and a g-string, which is exactly why I need to keep my pink, fuzzy slipper-wearing woman away from the knife drawer until I'm one hundred percent sure she isn't a killer.

Chapter Thirteen

Tiger

PURSUING FAITH, SOMETHING I'VE BEEN DOING SINCE I first learned she existed but she just doesn't know it, I follow her into the living room. I find her snuggled under a cream-colored blanket I saw on one of the chairs, her ice cream already by the fire. I join her and sit down with my back against the stool I'd had her sprawled over earlier, and set my pint next to hers by the fire.

She gives me a thoughtful look. "You *know*," she says. "I'll believe you're staying when you take your shoes off."

I chuckle. "Is that the way you know a man's staying the night?"

"It seems like a good marker," she says. "Not that I've had to make that determination any time in recent history."

I'm not sorry at all, nor am I chuckling anymore. "Do you want me to stay, Faith?"

"Hard limit," she says, her voice a bit raspy. "I get tonight." And when I arch my brow at the less than conclusive answer, she adds, "Yes. I do." Definitive. No shyness to her.

I don't even try to hide the satisfaction in my stare. I reach down and unlace one of my shoes. She unlaces the other for me, tugging it off. I toss the other one. "How's that?"

"Better," she says, giving me a once over. "It somehow makes you less assuming and down to earth."

"Assuming," I say dryly. "That's right up there with arrogant."

"But arrogant works for you," she says. "You said so." Her brow furrows. "And how are you here when you have a big case next week?"

"I do my best prep work locked away from the rest of the world," I say. "And I've got another situation here. I actually rented a house for three months."

"Three months," she repeats, and this time she looks away, reaching for her ice cream, but I lay down beside her on my side, resting on my elbow. "Faith."

She inhales and looks at me, her expression guarded. "Yes?"

"The ice cream hasn't had time to thaw and what you're really thinking about right now is the fact that I'm here for three months."

She sets the ice cream back down. "You didn't tell me that."

"I'm telling you now."

"I don't know what to say to that."

"There's a first. You usually snap right back."

"I still don't know what to say to that."

"Well then, just remember this. You can hate me in the morning just as easily if I have a rental house here or if I don't."

"Am I *going* to hate you, Nick?"

"*No,* Faith. You are not."

She studies me for several beats, and then says, "You owe me a story."

"A story? I thought I owed you an orgasm."

"I'm pretty sure you owe me three orgasms, but just one story."

"What story are we talking about?" I ask, and it hits me then that she doesn't blush when we're talking sex, and yet, her art, her beauty…these things make her blush. She's sterilized to sex, not so unlike myself. It's physical. It's not emotional.

"Your trial story," she replies. "The one that made your opposing council on your new case your enemy. You said you had to throw out good evidence because he obtained it illegally, but you still won the case."

"What interests you about that story?"

"Aside from the fact that I like stories where people beat the odds, how you handled that case seems to me to be a crossing road for you. You chose to go the hard road rather than the easy road, and still you're a success."

I narrow my eyes on her, certain this is a masked reference to herself, maybe even to her walking away from blackmail and murder.

"What kind of case was it?" she asks.

"Insider trading," I say. "We were representing the CEO of a large tech company. I'll spare you the dirty accusations against him, but he was set up by a competitor. I managed to find someone who not only testified to the set-up, she had documents and recordings to prove it. But I found her in the hundredth hour, let me tell you."

"And you and your co-chair became eternal enemies."

"Considering I went to the board afterward and reported him, yes."

"After telling him you wouldn't?"

"The devil is in the details, sweetheart. I didn't lie to him. I never told him I wouldn't go to the board. But he lied to me. He told me he'd destroy the illegally-obtained evidence, but he kept it until the day of closing. And I already told you. I can't stand a damn liar, and I damn sure wasn't giving him another chance to burn me or the firm."

"And you got him fired," she assumes.

"That's the insanity of this story. The board chose to reprimand him instead of fire him."

She blanches. "After he broke the law?"

"Yes. After he broke the law. They also offered me partner, and at twenty-eight that would have made me the youngest in their history."

"And you declined."

"In two flat seconds. If they felt his behavior was appropriate, I damn sure wasn't signing up for a bigger piece of that liability."

"And he's still with them?"

"They gave him my partnership spot, which tells you, they're born of his same cloth."

"So this case is personal to you," she adds.

"No case is personal to me," I say, my own words an unfriendly reminder of the fact that I've made her personal. "When you get personal," I add, a warning to myself as I speak it, "you end up on the bottom with everyone else on top."

"Yes," she agrees, and when she says nothing more, again reaching for her ice cream, that one word becomes loaded.

"Yes?" I prod, as she removes the lid to her ice cream and jabs her spoon inside.

"Yes," she says, offering nothing more but my pint of ice cream, which she shoves into my hand. "It's ready." And then before I can press further, she moves on, "Did you leave and open your firm, or did that come later?"

I pull the lid off my pint. "I left and opened my firm. Ten years ago next month."

She hands me a spoon. "Why San Francisco, and not L.A.?"

"I can do everything I can do there in San Francisco, with fewer assholes and less traffic."

"Yes," she says. "There are."

"You're very agreeable," I say. "That's different for you."

"You haven't said anything outrageous for me to call you on in at least fifteen minutes. But I'm sure you can remedy that if you try really hard."

"That's more like it," I say, watching as she scoops up ice cream and takes a bite.

"Hmmm," she sighs. "I love this stuff." She motions to me with her spoon. "Try yours. I'm dying to know if you like it."

I reach over and take a bite of hers. "Yes. It's delicious."

She smiles and sticks her spoon in my ice cream before taking a bite and then says, "A spoon for a spoon."

"Like trust for trust?" I ask.

Her mood is instantly somber. "Trust does matter to me, Nick."

I feel a punch in my chest with those words and my betrayal, but I have to know she's innocent, and this is about murder. Evidence is everything. "No lies," I say, hoping like hell mine are the only ones between us. "Tell me something about you."

She settles back underneath her blanket, the withdrawal in the action easy to read, even before she says, "You already know about me. You researched me."

"Tell me what documents and the internet can't. The important parts. Who are you, Faith?"

She takes a bite of ice cream and I do the same times three, its sweetness easier to swallow than the idea that she might not be what she seems, what I want her to be. "Faith?" I press, when she doesn't immediately reply.

"I'm just trying to figure out what there is to tell outside what you know. I mean the checklist is pretty obvious. My father died two years ago. My mother died two months ago."

"That's how you define yourself?"

"Death does a lot to define us."

"I disagree," I say. "Life defines us. And yes, before you ask. I've known death. My mother died in a car accident when I was thirteen. My father died a month ago."

She stares at me, her expression remarkably impassive. "I'm not going to offer you awkward condolences."

"I appreciate that, but most people *don't* offer me condolences."

"I guess that's the difference for women than men, which is really pretty messed up."

"The difference is, I not only wasn't close to my father, but no one around me even knew him. And I'm an obvious hard-ass."

"My mother was well-known in Sonoma," she says. "You said you weren't close to your father? Didn't he raise you after

150

your mother died?"

"The many versions of a nanny my father wanted to fuck raised me after I ended up back with him."

"I see," she says, and I sense she wants to ask, or say, something more, but she's too busy rebuilding that wall to let it happen.

"Why'd you leave L.A.?" I ask, before she finishes shutting me out.

"My father died and my mother was struggling to handle the winery. I came back to help."

"For two years?"

"It was supposed to be a few months. At six months, I figured out she just couldn't handle it."

"And you bought this house."

"Yes. I spent my inheritance on it, which in hindsight, was a poor use of my cash. But at the time I needed something that was mine. I had it remodeled, actually. The entire top floor is my studio."

"Because your art is everything to you."

She sets her ice cream and her spoon down and I do the same and when she refocuses on me, she says, "You didn't ask about why I might admire you."

"I promised to stop pushing you before I got the chance."

"All right then. I'll tell you now. When I saw the tiger tattoo, and despite now knowing the meaning, even the 'an eye for an eye' tattoo, they told me a story about you. They told me that you know who you are. You own it. You claim it. You have the tattoos to prove it."

"You're an artist, Faith."

She picks up her ice cream again. "I think I'll eat the rest of this pint before I respond to that."

"That statement was a fact. It doesn't require an answer. Why black, white, and red?"

"Black and white is the purest form of any image to me. It lets the viewer create the story."

"And the red?"

"The beginning of the story as I see it. A guide for the viewer's imagination to flow. I know it sounds silly, but it's how I think when I'm creating."

The red isn't blood. It isn't death. It's life. "You mentioned your new work to Josh."

"It's really six months to a year old," she says. "He just thinks it's new. I haven't painted recently."

"You paint about life."

"Yes."

"And yet you just defined yourself by death. No wonder you can't paint."

Her eyes go wide. "I…I hadn't thought of it that way." She glances away from me and back again. "I painted today. It was amazing."

"And what music did you paint to today? Elvis?"

"No Elvis today. No music today. I was inspired before I picked up the brush."

There is something in her eyes, in her voice, that I can't read, but I want to understand. "By what, Faith?"

"Life," she says, indicating my ice cream, her brow crinkling in worry, with the cutest dimple in the center. "You've hardly eaten that. Do you want the Doritos?"

"No." I laugh. "I do not want the Doritos. I'll stick with ice cream." I set my pint down, spoon as well, and move closer to her, taking *her* spoon from her again. "I'll share yours."

"Okay," she says, awareness spiking between us. "I'll share."

I take a bite of the ice cream, sweet cream and praline exploding in my mouth, and I cup Faith's cheeks and pull her mouth to mine. My tongue licks into her mouth, and she sighs into the kiss the way I've come to know she will, as if it's everything she's been waiting on. And it is fucking hot as hell. I deepen the kiss, drinking her in like the drug she is, and then slowly pull back. "You taste good," she whispers, stroking the edge of my lip.

"So do you, sweetheart." I pull away the blanket, her robe parting, one rosy nipple peeking out of the silk, and I'm inspired. I take a bite of ice cream, set it aside, and with the cold sweetness in my mouth, pull Faith down to the ground with me, aligning our bodies, my mouth finding her exposed nipple.

I suckle it, while she sucks in air, her hands going to my head. "It's cold," she pants, arching her back.

"I'll warm you up," I promise, taking another bite of the ice cream and kissing her again, and damn, every moan and sigh she makes affects me. She affects me. For once, I'm with a woman and not thinking about tits and ass and fucking her to take the edge off before I get back to what's important: work. I'm thinking about Faith's next moan and sigh. And my mouth and hands are on a journey for more of everything Faith will give me. A journey that leads me to that sweet spot between her legs and a promise I made: Next time I won't stop. And I don't. I lick her clit. I lick into her sex. I fuck her with my mouth and pull back. Then I tenderly lick again, teasing both of us in the process. And do it all over again. I take pleasure in driving her to the edge, but this time, I take even more pleasure in that last desperate lift of her hips, and the way she trembles with my fingers inside her, right before she shatters under my tongue. And what I'm left with is a journey that hasn't changed. It's still the quest for more. I want more from this woman, who might just literally be the death of me if I'm not careful. And yet, that doesn't matter.

I still want more.

Chapter Fourteen

Tiger

I BLINK AWAKE TO THE SCENT OF VANILLA AND AMBER, and the silky strands of Faith's blonde hair tickling my nose, the sweet press of her naked next to me. The fireplace is also burning to my right, the rug is beneath me, and the sun is burning through a window in a blinding bright light. Someone is also holding their damn finger on the doorbell.

Faith jolts awake and sits up, the blanket falling to just the right spot to expose her creamy white back, and to cover my morning wood, I'd have claimed her if not for the incessant doorbell ringing. "Any idea who that asshole is?" I ask irritably, preferring to wake up with this woman in a much different way.

"I'll handle it," Faith says, avoiding my query, her fingers diving into her hair before she pops to her feet and takes the blanket with her. The result: my wood is officially on display, while someone is now pounding on the door.

Faith lets out a low, frustrated sound. "I need to throw on clothes," she says, rushing toward her bedroom, sadly never even noticing said morning wood, which only makes me more irritated at the incessant knocking now consuming the entire damn space.

I push to my feet, grab my pants, and in the thirty seconds it takes me to pull them on, the door bell has stopped ringing and started again. Running hands through my tangled hair, compliments of Faith's fingers, I walk to her bedroom, my gaze landing on that card on the bed, before the empty space leads me through to the bathroom. I find Faith standing in her closet, pulling a t-shirt into place and already wearing black sweatpants. "Who the hell is that?" I ask again.

"I don't know," she says, shoving her feet into Keds, "but as embarrassing as this is about to get, I'm guessing it has to be one of the bill collectors from the winery."

"As in plural?" I ask. "There's more than the bank chasing you for money?"

Her expression tightens, right along with her reply. "Yes. It's every vendor we use, and no one would stay this long, and this rudely, that wasn't here to collect money."

Protectiveness, as unfamiliar as the possessiveness she stirs in me, rises in me and I go with it. "I'll handle it," I say, heading back to the bedroom and onward toward the front of the house, my mind processing the implications of Faith's embarrassment and circumstances. And I come to the obvious conclusion that has nothing to do with my rapidly growing interest in this woman. No one with access to the funds my father wrote to her mother would put themselves through this with such genuine emotional response. If Faith was involved in whatever scam occurred, which I highly doubt, she doesn't have the money now. And if she wanted to take the money and run, why put herself through this? Why not give the winery to the bank?

"Nick," Faith calls after me, her voice echoing from the distance. "Nick. Stop."

"Not on your life, sweetheart," I murmur, doubtful she can even hear me, but my actions speak for themselves.

The pounding grows louder right about the time I reach the foyer, as if the asshole just took his boot to the door, or his fists. I disarm the alarm, unlock the door, and right when I'm about to open it, Faith calls out from behind me, "You have on no shoes, no shirt, and no underwear, and your pants are unzipped."

I open the fucking door and there stand the two stooges I'd called suits at the winery two nights before. This time they wear matching khakis and white-collared shirts, because apparently khakis are supposed to be intimidating. "Mr. Rogers," Stooge Number One says, and while I can remember his name, I just don't care to give him that credit. "I…We…"

Stooge Number Two tries to fill in the blanks. "We didn't know you were personally involved in this."

"Card," I demand.

They both blink at me like I've just spoken another language they don't understand any more than their own.

"Business-fucking-card," I say. "Now."

They both fumble with their pockets, and I have two cards shoved at me. I grab one, and look at it. Then the other. Both employees of a collection agency which I happen to know that the bank that holds Faith's note hires often.

"We both know the ways you've broken the law," I say. "Don't do this again." And with that order, I slam the door on them and lock it. I don't immediately turn to Faith, who is hovering nearby. I step to the slit of a window beside the door, and watch the stooges all but run to their car.

Rotating, I find Faith standing under the archway dividing the hall from the foyer. "They won't be back. I'll buy you some time at the bank, but we need to sit down and talk. I need to be fully armed with information when I talk to the bank."

"No," she says. "No. I can't pay you."

I give her a once over, her nipples puckered under her pink tee, her hair a wild, sexy mess. Her lips are natural, and swollen from my kisses, for which I plan for many more. "I'm doing this for you, Faith. Not money." I take a step toward her.

She backs up and holds up a hand. "Stop. You don't get to fuck me and then take over my life, Nick. I didn't even invite you into my life. I invited you for one night. Hard rule, Nick."

"I've had my share of one night women, Faith," I say, voicing what I've only just concluded myself. "You aren't one of them." I firm my voice. "I'm not leaving. You need my help, and you're going to take my help."

"You don't get to just decide that. I'm not some girl that's gaga over you, Nick. I'm a grown woman who lives her life and makes her own decisions."

"Who now has help. There is nothing wrong with needing help besides not having it."

"You can't bulldoze me, Nick. I won't let you."

"If I could, you wouldn't be interesting to me, Faith. And you are. More now than the moment I met you, and that's new for me. Usually, a fuck does the job and I'm not interested anymore."

"There it is. The exact reason I'm reacting like I am. You basically just confirmed my thoughts. You'll help me until the interest fades. I pay not in money, but by entertaining you and fucking you, until I have the misfortune of sating your appetite. I don't need what you just made me feel in my life right now or ever again. Leave, Nick." She turns on her heel and starts marching away.

I stand there, mentally dissecting all the reasons she's just kicked me to the door, that I don't plan on exiting. Something to hide. Embarrassment. The something to hide might not even be about a crime, but that embarrassment. Macom. He was obviously part of her life and a bad one, and I've stormed into hers without giving her time to breathe or to reject me. But I don't have a choice. I can't let that happen. Not under these circumstances, and as it turns out, I don't want it to happen for my own personal reasons, of which I'll examine when the heady scent of her isn't driving me fucking insane.

I pursue her yet again, finding her in the kitchen, her back to me while she stares at a Keurig dripping coffee into a cup. She knows I'm here. I can sense it, but she walks to the refrigerator and pulls out some kind of flavored creamer. I want to storm around that counter, pull her to me, and kiss her until she melts for me. I want to strip her naked and fuck her right here on the solid wood island I didn't fuck her on last night. But doing those things would only drive home her accusation that I just want sex from her.

Clamping down on all those male urges, and a hell of an overload of testosterone, I walk to the barstool opposite her at the island and sit down. She walks to the Keurig, fills her cup with creamer, and then turns to face me, that cup cradled in her hands. "I am not your plaything."

"No," I say. "You are not. And I'm not yours either, Faith. That isn't what this is."

"It feels like it is."

"We are, as I said before, red hot together. That doesn't make it all we are."

"You can't just come into my life and try to take over," she repeats.

"I'm not."

"You *are*. It's your way."

She's right. It is. "Usually people are relieved when I want to help them."

"Aside from the ridiculous arrogance of that statement that isn't working for you right now, Nick Rogers, have you just fucked and spanked *those* people?" She holds up a hand. "Don't answer that. I don't want you to tell me what I want to hear."

"What do you want to hear, Faith?" I ask, her statement speaking volumes about where her head is, and it isn't focused on kicking me out.

"Nothing," she says. "I told you—"

"Let's talk about m*y* hard limits with women," I say. "They're really quite simple. No tomorrows. No conversation. No confession over my many nannies I tell no one about. For me, I just want to fuck."

"Why did you tell me about the nannies?"

"Because my gut said that you needed to hear it. Fuck. Maybe I needed to say it to someone who needed to hear it. I don't know what this is between us, Faith, but it's not what you're trying to turn it into."

"You said that we just needed to fuck each other out of our systems."

"I know what I said."

"And now—"

"And now I want more. That is exactly what I keep thinking with you. I want more. What the hell does that mean? I don't know, but I need to find out and I think you do, too."

"Arrogance again?"

"Not this time. Just facts. Just possibilities. And I can't promise where that leads, but I can tell you that for me, it's not just sex. If it was, you'd be naked and on the counter right now, because that's exactly where I wanted you when I walked into this kitchen."

She doesn't blush. She looks me in the eye. "You said you didn't want more."

"I didn't, but I have learned in life not to run from the unexpected. And I'm not running from this and I'm not letting you run from it because of a past that I'm not a part of."

"The past is a part of me."

"But I am not," I say, "and you responded to me like I was in the foyer."

She turns her head, obviously struggling with where this is leading, seconds ticking by before she sips her coffee and then sets it on the island, her eyes meeting mine. "You are very assuming, Nick."

"Agreed," I say, reaching for her coffee cup. "But only about things that matter to me, and it appears you do." I turn the cup so that my lips are aligned with the exact spot where hers were moments before, the act telling her we're connected now, that possessiveness I've felt on numerous occasions with Faith back again.

I drink, taking a sip of the chocolatey concoction that would taste better on her lips, against my lips. "I'm beginning to get the idea you have a sweet tooth."

"I do," she says. "And yet there is nothing sweet about you, Nick."

"You might be surprised. If you give me a chance."

"You aren't going to bulldoze me."

"So you told me," I say, sipping her coffee again, and then setting it back in front of her. "And since you seem to need to hear it again, if I could, you wouldn't be interesting to me." I soften my voice. "Don't let pride, or fear of us, get in the way of a solution to a problem you need to solve."

She picks up the coffee, takes a drink, and then another, and when she sets it back down, I arch a brow at her interest in drinking, that she's called nerves. I like that she can be nervous and overcome those nerves. That makes her strong, as proven by her next smart question. "Isn't sleeping with me and representing me some kind of ethical issue for you?"

"Not so long as the relationship existed prior to me becoming your counsel."

"Frank is my attorney already. I have him on retainer."

"Frank's an estate attorney on the verge of retirement. He is not going to make the bank his bitch. I will." I soften my voice. "Talk to me, Faith. Let me help and I promise that help comes with no conditions. Whatever happens with us personally, I'm with you on this until the end."

"I *hate* airing my dirty laundry to you. And it's not even that I barely know you. It's that I don't want this to be how I know you."

It's an honest answer. I hear it in the rasp of her voice. I see it in the torment in her eyes. And every honest answer she gives me makes me trust her more. "We all have our dirty laundry, Faith. I told you my father fucked all of my many nannies. I don't talk about my father. Or the many nannies."

"You don't?"

"No, Faith, I don't."

"You thought I needed to hear that," she says, but it's not a question, and she reaches for the cup again, withdrawing.

"Why did you just try to shut down on me?" I ask.

She sets the cup down, a few beats passing before her eyes lift and meet mine. "I appreciate that you shared that with me."

"But you withdrew."

"No. I just...I was taking in the impact of your statement. Taking stock of myself, too, and my reaction to...you, Nick. And I don't mean to seem unappreciative of your offer to help. I'm sorry. I am embarrassed about this. And you *are* very unexpected."

"I met you while those two assholes were trying to collect from you at the winery. I knew what you were going through when I pursued you."

"You knew you wanted to get me naked," she says, giving a humorless laugh. "There's a difference."

"I repeat. I'm here. I'm not leaving. I'm helping you. If that makes me a bull, let's fight about it and get past it."

"I don't want to fight with you, too."

It's not hard to surmise the "too" means the collectors, but my gut says it's more, but avoiding an emotional trigger right now, I focus us on business. "If you don't want to replace Frank, I'll manage Frank. But I need details from you first."

"Details," she repeats.

"Yes. Details. If it's easier, I can tell you what I learned when I was researching you."

"Please don't. I'd rather not know. Bottom line, without the family drama. My father left the winery to my mother on the condition I inherit on her death. She had no will and she was apparently four months behind on a note my father took from the bank five years ago. Actually, she was behind on most things. Taxes, vendors, the bank."

"Has the winery been losing money?"

"No. That's just it. She didn't run it. I did. All of it for most of the two years since my father died and I had a tight rein on our profit and loss. We were—are—making a net of forty grand a month before her income."

"But she wasn't paying the bank note and obviously select vendors."

"Several months before she died, I started getting collection calls. I confronted her and she said she had it handled."

"Define handled?"

"That's exactly what I said, but she shut me out."

"And you have no idea where the money is?"

"I'm locked out of her accounts because the bank keeps rejecting every executor we try to name with a conflict of interest claim."

I tap the table, my mind working. If her mother needed money, blackmailing my father makes sense. But she clearly didn't use it to pay the bills. Was Faith's mother being black-mailed along with my father? Was her mother planning to leave the winery behind and run off with someone?

"It's bad, right?" Faith asks, when I don't immediately respond.

"We'll back the bank off," I say. "And we'll get you your executor and buy you some time. I can't promise how long, but some time. Have you paid the taxes?"

"Yes. I used what I had left of my inheritance from my father. And I'm paying the vendors for current services and then some, which worked for some. Not all. I would have taken a loan on this house, but the note is too small and I can't sell it with a profit."

"How much are you behind with the bank?"

"Sixty thousand dollars and there's another hundred thousand owed to vendors."

And yet, my father wrote her mother a million dollars in checks. It just doesn't add up. I glance at the loan papers she's given me. "This note isn't even close to what your property would be worth. Have you had the winery valued? Once I clear this probate issue, have you considered—"

"No," she says, reading my mind. "I can't sell it. I promised my father it would stay in the family and I'd never sell it before the bank foreclosed anyway."

"So your mother knew that if you didn't take care of the place, you'd inherit a disaster."

"Yes. She knew. But it wasn't about the inheritance to me. This was never my life, or my dream, but she knew that my father's wishes were, and are, sacred to me."

And so Faith gave up her art and her life, which to some would be a motive to kill her mother, grabbed the reins, and tried to end the hellish cycle of the past two years, but that just doesn't ring true to me. But the ways I could fit my father into the equation are many: that he found out about the murder, for instance, doesn't support a reason for the checks he wrote to her mother.

"My mother has to have money that I can get to and handle this," she continues. "And even if she doesn't, which is completely illogical, I have a great manager at the winery.

We're a great team. We're making money. As long as I stay involved, I have the tools to keep succeeding. I just need time to catch things up."

"You're sure you're making forty thousand a month?"

"Yes. Very. Forty thousand after expenses, which means with my mother's love of men, Botox, and clothes, she had to have savings on top of the money she hadn't spent on bills."

"Men," I repeat. "Was there some young thing she was spending the money on?"

"There was always some young thing, Nick, even when my father was alive. At least your father's affairs were not when he was married to your mother."

"The only difference between you and me, sweetheart, is that my mother left my father and I wasn't blind, or young enough, not to know why."

"At least she has self-respect. My father knew about my mother's affairs, but he wouldn't leave. He made excuses for her. That's why I went to L.A. for school and stayed there. I loved my father, but it hurt me to watch him get hurt over and over again. And the behavior didn't fit what I knew of him."

In other words, her mother could have partnered with any number of men to blackmail my father, with an end game that might, or might not, have included a bigger plan. For instance, running off after draining the winery's funds, and leaving Faith to suffer, which ironically is what she did, anyway.

"Nick," Faith pleads. "You keep going silent and it's making me a little crazy. What are you thinking?"

"Has there been a recent man you know of?" I ask, looking for a suspect that isn't Faith.

"Her attention span was short, but she also knew I didn't approve. She didn't bring them around me. She'd taken a number of trips to San Francisco this past year, though.'"

To see my father, I surmise, and in that moment, I wish like hell I was in a place where I could say that to Faith, but I'm not. Even if I were certain she was innocent, if she knew the truth of why I sought her out, she'd shut me out before I could help her. "You have no idea where she went or who she saw?"

"No. I don't. I asked but she'd simply say 'a friend' lived there. *Nick*. What are you thinking?"

"Something doesn't compute, Faith. You have to see that."

She inhales, her lashes lowering. "I do," she says, looking at me again. "I'm going to find out she gave the money to some hot, young thing, just like you've inferred, and I'm angry. I'm really damn angry." She straightens, determination in her face. "But whatever she's done or not done, I return to my certainty that I can still save the winery. I just need time."

I study her for a long few moments, and there are some cold, hard facts about how the bank may have handled this that I decide to save for later. "I need to talk to Frank. I need us both to talk to Frank so he knows you're on board with this." I glance at my Rolex. "It's only eight and it's Saturday. Unlike the two stooges that just came by here, let's give him a few more hours to sleep. Not to mention, I have a call with North that I need to prep for." I glance at my watch. "I'm going to set it up for noon."

"Oh God," she says. "Your deposition. Please, just put this aside until it's over. I've made it this long. I can make it another week."

I don't tell her the bank might try to pull a dirty trick I'm not going to give them a chance to pull. "I have my work in the car. I'll sit down at your kitchen table, and we'll call Frank after I finish up with North," I say, walking around the island,

and pulling all her soft, tempting, fuckable curves to me. And when her hand settles on my chest, that morning wood is back. I'm hard. I'm hot. And I want her. "But I'm going to need something to eat other than ice cream," I add, "and a cold shower, since I don't have time to fuck you properly right now, and I really want to fuck you right now."

"You know," she says, her hand flattening on my naked stomach, her eyes lighting with mischief, the worry and anger of the past few minutes, at least momentarily lost, if not gone. "I considered telling you we should cool things down. But your pants are open and your cock is right," her fingers touch the head of my shaft, "here. And you really need the edge off if you're going to do a good job for you and me. I feel obligated to help."

"Do you now?"

"Yes," she says, and holy fuck, she is going down on to her knees, and she already has my cock out of my pants and wrapped in her hand. "And I feel that this is the way to it." She strokes the head of my cock with her tongue and smiles up at me. "Salty. You really did need this, didn't you? And just in case you're wondering. Don't hold back. I intend to swallow." And with that evil, seductive comment, she draws me into her mouth. And damn, Faith is good. She suckles. She licks. And when my hand goes to her hair, my body pumping into her, she makes these hot little sounds, like she needs this as much as I do, which has my balls tight, my body burning in all the right ways.

She wraps her hand around my thigh for leverage, and I'm close. So damn close. "That's right, sweetheart," I murmur, my voice low, gravelly. "That's good." My hand twines into her hair, urgency surging through me. I pump harder, pushing my cock deeper into her throat and she takes me, sucks me harder even, and that does it for me. She does it for me. I'm there, a hoarse moan sliding from my lips with the release that follows. My shaft spasms in her mouth and she does exactly what she said she would. She swallows, but she is in no rush to end this. She drags her tongue and lips up and down me, slowly easing me to the completion of the best damn blow job of my life.

Only when my chin lowers, my eyes finding hers, does she slide her mouth from my body. She pushes to her feet, and I drag her to me. "You know that wasn't—"

"Payment for services? Damn straight it wasn't. Free will, Nick. And now, I'm going to shower, and go pick up food so you can get your work done." She pushes away from me and takes off walking. Damn that woman rocks my world. I hope like hell she's innocent because I'm in deep now. And about to be deeper, because she's about to be naked in that shower and so am I.

Chapter Fifteen

Tiger

I T'S NEARLY ELEVEN BY THE TIME FAITH IS READY TO leave to pick up food, and I walk her to my BMW outside her house, while her car waits for the tow truck we called a few minutes ago. Both of us are in faded jeans and boots, me in a black t-shirt with the classic royal blue BMW logo on it and her in some sort of pink, long sleeved lace t-shirt that hugs her breasts just right. Which I notice, because unlike my hair that is knotted at the back of my head, her long blonde hair is not only free and smelling like vanilla and amber again, it's resting over her nipples, which I just had in my mouth fifteen minutes ago.

She dangles my keys between us. "I'm nervous about driving your car."

"Don't wreck it and everything will be fine."

"Thanks for that comforting thought and vote of confidence."

"That's what people like about me," I say. "I'm warm and fuzzy *all the damn* time."

Her sexy mouth curves, and damn, I'm thinking about it on my cock again. "Like I said, Nick Rogers," she says, as if she's just heard my thoughts. "There's nothing sweet about you."

I pull her to me and give her a long, drugging kiss and I swear I can taste that amber and vanilla scent from her hair on her lips. "How's that for sweet?" I demand.

"Your kisses aren't sweet, any more than you're a nice guy," she says. "But you're right. Nice is overrated and so is sweet."

I give her pink painted lips a glance. "Why the *fuck* does your lipstick never come off?"

She laughs. "Such fierceness over lipstick. It's not supposed to. They make it that way."

"Hmmm. Good. I think I like a challenge."

"Your challenge is your deposition next week. Let me get to the grocery store and pick up that Italian food I promised, so you can get your job done."

"I don't think I've ever had a woman scold me about my work," I say. "It's surprisingly arousing. But I'm pushing my call back to one." I release her and open the car door. "But go now before I need to push this call back to noon."

She starts to climb inside but pauses. "Make yourself at home. Just don't burn down the place and everything will be fine."

Laughing at her play on my warning, aware that she manages to keep the playing field even at all times, I watch as she disappears into the BMW. I shut her inside, backing up to watch her depart, and as she puts the car into gear, I decide there's something very wrong, and yet right at the same time, about a woman I'm fucking in my pride and joy, my custom BMW Hurricane. But then, there is something about Faith that's both wrong and right, all the way around. She disappears around a curve and I sigh. All I can do is hope like hell she's as good at driving it as she is riding me.

I cross the drive and march up the stairs. Entering the house, I shut the door and prepare to start a search. But damn it, it's impossible not to feel the betrayal of Faith's trust in that act, which feeds my need to prove her innocence and not her guilt, which I've already established as a problem. At this point, I'll take innocence any way I can frame it, and she's logical and smart. It will be a blow to find out why I sought her out, but she'll understand. Forgiving me might be another story, but right now, I just need to find a murderer that isn't her. I glance at my watch: eleven-fifteen. I need time to review the material North has certainly already emailed me, but by the time I do this search and eat with Faith, that's not going to happen. Not willing to compromise the prep for the deposition or my management of North, I snag my cellphone from my pocket, and text him: *Move to two o'clock.*

He responds so damn fast I don't know how he has time to type: *Copy that, boss.*

I smirk and shove my phone back in my pocket. "The kid's eager," I murmur. "I'll give him that."

In the interest of time, I head for Faith's bedroom, where most people keep their secrets. Once I'm there, I place my hand on a dresser drawer and hesitate. Damn it, I hate doing this, but I have no other option. I pull open one organized drawer after another, finding nothing out of the ordinary. The nightstands are next, and I find more of the same. The bed's a platform, which means there's no hiding spots beneath it but my gaze lands on the painting above Faith's bed, one of her own works, this one of a vineyard, with a streak of red on one vine. She's talented, stunningly so, which brings my attention to that card from Faith's father she didn't want to open. Why do I know that card is all about his confidence and pride in her for taking over the winery, with a negative spin on her art, her passion? And yet, even in death, she wants to please him, craving his love. Not a problem I had with my father. I never craved anything from the man. Hell, he probably only gave Meredith Winter a million dollars so it was a million less that I'd inherit.

Rejecting the grind in my gut with that thought, I turn away from the bed and head into the bathroom, searching the drawers there, and then I move into Faith's closet. My digging there includes checking pockets and shoes, but the results are the same. Nothing. From there, I make my way to the opposite side of the house where I find a small library, with a couple of overstuffed chairs, and art books filling the shelves. I don't have time to check those books. I need to find an office. There has to be one, or a place where she keeps her documents and this isn't it.

Glancing at my watch, I estimate I have thirty minutes before Faith returns and I track a path to the kitchen, do a quick search. Realizing that I have no place but Faith's studio left to search, I hesitate. That feels like a place she should take me, but there could be an office up there somewhere, and I have to look for that. For now, though, I walk into the dining room, where I've left my briefcase that I retrieved from the car before Faith left. I sit down at the rectangular dark wood table, and glance at the credenza that has no drawers before I unpack my MacBook and files to make it look like I've been working.

Next, I have to make a phone call before Faith returns, even above searching the studio for an office. Moving to one of the floor-to-ceiling windows framing the credenza, I pull back the curtain to keep an eye on the driveway before removing my phone from my pocket, dialing Beck Luche, a tattooed up former CIA agent who now does private hire work, and not for a small price. He also did five years undercover as a rogue US hacker deep inside a Russian hacking operation. It's a detail about his past I learned when he was under consideration for a hundred-thousand-dollar paycheck for one of my high-tech clients. He got the job and I hired him personally three days ago after waiting two weeks for him to be free from another job. But I didn't want this screwed up.

"Nicolas," he answers, using that name despite me explicitly telling him not to. "How's the meeting with the would-be black widow if she ever got married?" he asks.

I grind my teeth at the dagger he's just thrown. "She's either innocent or a damn good actress."

"The best criminals are always the best actors."

He just keeps on throwing daggers. "Macom Maloy. Have you checked him out?"

He snorts. "If you thought I was an amateur, why'd you hire me and pay me so damn much money?" He doesn't wait for a reply he has no intention of getting in the first place, moving on. "Of course I checked out the ex-boyfriend. And that dude is a tool, but he's not smart enough to pull off the blackmail and murder, especially living in another city."

"But he's got money to pay someone else to do it."

"That man isn't thinking about Faith Winter and he has no connections to Meredith Winter at all. That man is thinking about money, art, and some private fuck club like the one you own. He used to take Faith to it, but now, he just takes himself, as in several times a week."

I had no idea Beck, knew about the "cigar club" that fronts for the sex club I bought from a friend, and client, last year when he went off and got married. But then if he didn't, he wouldn't be worth hiring. And the fuck club Macom took Faith to, and replaced her with, explains much of Faith's references to her sexual past. It also indicates another uncomfortable disclosure with this woman I'm not looking forward to anytime soon.

"Let me run down what I know," Beck says. "Thanks to the security feed from your father's house, I've determined that Meredith Winter visited your father once a week for six months before she died. The checks he wrote her began at four months."

I inhale a jagged breath. "So she did visit him."

"She went to his home during those visits, and stayed there for hours when she did. I have a few instances of them kissing by his door. He was banging her, but it went further than that. They had regular phone conversations in between their visits. No emails, unfortunately. But the bottom line here. A relationship between the two pokes holes in the blackmail theory. He sounds like he was giving her the money by choice. Paid sex perhaps."

"My father liked his women thirty years his junior," I say. "He wasn't paying a fifty-something-year-old woman for sex."

"She was still a gorgeous woman."

"That's not it. Moving on. Meredith wasn't paying the bills at the winery. She was taking his money and the money made at the winery and doing something with it."

"I was coming to that. Her bank accounts were dry for that four-month window she was taking checks from your father. She'd deposit those checks, let them clear, and then clean out every penny of her accounts. I don't know yet where it went, but I'm working on it."

"She was giving it to someone," I surmise.

"Or stashing it," he says. "Meredith had a revolving bedroom door. She'd have a great many candidates for cohorts or enemies but one option stands out. Jesse Coates was seeing Meredith for the few months before your father. Twenty years her junior and a successful stockbroker who moved from New York to San Francisco. He might be behind a scam."

I scrub my jaw. "My father was too smart to be scammed. Blackmailed yes, but not scammed."

"Blackmail is a scam."

"Blackmail is blackmail. Being seduced by a woman and stolen from is another."

"You wouldn't believe the people I've seen scammed, my man," Beck says. "It would blow your mind. And if that's what went down, it was done smartly. I see no contact between Meredith and Jesse in the six-month window that she was seeing your father, but that really doesn't matter. That could be part of an end game."

"What are we thinking was the big end game?"

"I don't make assumptions I can't back up. And what doesn't add up to me is that Meredith wasn't paying the bills at the winery. She could have sold the place for a small fortune."

"Faith inherited on her death as a stipulation of her

mother's inheritance, which would mean her mother could not sell without Faith's willingness. And I can tell you that woman appears to be holding onto a sinking ship because it's her father's wishes."

"Yes, Faith. I'm still working on figuring out that hot little number."

That possessiveness flares in me again. "And?" I ask tightly.

"And right now she looks clean, but so does Jesse. Not to mention the fact that you just gave her motive. She wanted to keep the winery, her mother did not. Maybe her mother was trying to force her hand into selling by not paying the bills and destroying the vines. The mother wanted the payday that property would be worth. Faith didn't. Maybe your father was in on the payday."

"Sell for the massive profit margin that property and operation are worth or have them taken away."

"That's the theory I'm going to work on."

"Working that theory, Faith would have to have connections to my father, who she'd have had to have killed, right along with her mother."

"Which I have yet to find."

"What about her sharing a link to anyone connected to my father?"

"Nothing and I dug through layers as deep as a phone book."

I consider everything he's said to me. "Meredith forcing Faith to sell and taking off with a hot young thing for the money makes sense to me. What doesn't is how my father fits into this. Why the fuck was he writing her checks? Wait. *Fuck.* He wanted in on the sale of the winery."

"Then why pay Meredith the money?"

"A down payment on him buying it is my guess."

"But they're both gone and so is the money."

"Which means you need to—"

"Find the money. I plan on it."

"Call me," I say, but when I'm about to end the connection, he says, "Nicolas."

"I'd tell you to stop calling me that, but it clearly won't matter."

"Be careful with Faith Winter. She could have the money. She could want to sell herself."

"Then why go through this hell?"

"Because not going through it makes her look guilty. Like I said, man. Be careful."

With that blow, he ends the call and standing there, aware that I am guilty of not wanting her to be guilty, but no matter how many times I warn myself of this danger, it doesn't change. I'm going there again. It is what it is. I want her to be innocent. I'm boring myself with the repeat of this conclusion. Accepting what is allows me to manage what is.

Moving on to what I just learned. Yes. Faith has motive to act against her mother, with financial gain, but I don't believe she wants to sell the winery. More like save it from her mother selling it, but she could have done that through the court system. But to believe that she would have, or could have, plotted out and killed my father and her mother is a stretch I can't make. I scrub my jaw. But I don't want to make it either. I just admitted that.

I glance at my watch and then scan the horizon with no sign of Faith. I estimate I have fifteen minutes until Faith will be here. Just enough time to nose around upstairs if I hurry.

Scanning the horizon one last time, I settle the curtain back into place, and waste no time making my way to the stairs. I don't hesitate when I start the straight climb up. I'm helping her. She just doesn't know it and I'd be fine with her never knowing it, but that's not possible.

At the last step, I turn right under an archway, and find myself, in a room with a steepled ceiling, that literally stretches the entire top level of the house. The wood floor has been glossed with some sort of finish I assume is easily wiped clean. There are two arched windows consuming the wall in front of me and both ends cap to the space. And there are random easels sitting around the room, all uncovered, all demanding attention I can't give them. My gaze lifts to a door to my left, which I hope is an office. Moving in that direction, I enter and flip on the light, and sure enough, I find a heavy dark wood desk, a deep leather chair in the corner and random works of art on the wall that are absolutely Faith's signature strokes and colors. And damn, there really is something sexy about a talent I'll never have.

Another arched floor-to-ceiling window sits behind the chair and illuminates the room, allowing me to round the desk and sit down without a light, and to quickly locate random financial documents. I pull out my phone, set my alarm for five minutes, and start snapping photos. It goes off right as I find her father's will, and I risk the extra minute to click shots of it. Out of time, and nowhere near done, I stand up and exit the office. I fully intend to hurry to the archway, but I notice the table and color palette sitting next to one easel, which means it has to be what she was painting yesterday. I take two steps in that direction and stop myself, some instinct in me telling me that looking at that painting is far less forgivable than searching her house, at least now that I have every intention of saving her from the hell she's in.

I turn back to the door, and that's when I hear the front door open and Faith's footsteps downstairs. *Fuck.* I run a hand through my hair and make an instant decision. I have to own up to being up here and if I let her walk around looking for me that's only going to make this worse. Inhaling a jagged breath, I walk to the archway and step to the landing above the steps. As if she sensed I was up here, she's at the bottom of the steps, looking up at me, her blonde hair tousled from the wind, her hand on the railing.

She doesn't speak. For long seconds, she doesn't move. And then suddenly she is walking up the steps toward me, her pace steady, controlled, anger crackling off of her. She stops in front of me, her eyes meet mine, and it's not anger that gets me. It's the wounded look of betrayal. "This is not my house. This is my private work place. This is my sanctuary." She doesn't give me time to reply. "You saw it, didn't you?"

"Faith-"

"I knew it." She cuts away from me and walks into the studio.

Fuck. What does she think I found? What the hell am I about to find out about this woman that I don't want to know. I follow her inside the room, but she isn't headed to the office. She's standing at the painting she started last night. She stares at it. "Do know why I painted this?"

I walk toward her. "Faith," I begin again. "I didn't—"

"Look at this?" She waves her hand in front of it and turns to face me. "You came up here and you didn't look at my work?"

"I am intrigued by your work, Faith. I was drawn up here

but I got here and realized it was a mistake. I knew this was your private domain and I—"

"A liar is not a better shade for you than fear, Nick Rogers. No. Tiger. Because that's who you are." She grabs the easel, struggling with it, and I move toward her, but before I can get to her, she's flung it around until it lands in the space left between us. My gaze lands on the painting of myself, and I suck in air, a reaction I'm not sure I've had more than a few times in my life.

"Do you know why I painted that, *Tiger*? Because I was trying to figure out why I want to trust you but can't."

Chapter Sixteen

Tiger

THE PAINTING OF ME LAYS BETWEEN FAITH AND I, OUR eyes meeting, hers still alight with anger and betrayal. And I want to call her reaction over the top, but she clearly senses I came to her without pure motives. "Faith," I begin, and for once in my life I'm not even sure how I'm going to finish the sentence. But I never get the chance.

"Leave," she orders, her voice as strong as her evident will. "I want you to leave."

I reject her demand not in words she won't hear, but actions. I'm around that painting before she can blink twice, pulling her against me, all her damn soft, fuckable, perfect curves pressed to my body. "You want to know me? Look into my eyes, Faith. See what's there, not what you choose to paint."

Her hand settles on my chest, elbow stiff. "You are such an asshole, *Tiger*. You are—"

"I know what you think of me," I say, cupping the back of her head. "But I don't accept it anymore." I lower my head and kiss her, licking into her mouth, the taste of anger and the betrayal I'd seen in her eyes on her lips, and it guts me. I *am* betraying her, and I have no way out of where I've gone, or why I can't tell her the truth. "And my name is not Tiger," I say, tearing my mouth from hers. "I'm Nick to you, Faith."

"You had no right to come up here, *Tiger*. You had no right—"

"You're right," I say. "I was wrong, Faith, but I swear to you, I didn't look at any of your paintings."

"Liar."

She's right. I am. Just not about this. "I *didn't* look."

"The best liars are the best actors."

That play on Beck's words hits a nerve that I reject like her command for me to leave, cupping her face. "I didn't look at your work, Faith," I say again, and because I won't lie where I don't have to lie, I add, "But I wanted to. And I wanted to because I too want to know who you are. I want to know your secrets. I want to know what the hell you are doing to me that no other woman has done."

"You barely know me."

"But I want to. That's the point."

"You are—"

"*Obsessed* with you," I say, and this time when my mouth closes down on hers, I let her taste those words on my tongue. I let her taste my hunger for her. I let her taste how much I want her and how much I don't want to want her, and yet, how high I am on this addiction. Maybe it's the forbidden.

Maybe it's her. I don't know. And in this moment, I don't care. And this time, she doesn't either. She answers every unspoken word I deliver on my tongue with conflicted need.

I pull her shirt over her head, and I have her bra off in seconds, touching her breasts, teasing her nipples, my mouth devouring her mouth. And her hands, talented, gifted hands, are pressed under my shirt, burning me where they caress my skin. I unbutton her pants, fully intending to strip her naked. "Your meeting," she pants out, grabbing my hand.

I pull back to look at her. "Are you actually thinking of my meeting right now?"

"Yes," she murmurs. "But with regret."

"I moved it to two," I say, scooping her up and carrying her toward the office, my steps tracking a path that doesn't stop until we're at that oversized chair where I sit her down.

I'm on a knee in front of her in an instant, and we're both removing her boots with hurried hands. The minute I'm over that obstacle, I pull her to her feet, unzipping her pants. My lips on her belly and the male in me, the man who is obsessed with every inch of this woman, revels in the trembling that quakes her body.

I pull down her pants, panties as well, wrapping my arm around her waist, before tugging them away. One hand at her hip, the other cupping her sex, two fingers sliding into her wet heat, where I press them inside her, a tease I quickly remove. She moans in protest, and I stand up, cupping her face again, and swallowing that tormented, delicious sound.

"Hurry," she pleads, reaching for my pants. "I need—"

I kiss her again. "I need," I murmur, reaching into my pocket for the last condom I have there, but come up dry. I search the other. I've got nothing and her hand has just made its way into my jeans and into my underwear, her fingers wrapping my cock with delicious pressure.

I reach down and cover her hand with mine. "The last condom I had fell out somewhere."

She pulls back to look at me. "Oh," she says, regrettably easing from my body.

My hands go to her waist, eyes raking over her naked breasts, before I promise, "We'll improvise."

"I have one," she says. "I have a condom. A birthday prank at work. They said I—it doesn't matter. It's here." She slips around me, and hurries to the desk, naked, beautiful and suddenly pulling the papers I'd shot photos of from a drawer, flinging them on top of the desk. And as hot and hard as I am, I can think of one thing in this moment. She has zero concern about something in those files exposing a secret or a lie. And I feel her actions as both a relief and a punch of guilt. "I can't find it," she announces, pressing her hands to the desk, her head lowered, long blonde hair draping her shoulders. Her back arches, backside in the air. Her beautiful body is exposed, but there is so much more of herself she's showing to me right now without knowing. "This is wrong on so many levels."

I move toward her and turn her to me, hands shackling her waist. "Back to improvising."

"I'm on the pill," she announces. "I stayed on despite Macom—okay. Why did I just say his damnable name?" She presses her head to my shoulder and raises it again. "I know you probably don't want to without one and I shouldn't, but I just—"

I kiss her, and no, I do not have sex without a condom. Not ever. But there is trust in what she just offered me that I have not given her. And the sweet taste of her tongue on my tongue is now a part of my new obsession, as is her body pressed to mine, and her—just her—I forget the condom. I forget everything but touching her, kissing her, and then there is that moment that I end up on the chair but she slips away, kneeling at my feet.

"My turn," she says, yanking at my boot and if the woman wants my boots off, they're coming off.

I reach down and take care of the other one before she slides her hands into my pants again. "We're going naked," she says. "I want *naked.*"

"Naked it is," I say, kissing her hard and fast before I undress and pull her to my lap, her long, sexy legs straddling me and she is sliding down my *naked* cock, the wet heat of her naked body gripping me, that is pure fucking bliss.

But more so is the moment that I'm kissing her, and then I'm not because we're just breathing together. I feel this woman in ways I didn't know it was possible to feel a woman, and I just met her. I feel her everywhere, burning me alive. And maybe I'm making the biggest mistake of my life with her, but if I die, I'll die happy. And when we do kiss again, it's slow, sexy kisses. And slow, nerve-stroking slides of our body, that meld our breathing, our tongues, our bodies, until we both shatter into release. Until I release inside her as I have with no other woman since I was a young fool, and I bury my face in her vanilla and amber smelling hair.

And I hold her.

When I never hold women.

It sends the wrong message.

And yet, I hold Faith now. I inhale the scent of her hair.

"Tell me you don't regret that," she murmurs against my neck.

I lean back to look at her. "What the hell am I supposed to be regretting?"

"Not using a condom."

"No man or woman has a regret over a missing condom unless the result is later regrettable, but since I don't fuck without a condom, you're safe."

"I don't either, Nick. Never with Macom. I...he liked...I didn't."

I want her to fill in those blanks but I sense that this is another one of those moments where pushing is the wrong choice. "We're naked in every way and safe," I say softly. "*Except* that now we have to get you off me and save your chair from our mess."

"Kleenex on the table," she says, and without warning, she leans over and she starts to tumble. I catch her but not without a lean that puts us both on the floor, her on her back, me over the top of her, and us both in an eruption of laughter.

And when that laughter fades, we don't move. We stare at each other, and I have this sense that we both are trying to read the other, I damn sure am her. That we both are trying to understand what this is between us. Sex? Really damn good sex? Or...what? I don't know what the hell it is, but it's a powerful force between us, a magnet with a pull that won't be escaped. Seconds tick by and I pull her to her feet, our gazes colliding before we both dress. And as we do, the reason for the explosion that led to taking our clothes off in the first place comes full circle, expanding in the air between us. The minute we're dressed, I pull her to me. "Faith."

"I probably overreacted," she says, reading where I'm going.

"You didn't," I say. "I had no right to come up here. And

I repeat, I didn't look at the painting. I am, however, as in-trigued by your art as I am you. It is you. It's a gift you alone possess."

Her lashes lower, her expression etched with torment be-fore she looks at me again. "Thank you for saying that." She covers my hand with hers. "Let's go heat up the food."

She's slammed the wall down again, evidence that I've hit a nerve. And as much as I want to push and know this woman, for right and wrong reasons, I let it go. But I've made my decision. I'm not letting her go. Guilty or innocent, she's mine now, even if she doesn't know it. And guilty or innocent, wherever that leads.

Chapter Seventeen

Tiger

Once we're downstairs, Faith sticks our food in the microwave, while I unpack the groceries she's bought, which includes milk, eggs, and... "Pancake mix?" I ask, holding up the instant mix. "I don't get your famous pancakes?"

"I guess I didn't mention that they're famous because that's all I ever make."

I laugh. "No, you didn't." I walk to the pantry and find the proper spot to stick them before turning back to her. "I might have to make you pancakes."

"You cook?" she asks, setting bottles of water on the island where we plan to eat.

"I picked up a few tricks from one of my many nannies

who had a thing for cooking contests."

She opens the microwave. "The food should be ready," she says, inspecting it and then removing the container. "We're good to eat." She sets our sealed containers on the table, and I move to the spot directly across from her, both of us claiming our seats before returning to our prior conversation. "As for cooking," she says. "I don't. Neither of my parents cooked and I didn't have to learn. Growing up at the winery, there's two chefs on staff. One for the restaurant and another for the staff." She lifts the lid to her food to display spaghetti and meatballs and I do the same.

"Looks and smells amazing," I approve, the scent of sweet and spicy tomato sauce almost as good as her amber and vanilla scent right about now.

"It is," she assures me. "An Italian family owns the place. And I'd offer you wine, but I don't keep it here."

I arch a brow. "Aren't you supposed to be a wine lover?"

"I like wine," she says, "but when I'm here, I just want to escape everything to do with the winery." She picks up her fork, and clearly makes a move to change the subject by adding, "I'm starving and real women eat everything on their plate."

"Sweetheart," I say, wrapping pasta around my fork, "you keep up with me on everything else. I'd be disappointed if this was different." I take a bite.

Faith watches me with intense green eyes. "Well?" she prods.

"Damn good," I say. "And I've eaten my share of pasta in Rome."

She sighs. "Oh how I'd love to go to Italy. My parents went a good half dozen times for 'wine research' as they called it.

My father loved those trips. My mother was all his then. I can't imagine wanting someone so badly that you'd allow yourself to be treated that way. I never understood."

Which, judging from what I know of her, is why Macom got kicked to the curb after only a year. "There's a fine line between love and hate," I assure her. "Lovers become enemies. I see it all the time with my work."

"But you do corporate law, right?"

"Personal relationships are common disruptors to business. The worst kind because they get emotional and dirty." I stay focused on her past. "Who stayed with you when your parents were traveling?"

"A friend of my parents who passed away a few years ago. And Kasey, the manager at the winery, has been there for twenty years."

I study her a moment. "Why, if he's good at his job, can't you paint, Faith?"

Her answer comes without hesitation. "Kasey and my father were a team. A few years back, we were just getting by, but they'd built our retail sales to a huge dollar figure the year before my father died. That's why I was able to buy this house with my inheritance."

"And your mother inherited well, I assume?"

"He had life insurance and money from the winery, which is why I need into her bank accounts."

That Beck tells me are empty, I think.

"When my father passed," she continues, "my mother insisted she was taking over that role my father held, but it was, as expected, a disaster. My mother angered customers and made rash decisions."

"You lost business," I surmise.

"A ton of business." She stabs a meatball. "That's when I took over and tried to earn the deals back. But it got worse before it got better. We lost one section of our vineyard to a bad freeze because she declined normal procedures as too costly. Kasey was at his wit's end and I convinced him to stay. That freeze," she says, stabbing a meatball, "makes the forty thousand a month a real accomplishment."

"Don't artistic types hate the business end of things?"

"I know this place," she says. "I bring knowledge and the name to the brand." She waves that off. "Enough about that place. Did you always want to be an attorney?"

"Yes. My father was an attorney and I wanted to be better than him. And I wanted him to know I was better than him."

"Are you?"

"Yes," I say, offering nothing more, and nothing more is how I always liked that man.

"How did he die?"

"Heart attack."

"My mother too, and I'd say that's ironic, but it's a common way to die."

"It *is* common," I say, and, I silently add, and the perfect cover up for a murder. Or two.

She sets her fork down. "Right. Common. And this is a bad subject. I think I'm done eating."

"You've hardly touched your food, Faith."

"I just…like I said. It's a bad subject." She starts to get up and I catch her hand. "Sit with me." She hesitates but nods, settling back into her seat. I glance at her plate, then at her, letting her see the heat in their depths. "I'm going to make you wish you ate that."

She studies me right back for several beats and then picks

up her fork. "I'll eat, and I'll do so because my growling stomach will distract me when I paint, and then I'm going to paint while you get ready for your call."

"Not about to let it be about me, now are you?" I challenge, but I don't give her time to fire back. "Are you going to finish painting me?"

"Maybe," she says, her eyes filling with mischief. "We'll see if you inspire me again."

I remember the way she'd thrown that painting on the ground, the way she'd shouted at me. "If inspiring you means making you think you can't trust me, I'd rather not."

"There are other ways to inspire me," she says, taking a bite of her food.

"How should I inspire you, Faith?"

"I'll consider letting you know when it happens."

"All right then. When did you first get inspired to paint?"

"I always wanted to paint. From Crayola to paintbrush at age five. And Sonoma is filled with art to feed my love."

Now she says love, but she's used the word "like" when talking about wine. "And you went off to college with a plan to turn it into a career."

"I did."

"And your parents had to be proud."

"They were supportive enough, but as an aspiring artist, I'm just like half of L.A. trying to make it to the big or small screen. No one takes them serious until they do it."

"And Macom? Did he take your art seriously?"

"He's an artist."

"So he understood the struggles."

"Yes," she says, reaching for the bottle of water. "I suppose you could say that." But something about the way she says those words, says there's more to that story than meets the eye.

I open my mouth to find a way to that story, when her cellphone rings and I finish my food, while she pushes to her feet and walks to the counter where her purse, which looks like it's seen better days, sits. She retrieves her phone and glances at the screen. "The mechanic." She answers the call.

I stand and dump my take-out plate into the trash, and Faith seals hers and walks to the fridge as she listens. "Okay. Yes. No. Just please tow it to the winery. Thank you." She ends the call and stuffs her phone into her jeans.

"That didn't sound good."

"All I heard was the price and I'm not spending that without another opinion and some time. I have another car at the winery. I'll just have to ask you to please take me to pick it up when you leave."

"And when am I going to leave, Faith?"

"According to my hard limit, before we sleep tonight."

"No sleep then," I say. "So be it." I don't give her time to argue. "Let's call Frank."

"My paperwork related to the winery is all upstairs. We should call with the documents in front of you. And if you want, you can just work up there while I paint. Or not. You're welcome to stay down here."

"Upstairs," I say, the significance of her going from not wanting me up there, to wanting me up there not something that I miss. Neither is the fact that she just invited me to sit at that desk, where I can nose around in anything I want. And she has to know this. I gather my work and we head up to the studio. Faith straightens the desktop, but sets a stack of files on the desk. "Taxes. My father's will. Collection letters. Random other items. If you need anything specific that isn't there, just ask."

I reach for a file that catches my eye and flip it open, looking at the forty-five-million-dollar valuation of the vineyard, with the note for thirty-five. "Faith, you could sell for ten million?"

"That evaluation was done before that freeze and the substantial loss of business that followed. I still believe it would sell for a profit, but nowhere near that. But I'm not selling, Nick. This is my family business."

"Did your mother know the value had gone down?"

"I tried to tell her that, but she didn't care enough to listen."

Or she did listen, and the freeze lowered the price and made the vineyard a steal for someone like my father, who would rebuild it. It makes sense, except for the fact that my father wouldn't put money down on something Meredith Winter had no right to sell. He was not that stupid. Not to mention the fact that both of them are dead now. "Let's call Frank."

She pulls her cellphone from her pocket and dials on speaker. "Faith," Frank answers. "What's happened? Is it the bank harassing you again?"

"I'm here with Nick Rogers."

"Ah yes. Nick. I knew this call was coming when you brought up his name. I might be old but I still have instincts. Am I being fired?"

"No," Faith says quickly, her eyes meeting mine, a silent plea for me to say the right thing right now.

"I'm going to play second counsel," I say. "But I need to be brought up to date."

Frank doesn't hesitate. "Well for starters, we have no will, and the bank sees this as a chance to make a profit, thus they have a substantial interest in claiming the property."

Speaking to Frank I say, "Which is an asinine claim that will never hold up in court. I can name five ways to Sunday how they're pushing the limits of the law."

"I couldn't agree more."

"Have we made it clear to the bank that you'll counter-attack?"

He gives a long, rambling answer that amounts to "no" and does not please me. "We need to order another evaluation of the property," I say.

"It's not her property until we clear this probate issue," he argues.

"The bank has an end game here," I say. "The way I see this, they're either representing a buyer who has some interest we don't yet know in this property thus wants to force Faith to sell. Or frankly, *Frank*, they're hoping you're weak enough to let them take it from her before she can sell for a big payday."

Faith's eyes go wide, and I hold up a hand, while Frank says, "I don't want to let Faith down."

Faith shuts her eyes and then says, "You won't, Frank. You won't."

"We need to get you out of probate," Frank says. "Then you can take a loan on your winery and pay off the debt your mother left you."

"But the bank won't let that happen," Faith says.

"They will," I assure her. "I'm taking care of this." Her eyes meet mine, shadows and worry in their depths, and I repeat, "I'm taking care of this."

She gives a tiny nod. "And I'm going to leave you two to your attorney talk." She tugs on her shirt to whisper, "I'm going to go change."

I nod this time, watching her depart, before I take Frank off speaker phone. "Tell me the players in this game."

He begins a detailed rundown of who is involved with what and what's happened, which on his part is a pathetic example of legal work. He has no fire left in him and Faith needs fire on her side right now. Fifteen minutes later Frank and I end the call just before Faith appears in the doorway, now wearing paint spattered jeans and a t-shirt. "Well?"

"He's not done enough. I will. We'll talk through a plan before I leave."

She studies me several long beats. "Thank you, Nick."

"Tiger on this, sweetheart. That's a promise."

"Tiger," she says. "There's a coffee pot in the corner. And a mini-fridge with random creamers which shouldn't be expired because they last a scary long time when you think about it."

"Thanks, sweetheart," I say. "You're going to paint?"

"I am."

"Will I get to see the results?"

She gives me a coy smile. "Maybe." She slips away and I glance down at the paperwork in front of me, craving time to review it in more detail I don't have.

I grab my briefcase from the ground beside me and pull out my MacBook and review what North has sent me. That's when Mozart fills the air, a sign that Faith remembers I work to classical music. And what's crazy is that no other woman has ever known that about me. I've only just met Faith, and I've let her see parts of me no one else has. I stand and walk to the door to find her standing at the easel, my painting no longer on the ground. It's in front of her, pleading for her brush, and I wonder if she's still looking for the lies that I've sworn I despise but can't stop telling her.

Chapter Eighteen

Faith

NICK AND I SPEND THE REST OF SATURDAY AFTERNOON and into the evening inside my studio, him in my office, and me sitting in front of a once-blank canvas with a brush in hand. And I do what I love, what I have denied myself for far too long.

I paint and I do so without hesitation.

I paint without what I now believe to be the fear of the past few months. Fear of failure. Fear of disappointment. Fear of seeing myself through my brush when I do not like who, and what, the past few months have made me.

I paint Nick.

His strong face.

His piercing eyes.

His tattoos. The Tiger. The words: *An eye for an eye.*

And I do all of this while trying to understand a man who seems to understand me perhaps too well. I also do so quite entertained by the way he paces my office, throws paper balls at a trashcan, talks to himself, and then repeats. *His* creative process. And what I like about seeing this is that the hard work beneath it shows me what's beneath the arrogance.

Amazingly too, at random times, I look up from my canvas to find him standing at the office door, his broad shoulder resting against the doorway, a force that consumes the room while he intently watches me work, and I do not withdraw. I'm okay with him being here. I'm okay with him observing my creative process when I have *never* allowed anyone to watch me work, including Macom. But then, Macom was always critical of every creative choice I made and Nick…is not.

But then Nick and I are new to each other and time changes people. I've often wondered when my father became my mother's man-child rather than her husband. Was it instant? Was it at one month? One year? Ten years? Every question leads me back to the paint on my brush, and the man in my office. That's the great thing about a one-night hard limit: It never has time to go sour. The person can never see too much or know too much. And yet, any minute now, Nick and I will be at two.

Unless I send him away.

As if he senses where my thoughts are, I feel him, rather than see him, step back into the doorway of my office. And after hours of this push and pull of wordless energy between us, I don't have to look at him to know that one of his broad shoulders rests on the doorway. Or that his piercing blue eyes are on me, not the sun fading and washing the green from the mountainsides, soon to disappear and leave them black. But this time, I do not allow him to watch me work.

Instead, I clean my brush and remove my smock. Then, and only then do I lift my gaze to meet his. He doesn't speak, but his piercing blue eyes are softer now, but still warm. So very warm. Not the kind of warm that says he's about to strip me naked and remind me why I can't resist him. But warm with affection, and that kind of warm, mixed with the fact that he sees too much and knows too much, should be exactly why I send him on his way.

Hard limit: *One night.*

Inhaling, I tell myself that limits are not made to be broken. My limit was meant to protect me.

I start walking toward him, and I know immediately why I need that protection. Because he affects me on every possible level, inside and out. Because as those warm eyes of his track my every step, I feel his attention like a touch when it's not a touch at all. I feel this man in so many ways, inside and out, that I have never felt with another. And I have only just met him. What impact might he have on me, what things might he see in me that I do not want seen, if he were with me beyond my hard limit?

There is little time for me to answer this question, as my path to him is short, and when I stop in front of him, he doesn't touch me. *Free will.* The decision about tonight is in the air.

"All done painting?" he asks.

"For now," I say.

"That's a good answer. It means you plan to pick up that brush again tomorrow. Do I get to see today's work?"

"No," I say without hesitation. "You already saw it before it was finished."

"And what, Faith, makes a painting of me 'finished'?"

"I'll know when it happens."

"But we've established it won't be tonight."

"No," I say. "It won't be tonight."

There's an inference there that he will be around to see it another day, or night, but unique for Nick, he doesn't push. Instead, his gaze lifts beyond my shoulder and he scans what I know to be the now shadowy horizon. "It's peaceful here," he says. "I see why you were drawn to this place."

"It's easy to feel alone here."

"Is that a good thing?"

"Yes," I say, my stare unwaveringly on his, my answer the truth, for so many reasons I will never explain to anyone.

His eyes hold mine as well, and that warmth I'd seen in his stare of minutes before expands between us. "Tonight, Faith?"

"No," I say softly, because while alone is good, he feels better. "Not tonight."

His big hands come down on my waist, and he pulls me to him, our bodies flush, and when his gaze lowers to my mouth and lingers, I know he is thinking about kissing me, I desperately want him to kiss me. But he does not. Instead he says, "How about those gourmet pancakes?"

"Mine or yours?" I ask, finding a smile isn't so hard to come by with this man as I'd once thought.

"I'm thinking we better go with mine," he says. "But we're going to have to make a run to the store."

To the store.

With Nick.

Hard limit number two: *Just sex. Don't get personal.*

I have to put the brakes on everything but sex.

I should tell him this, but he's laced his fingers with mine, and he's leading me toward the stairs.

I repeat my new hard limit often for the next hour. In my head, and not to him, and I do this for what I consider a logical reason. He likes a challenge. I'm not going to issue him one on something I can't afford for him to win. So over and over, I mentally recite: Hard limit number two: *Just sex. Don't get personal.*

The first road block to maintaining that limit is that I go to the store with Nick in the first place. I should have said no to this trip, but the fact that he's absolutely consuming, assuming, and arrogant while there, should have made limit number two easy to follow. The opposite proves true. I learn little things about him and he learns little things about me, like that I hate mushrooms, and he hates olives. He loves orange juice and so do I. Cereal is a necessity, the more marshmallows the better.

In other words: Hard limit number two is a *failure*. And when it comes to Nick Rogers, resistance is futile.

The man finds ways to touch me the entire time we're in the store, drawing attention to us that he seems to enjoy, while I dread the wagging tongues to follow. And I know every moment that I should tell myself to back him off, but I don't. Instead, I help him load up bags with nuts, strawberries, cream, and various other items, and before long we are back in my kitchen, both of us working on his specialty pancakes. And we're talking too much. We have on too many clothes. This is not what I signed up for, but I don't stop it from happening. Somehow, we end up on my bed with our clothes on but no shoes, eating pancakes. Talking again.

There is so much—too much—talking going on. And yet I'm doing a lot of the talking. What is wrong with me? "Tell me about your most memorable courtroom experiences," I prod, my excuse for prodding, my need to finish my painting, to finish the story in his eyes.

Nick laughs. "Where to start?" He considers several moments. "Okay. How's this for memorable? I'm giving the biggest closing argument of my very young career at the time, and I have enough adrenaline pumping through me to fuel an eighteen-wheeler. I'm halfway through it and it's going well. Really damn well."

"And you nailed it."

He laughs again, that deep, sexy laugh that seems to slide up and down my spine, before landing in my belly. "No. I would have, or so I tell myself to this day, but the judge let out a burp so loud that the entire courtroom went silent and then burst into laughter that went on eternally."

"Oh my God. Did you—what did you do?"

"I had to finish, but no one was listening. Thankfully no one listened to the opposing counsel either."

"Did you win?"

"I won," he says, setting our empty plates on the nightstand behind him, before adding, "and I was proud of that win then, but looking back, the case was a slam dunk anyone could have won."

I study him, charmed by this man who gave me humor over the grandeur I've expected. "Humble pie from Nick Rogers? Really?"

That warmth is back in his eyes. "There's much about me that might surprise you, Faith."

"So it seems," I say, but I do not tempt fate, or his questions, by once again telling him the same is true of me, nor do I have a chance to be lured into that misstep. He reaches for me and pulls me to the mattress, his big body framing mine, his powerful thigh pressed between mine. "There is much about you that has surprised me, Faith Winter, and I should tell you that I am so far from fucking you out of my system that I haven't even begun."

He doesn't give me time to react, let alone speak, before his lips are on mine, and he's kissing me, a drugging, slow kiss. And it seems now that I feel every new kiss he claims deeper now in every possible way. He is the escape I'd hoped for, but he is so much more. And eventually we are once again naked, but it's not kinky spankings and naughty talk. It's not *just sex* at all. It's passionate, and intense, yes, but it's softer and gentler than before, in ways I don't understand but feel.

Until we are here and now, in this exact moment when the lights are out, the TV playing a movie with barely audible sound. His heart thunders beneath my ear, telling me that he is still awake as well. I inhale, breathing in that woodsy scent of him, wondering how one person can feel so right and so wrong at the same time. Macom had felt right and then wrong, though the wrong took me longer than it should have to admit, but he was never both at once. Ironically too, when I look into Nick's eyes, I believe he feels the same of me.

I'd told Nick that it's easy to feel alone here in this house, but I didn't tell him just how good that usually is to me. I didn't tell him that alone is safe. I didn't tell him that alone allows me to be me without fearing what someone will see or judge. Alone is a place where I take shelter, and can breathe again. But as necessary as being alone feels right now, Nick has awakened something in me and not just the woman. I am painting again, and suddenly I realize that painting is how I learn, grow, cope.

My mind starts to travel back to the past, to how solitude became my sanctuary, and I meld myself closer to Nick, and somehow find myself asking, "Did you speak to your father often?"

"No," he says simply.

"Do you feel guilty about that?"

"No," he says, no hesitation. Just straight up. This is how it is. This is what it is.

"Have you cried for him?"

"No," he says again. "I have not."

"Me either," I say, and I don't mean to say more, but in the safety of darkness, my eyes hidden, my expression with them, I do. "And it feels bad," I add. "Like I'm supposed to be crying for her."

"If the person didn't deserve your love in life," he replies, "they don't deserve your tears in death."

I know he's right. My mother doesn't deserve my tears, but death is her friend and my enemy. Death is the gaping hole in your soul that just keeps spiraling into blackness. "Do you have siblings, Nick?

"No."

"Other family?"

"No."

"Then you're alone now, too."

"Sweetheart, I was alone when that man was in the room."

As was I with my mother, I think, memories trying to invade my mind, I do not want to revisit. I shut my eyes, inhaling Nick's woodsy scent, losing myself in him. In sleep, I hope. And the shadows start to form. The darkness, too, but then suddenly, I don't smell Nick any longer. That woodsy scent is replaced by flowers. So many flowers. Daisies. Roses. Lilacs. The scent of the Reid Winter Gardens. The scent of my mother that clings to my hair and clothes almost daily. I will my mind away from the place I sense it's taking me. I fight a mental war I lose. I am back in time living my tenth birthday.

My father has just picked me up from school and we've returned to the mansion, and I cannot wait to find my mother, a drawing in my hand, a present for her, while my father has promised mine will come soon. I push through the doors leading to the garden. I drop my drawing, and gasp when it starts to blow. I run and catch it, picking it up and staring down at the colors. So many colors. So many flowers. I've drawn my mother's garden and I know she will be proud.

With my prize back in hand, I rush to the gazebo where I always find her, but stop short when I spy a tall, dark-haired man with her. "I told you not to come here," my mother says.

"Return my phone calls, Meredith, and I won't."

"You do understand I'm married?"

He grabs my mother's arm and pulls her to him. "I also understand you want me," he says, and then he is kissing her, and I open my mouth to scream, but nothing comes out. I turn away and start running and just when I reach the door to the mansion, it opens and my father steps outside. And he's big and tall and like a teddy bear that loves and loves and I want to protect him like he protects me.

"Daddy!" I shout and fling myself at him, hugging him.

"Hey honey. Did you find your mother?"

"She's inside," I say. "We have to find her. I need cake."

He laughs and takes my hand, leading me to the mansion.

"Let's find her and have cake."

My lashes lift, my eyes pierced by sunlight, and I blink away slumber with the sudden realization that Nick is gone. I jolt to a sitting position, pulling the blanket over my nudity, a ball of emotion I refuse to name in my chest. Of course he's gone. Why wouldn't he be gone? That ball in my chest expands and I reject it, refusing to name it. Glancing at the clock, I'm appalled to discover it's after nine. I have the rest of today here before I go back to the mansion, and I'm wasting it in bed, which admittedly was more appealing when Nick was in it, but I'm damn sure not letting today suck because of him leaving without saying a word.

Throwing off the covers, I walk into the bathroom and pull on my pink robe and shove my feet in my pink fluffy slippers. By habit, I brush my teeth and hair, and note the smudges of mascara under my eyes. "No wonder he left," I murmur. I look like the scary chick from that horror movie, *The Grudge*, or something like that. Only she had dark hair, meant to be Goth and scary. At this moment, I'm a close second to her though, for sure. I decide I don't care either. There is no one to care but me and I just want coffee. And I think I might make me some gourmet pancakes my way. I need to stick to doing things my way. And bill collectors or not, I need to stop staying at the mansion. I need my space. I guess that is the gift Nick Rogers left me with.

Me again.

Or maybe that will turn out to be a curse, and I will in turn *curse him* for months to follow.

I walk back into the bedroom, and note that he is, indeed, polite. He took our plates to the kitchen when he left. For some reason, that really irritates me. I walk into the living room, and my mind goes back to the dream, to my tenth birthday, and without a conscious decision to do so, I cross the living room and enter the library. Once I'm there, I walk to the bookshelf and pull out a worn brown journal and sit down on the chair beside it, opening it to pull out a piece of old, worn paper that was once balled up like one of the pieces of paper Nick used for paper basketball in my office yesterday.

"Faith."

I jolt at Nick's voice, looking up to find him standing in the doorway.

"You scared the heck out of me, Nick," I say, my hand at my chest, while his chest is hugged by a snug black t-shirt he's paired with black jeans and biker style boots, the many sides of this man dauntingly sexy.

He starts laughing in reaction, his jaw sporting heavy stubble, while his hair is loose and damp, because apparently, he took a shower and I didn't know.

"It's not funny," I scold.

"No," he says crossing the room to sit on the footstool in front of me. "It's not funny, but I hate to tell you Faith, as beautiful as you are, right now you look like the girl from—"

"*The Grudge*," I supply, remembering my make-up. "I noticed that but I thought...I noticed."

He narrows those too blue, too intelligent eyes on me. "You thought I was gone?"

I could deny the truth but he already knows and games are better when naked or trying to get naked. "Yes," I say. "I did."

His eyes fill with mischief. "And miss a chance to see how you look this morning?"

I scowl and he leans in to kiss me, before saying, "Minty

fresh. I find it interesting that you brushed your teeth and left your mascara like that."

"Maybe I wanted to scare you away," I say. "And fair warning. I'm cranky without coffee."

"We can fix that in about two minutes." His gaze goes to the drawing. "What's this?"

It's a testament to how this man distracts and consumes me that I've forgotten what I'm holding in my hand. "The past," I say, and when I would fold it, Nick catches my hand.

"Was this your work as a child?"

"Yes," I say. "It was."

"You saw things in color then. When did that change?"

That day, I think, but instead I focus on the next time I created anything. "Sixteen."

"What made you change?"

"Life," I say, and because I have no intent of explaining, I add, "I really need that coffee. Actually, I really need a shower."

He studies me several beats, and then releases my hand. "I'll be armed with coffee in the kitchen." I shut the journal and Nick glances at it. "You're a journal writer?"

"No," I say. "I paint. I don't write. It's actually my father's."

He tilts his head. "Did you read it?"

The question cuts right along with the answer. "Every page many times over and I understand him less now that I ever thought possible." I stand and shove it back on the shelf, thinking of the words inside with biting clarity. "He loved her so damn unconditionally." I look at Nick, who remains on the stool. "And affection to me is as you said, with tears. It has to be earned."

"As it should be," he says, and this leaves me curious about him but I tell myself it's time to just stay curious about Nick.

To stop talking.

I walk toward the door, but that curiosity wins. I pause before exiting. "Has anyone earned that from you, Nick?" I ask, turning to find him standing by the stool now, facing me.

"There were a few swipes I tried to turn into something right, but they were always wrong."

"Why?"

"The only answer I have is that I don't believe in happily ever after," he says. "That doesn't sit well with most women."

And just like that he validates an acceptable reason for me to continue to bypass my hard limit of one night. "Since I don't either," I say, "then we really are the perfect distraction for each other, now aren't we? It's really kind of liberating. I don't have to worry about you falling in love with me and you don't have to worry about me falling in love with you."

I don't wait for a reply. I exit the library.

Chapter Nineteen

Faith

NO LOVE.

No happily ever after.

In these things, Nick and I are kindred souls, but that begs the question: Can one soul know another before the two people realize that to be true?

This is what is on my mind as I shower, then dress in faded jeans and t-shirt, concluding that with Nick and I this must be the case. It's the only explanation for the right and the wrong of us together. We aren't so much about dark lust as I'd started out thinking, as we're damage attracting damage. He's damaged. I'm damaged. We see each other. We know each other. The understanding between us, of each other, exists beyond the short time we've known one another. But do

215

damaged people cut each other deeper? Or do they heal each other when no one else can? I don't know this answer but I do know that in a short time, Nick has changed me. Or maybe just opened my eyes.

As if it's not enough to feel this, I am staring at the logo on my t-shirt that reads: Los Angeles Art Museum. My ex-employer, where by day, I embraced art, and then by night, I went home and embraced it again with a brush in my hand. I've let the past invade the present. No. I've let me be me. I'd say that is a good thing, but it exposes things I can't afford to expose. I think it's bad, like Nick, but also like Nick, it feels good. But bad is bad. Why can't I remember that with this man?

This thought lingers in my mind as I finish flat-ironing my hair and apply light make up, a brush of pink here and there, and no more. Satisfied that I no longer resemble a chick from a horror flick, I walk to the closet, stick my feet into black UGG sneakers, and then head toward the bedroom, only to stop dead in my tracks. On the white tiled ledge that frames my equally white tub, is Nick's bag. I just didn't look for it. Maybe I didn't want to see it. Maybe I just wanted him to be the asshole I've called him because that would be simple. But he's not simple and I don't feel like *we're* simple together at all. I like simple. It's easy to explain and control, and yet, I find myself walking toward the living room, seeking Nick out, with simple feeling overrated for the first time in my life.

I know he will make demands. I know he will want too much. I know everything for me should be too much right now. And I don't care. I just want to find him again, and inhale that scent of his, that is positively drugging in all the ways Nick is right and wrong. God, I love it.

216

Exiting the bedroom, the low rumble of Nick's confident voice draws me toward the kitchen. Rounding the corner, I find him sitting at the island in profile to me, his hair now tied at his nape, his orange and black Tiger tattoo displayed as he holds the phone to his ear. The art is detailed, exquisite really, but somehow simplistic and fierce, while the man too is fierce, there is nothing simple about Nick Rogers or what he makes me feel.

"Damn it, North," he scolds into the phone, glancing in my direction his eyes warming as they find me, and when I might expect him to somehow make this moment sexual, he does not. He lifts his cup to offer me his coffee, an intimate gesture that does funny things to my belly. I start in his direction and he scowls at something North has said. "Think like the enemy," he scolds the other man. "I would have prepped my client for every question you gave me for this witness."

I reach the island and pick up Nick's cup, my eyes meeting his as I place my lips where his lips may well have been moments before, but the instant the hot beverage touches my lips, the harsh taste of plain black coffee has me scowling. Nick laughs and apparently North is confused, because Nick says, "No. That wasn't funny and you will get your ass handed to you by opposing counsel and then by me. "

Yikes. North is in hot water and I decide to let Nick focus. I set his cup back down, and I walk to the coffee pot and get another cup brewing for me, listening as he goes back and forth with North for the next couple of minutes. My coffee has brewed and I'm just pouring white chocolate creamer in my steaming cup, when Nick says, "Just meet me at my place at five. We're going to be ready in the morning if we're up all night." He ends the call.

And I feel the end of the weekend like a punch in the chest.

I stand at the counter, my back to him, not about to turn until I figure out what the heck this reaction is that I'm having. What I'm *feeling*, which I guess is another curse and gift, Nick has given me. I am feeling things again because of him but he's about to leave. And, of course, he is. It's Sunday. And rental property or not, he lives and works in another city, and I'd planned on telling him to leave anyway. Hadn't I? No. I hadn't. I'm just trying to make myself feel simple and in control. And I am those things. This is a fling. This is a *weekend* fling. It was supposed to be one night. It's just a—

Nick steps behind me, his hands at my waist, his touch radiating through me with more impact than any man should ever have over me, especially since this is the last time I might ever touch him. And it *feels* much worse in premise than I'd imagined.

He leans in and nuzzles my hair, inhaling like he is breathing me in. And God, I really love when he does that. "Come to the city with me," he says.

Shock rolls through me and I face him, my hands landing hard on his chest. "What?"

"Come with me, Faith. I have to go back to San Francisco. If you're with me, then we can deal with the bank together. And you need a break from all of this. We'll come back here for the weekend."

"I have to run the winery, Nick."

His eyes darken, and not with disappointment, but rather awareness I have not yet realized. "At least you didn't decide your new hard limit includes me leaving and never seeing you again."

He's right. I didn't. This man is unraveling every carefully crafted plan I had and I can't seem to care. And I should care. This is trouble. He's trouble. *I'm* trouble. "What are we doing here, Nick? What is this?"

His hands settle on the counter on either side of me, his big body crowding mine without touching me. "I don't know, Faith," he says, "but let's find out."

"You don't—we don't—"

"I could supply a number of phrases to end that statement, but it would be words. Just words. I'm not done with you and I hope like hell you're not done with me, Faith."

"I wish I was," I say, angry at him for complicating my life. Happy that he has at the same time, because yes. I'm still fucked up.

"Ditto, sweetheart. We're here now, though. Agreed?"

"Yes," I say. "Agreed."

"Then let's make a new hard limit. The only hard limit that exists until we decide together otherwise, is we take this one day at a time."

Until we decide together. I realize with those words part of Nick's appeal. He's this uber alpha male. He's sexy. He's demanding. But he has this way of knowing when to back off, when to ask. This is new to me. This is right, not wrong. "One day at a time," I agree.

"Come to San Francisco with me."

I want to, I realize. I want to know who he is in his own domain, but want doesn't equal need. And I need to be here. "I can't just leave the winery."

"You have a manager. A good one, you said."

"Kasey is amazing," I say, "but I do my best to protect him and the staff from the bill collectors who stalk us during the week. I can't leave, Nick. I won't. Not now."

The doorbell rings. "Holy fuck," he says. "This isn't helping my case." He starts to move away, but I catch his arm.

"Damn it, Nick," I warn. "Just because we agreed to take this day by day is not an invitation for you to take over my life. I run my life."

"I know you run your life, sweetheart. I can't tell you enough times, I get it. Let me be clear. It makes me hot. It makes me want to bend you over the counter. But let me also be clear. I'm now your attorney, Faith. Unless we've deviated from that plan, I'm getting that door."

I purse my lips and release him, only to have him lean over, kiss me, and then he's on the move in about two flat seconds. "At least he has his pants zipped this time," I murmur, taking off after him, overwhelmed by Nick's desire to protect me and I tell myself to be smart enough to accept it, but to be strong enough not to count on it, now, or ever.

Clearing the hallway, I enter the foyer at the same moment that Josh, dressed in khakis and a button down, walks in the front door, but he doesn't seem to notice me. He shuts the door and faces Nick, the two men crackling with opposing male energy. "Nick Rogers, was the name, right?" Josh asks, and I'm not sure if he's being a smart ass or playing coy, considering he knew Nick's name immediately at the art gallery.

Nick doesn't respond. As in, at all. Seconds tick by and then more, and I can't take it. I have to break the tension before Josh does, and it ends badly for him. "Josh," I say, hurrying forward, remembering now. "I forgot you were stopping by."

"Obviously," he says, his tone acidic. "And clearly this isn't the time to have a serious business discussion. Call me

Monday and we'll talk through decisions that need to be made, or perhaps, forgotten." He turns and walks out of the door.

Certain this is about Macom, that this is personal not professional, I'm instantly angry and indignant, and I charge after him, not bothering to shut the door behind me. "Stop," I call after him, a cold gust of morning wind blasting me but I'm too hot-tempered to care.

Thankfully, he does as I've ordered, halfway down the stairs, turning to face me. "Now is clearly not the time, Faith."

"Because I dare to have a life again?" I demand, walking to the edge of the porch.

"That man in there is none of my business," he says. "But you are."

"My work is your business," I snap back.

"Exactly," he agrees. "And when I find out you've finally started painting again, that's a good thing. A distraction is not." He motions to my shirt. "You're wearing an art shirt. This gives me hope that we're back on track. You need to stay focused and get your career back on track."

"I painted *Nick*," I snap back before I can stop myself. "He inspired me to paint. Having a life again inspired me to paint."

He goes very still. "You painted a portrait?"

"Yes. I did. And I might do more. I might do a lot of things, but not now. Now, I have to save the winery and you know what, Josh? I know you need people who make money for you. I understand if you can't wait this out with me."

"I do need to make money, Faith. But more than anything I need clients who are actively involved in the career I'm representing them for. You need to be painting. I need to be placing your work. I got a call after the show from a representative of the L.A. Art Forum. They're interested in your work for next month's show."

My eyes go wide at the mention of one of the most prestigious events in the art world. "They are? They never—"

"They are now because you actually got out there and did something for your art. But I'm not saying yes when you're telling me now is not the time. So think about that, Faith. How much can you fit in your life right now? Cut what won't work, and if that's your art and me, I need to know and know quickly." He turns and walks away.

And I stand there, watching him cross to his white Porsche, because why wouldn't my agent drive a Porsche like my ex, who he's best friends with. Still pissed, really baffled about what just happened, I don't wait for him to leave. I walk into the house. The minute I'm inside, Nick shuts the door and pulls me to him.

"That wasn't about your art, sweetheart," he says, his hands at my waist. "You know that, right?"

"I don't know what the hell that was."

"He wants to fuck you. He's probably in love with you."

I blanch. "What? No. No. No. He's best friends with my ex."

"Come on, Faith. Some part of you knows that man wants you. And you need a new agent."

"Because you think he wants to fuck me?" I demand, angry all over again at these men trying to run my life. I push away from him, darting down the hallway, where I can have some coffee and get more wired and angry at the rest of the world.

Nick's on my heels, I can feel him, a heavy force of alpha pain-in-my-ass man right now, that while sexy as hell at moments, is not now. I enter the kitchen and round the island, fully intending to keep it between us, but he has other ideas. I turn and he's already with me, pressing me against the counter, his big, delicious, pain-in-my-ass body, crowding mine.

"He wants to fuck you, Faith. He's thinking with his dick, not his head. That isn't good for you."

"And what are you doing, Nick?"

"Sweetheart, I have no hesitation in telling you that I want to fuck you, and then do it all over again. But this isn't about me and you fucking. This is about your career."

"You don't know me enough to care about this."

"When do I get to care, Faith? One week? One month? Two? Tell me. Because this is new fucking territory for me."

"You can't—"

"I do and the one thing that your dickhead agent and I agree on is the fact that you need to paint. And I'm going to make you paint. And when you do, you need an agent who isn't thinking about fucking you instead of selling you."

"He's my ex's best friend," I say, returning to the explanation I've given myself every time I felt awkward with Josh.

"You said that already and it still changes nothing."

"You want me to change agents because he wants to fuck me and so do you."

"Sweetheart, I'm going to make sure you're well enough fucked that he never has a shot. And that's only going to piss him off more. Be ready. His wrath is coming but before it comes. Tell him to set up that show he mentioned."

"It's not that simple," I argue. "You don't understand."

"I understand that I want to fuck an artist. So you're going to be an artist."

I blink at the ridiculousness of that statement. "So I have to be an artist because you want to fuck an artist?"

"You *are* an artist, Faith. End of story and everything else you do is simply a distraction."

"Including you?"

He strokes a lock of hair behind my ear. "I'm okay with being second to your art."

Once again, Nick surprises me, delivering an answer that is nothing that I expect, and everything I didn't even know I wanted.

"Second to your art," he adds. "But not another man. New hard limit." He cups my face. "Whatever this is, it's exclusive. You fuck no one else until we decide it's over."

"And you, Nick?" I ask. "Will you fuck someone else?"

"Sweetheart. You have my full attention and not only do I want no one else. I want all of you and I'm not going to settle for any less."

I'm not sure what he means by this. *All of me.* And I don't ask because he can't have all of me. Which is why this should be the end. But when he kisses me I'm alive. When he touches me I'm on fire. When he's with me, I'm not alone, even though I would be with anyone else. So when he says, "Hard limit, Faith. Only us," I don't push him away and I don't push back. I live dangerously. I say, "Hard limit. Only us."

And just like that, Nick has proven I was right about him from the beginning. He is dark lust. He is all-consuming. He is an escape I crave. Maybe he's even an obsession as he'd called me. But more so, he *is* dangerous. I sense it. I feel it like I feel this man in every part of me inside and out.

But then, so am I.

Chapter Twenty

Faith

NICK PACKS UP HIS WORK AND MOST OF MY documents, and we head to the winery with the intent of having lunch there and reviewing his legal plan with the bank. And now, sitting in the passenger seat of his car, I am aware of this man next to me in ways I have never been aware of another man. It's not about looking at him and being aroused. Or looking at him and thinking about how sexy he is. It's about how I feel him inside and out. The way I know him beyond logic and reason. And maybe that means things are going too fast, but to where? We agreed. No love. No forever. This is just "us" and "us" makes me *feel* something that isn't guilt and pain. And I need that. I guess that means I need him, and that's a terrifying thought, to need someone else. My father needed my mother and that made him a fool.

"What are you going to do about Josh?" Nick asks.

I breathe out. "Have a heart-to-heart with him."

"You can't reason with a man who's thinking with his dick, sweetheart."

"I really hope you're wrong about his feelings for me, but even if you're not, he kept me on despite Macom telling him to drop me, *and* he placed my work when I was doing nothing to support it myself. No agent would have done that."

He glances over at me. "Macom told him to drop you?"

"Yes," I say. "I learned that he's all about an eye for an eye. I left him. It wounded his ego. He lashed out. And as much money as he makes Josh, Josh had the courage to tell him that professional and personal are two different things. I'd like to think that's about my work, not some personal agenda."

"Your work is exceptional, Faith," Nick says. "And any inference you took from my evaluation of Josh's interest in you otherwise was not intended. I also know his reputation. He's a good agent, but he's a good agent acting badly. He indirectly threatened you today when he said he'd cancel your art in the forum, and he did so because I was at your house."

"You're right. He did, but he deserves to have me talk to him not drop him right when I might find some success that he helped create. Like I said, and this is big: That man kept me on and helped place my work, when I was doing nothing to support that work."

He turns us into the winery property and glances over at me again. "Loyalty is a good quality, but once a man is in the place he's in with a woman, there's no room for delicate conversation. My advice that you didn't ask for: Be frank."

"You say this like it's from experience."

"I've never been shameless over a woman. Ever. But as I said. Love and hate wear a fine line and I've fought many a battle in court over that line."

"Noted, counselor," I say. "Be direct. I really don't have a problem with direct."

He gives me a sexy, half smile. "And yet you're damn good at talking in circles. You would have been a hell of an opponent in court."

"Oh no," I say. "I hate the spotlight. I would have hated the way people would stare at me and be hanging on my words."

"And yet your art puts you in the spotlight."

"My art is the spotlight," I say. "And that's how I like it." He turns us into the drive of the mansion. "And speaking of the spotlight. Because I've never brought a man here, everyone is going to be talking about the two of us."

"Not even Macom?"

"No," I say simply, saved from more when we pull to a halt at the front of the mansion.

But Nick still tries. "Just no?"

"Just no," I say, as the valets open both of our doors, but my mind is already on the way my father hated the idea of me with an artist, and how much I was certain my mother would like me with Macom a little too much. Not for the first time, I wonder how my father would have justified forgiving that one.

I make small talk with the valets, and Nick rounds the car to join me, his hand settling at my lower back, and the heavy weight of their stares stiffens my spine. "They'll get used to me," Nick promises, and the fact that he knows what I feel, and that he's made it clear he's sharing that burden with me, is more impactful to me than anything else he's done to this point. It's not about sex. It's not about legal matters. It's about a small moment of time that he recognized as mattering to me.

We walk the steps and as we reach the top level, the doors are opened for us, and just inside the foyer, Kasey greets us. Tall, and silver-gray at fifty, he is a good-looking man who is friendly, well-liked, and still manages to be reserved in his personal life. "Fair warning," he says. "We have a bridezilla in the house. I'd recommend taking cover."

I laugh. "You are a bridezilla expert," I say and as he glances at Nick, surprise in the depth of his stare, Nick offers him his hand.

"Nick Rogers."

"Kasey Gilligan," Kasey greets, and the two men shake hands and exchange small talk that doesn't last. Kasey's walk-ie-talkie goes off on his belt. "Trouble in the garden," a voice says.

"That's about the bridezilla," he says. "I need to go focus her on her vows."

Guilt over his dilemma, and my weekend away, wash over me. "Do you need—"

"No," he says. "I do not need your help. I'm quite capable of running this place."

"I know that."

"This weekend gave me hope that you might mean that statement."

He leaves me no room to argue. In a blink, he's gone and Nick glances down at me, arching a brow. "It's not about how he handles the management of the winery. It's about the challenges that were my mother, and now the bank."

"Then let's go talk about overcoming those things," he says. "Because my hard limit was made with an artist." He urges me forward and I guide him to the stairwell and a path behind it with a second stairwell leading down. The way he pushes me to paint, affects me in ways I'll analyze later, alone.

Once we're in the basement level, where there is a gift shop and a restaurant, we find our way to a rare vacant table among the fifteen that are mostly occupied, the floral table-cloths and designs in the center my mother's choice.

"What do you recommend?" Nick asks, grabbing the menu on the table, and I wonder if he knows the way he fills the room, or the way men look at him with envy, and the women with desire.

"Any of the five quiche choices," I reply. "The chef trained in France, and apparently, that's a thing there. She knows her quiche."

"Quiche it is," he says right as Samantha, our waitress appears.

Nick turns his attention to her, and I watch, waiting for her gorgeous brunette bombshell looks to affect him, but if he notices, he shows no reaction at all. In fact, his hand finds my knee under the table, his eyes looking in my direction more than not.

And it's only moments after we've ordered that, compliments of another waiter, we have coffee in front of us, and I find myself in the center of Nick's keen blue eyes. "I can't believe you've never been to Paris, considering the wine culture."

"My parents went. I stayed home."

Awareness that shouldn't be possible flickers in his eyes. "They invited you. You didn't want to go."

"I wanted to go," I say. "Just not with them."

"How bad was your relationship with your mother?"

"I'd say it ranked about where you describe that of yours

with your father."

"And everyone here knew?"

"No," I say. "We put on a good show."

"But Kasey knew."

"Kasey didn't know until after my father died and I was forced to become the wall between the two of them. Honestly, it's made Kasey and I closer. He loved my father and was confused by his relationship with my mother as well. I mean, my father was tough, charismatic and dynamic in business. His willingness to take my mother's abuse was illogical."

"Love is blind," he says wryly. "Or so it seems." He changes the subject. "I like Kasey, by the way."

"He's a good man," I say. "And a friend."

"How have you explained the bill collectors?"

"He knows there are probate issues, which knowing my mother as he did, does not surprise him."

"So you aren't going to lose him?"

"No. Not now. But I'm nervous about this dragging on too long and giving him cold feet."

"I'd like to talk to him next week, if you're okay with that?"

"Why?"

"I'm looking for any insight into your mother's activities he might give me that, as an outsider, might stand out to me, and not you."

"Of course," I say. "That seems logical. I'll tell him you'll call, but you have your deposition, Nick. You need to focus on that."

"I can walk and chew bubblegum at the same time, sweetheart. I do it all the time."

Our food is set in front of us, and in a few moments, we are both holding forks and Nick takes a bite. "Well?" I ask.

"Excellent," he approves. "No wonder you never learned to cook when you could eat here."

We chat a moment and I'm struck by the easy comfort I have with this man in any setting. It's not something I have with people and I've often thought that I stayed with Macom so long because I needed a connection to another human being. Not because I needed him.

"Tell me about the show Josh mentioned," Nick urges, a few bites into our meal.

The show again. He's mentioned it twice, and I haven't even let the possibility of being in that show sink in yet, nor do I want to talk about it. "You listened in on the entire conversation between myself and Josh, didn't you?"

"Unapologetically," he says, his eyes challenging me to disapprove.

But I don't. I feel envy instead at his ability to be frank and unapologetic about pretty much everything. Who he is. What he is. How he feels about his father. God. To be that free. What would it be like?

"You told him you painted me," Nick says.

"I shouldn't have," I reply without hesitation.

"Why?"

"Because I used it to justify me being with you."

Surprise flickers in his eyes. "I realized that," he says. "I wasn't sure you did."

"Otherwise, I'm not sorry I told him. You did inspire me to paint, Nick."

"By being an arrogant asshole you aren't sure you can trust?"

He's right. That is what happened, but somehow that feeling I'd had about him no longer weighs on me as it had. "I

231

don't trust easily."

"Those who do, get burned," he says, and there's something in his eyes, in his voice, that I cannot name, but wish I could and I never get the chance. He circles back to where this started. "The show, Faith."

"The show," I repeat, my mind tracking back to those years in L.A. "Being picked for it has always been a dream for me. For years, my work was presented to them. For years, I was declined."

"And this time they came to you," he observes.

That hope and dream inside me rises up with painful insistence and I shove it back down. "An inquiry means nothing."

"Have they inquired before?"

"No, but they may rule me out."

"But if they want you, you're not going to decline."

It's not a question. It's a command, and while I don't take commands well, this one is well-intended, but also ineffective for reasons out of his control. "They aren't going to accept me. It's a month away."

"Don't do that, Faith." His tone is absolute.

"Don't do what?"

"Downplay how big this is for you. Don't find a way to make it not matter."

I stare at him, trying to understand how this man I barely know can be this supportive. Is it real? Is it just a part of his temporary obsession with me? He arches a brow at my silent scrutiny, but I am saved a real answer when more food appears. But it's not a true escape. The moment we're alone, Nick returns to the topic. "What does the show do for you?"

"If you're spotlighted, you've made it. Those are the artists people want to have in their stores and on their walls."

Unbidden, my mind goes back to the day I'd told my father I had a full scholarship to UCLA. There had been hugs. Excitement. Smiles. Then he'd said, "I can see it now. Our wine will be in every gallery in the country because you know the wine that pairs with the art." And I'd been devastated. My art was never going to be more than a hobby to him.

Nick's knees capture mine under the table and my eyes jerk to his. "What just happened, sweetheart?" he asks, that tender warmth back in his eyes, and a knot forms in my throat.

"If I can get into the show, I can sell my work, and save the winery."

Nick's eyes narrow on mine, and I swear in that moment, it feels like he's diving deep into my soul and seeing too much again. "When you get into the show, it's about you, not the winery."

"But the money—"

"Let's talk about the winery and money with my attorney hat on."

I shove my plate aside and Nick does the same. "Okay. I don't like how that sounds."

"Money isn't your issue," he says. "If that were the case, I'd take advantage of a good investment, write you a check, get a return, and we'd be done with this."

"I'm not foolish enough to miss the way you framed that in a way you think I'd find acceptable, but you giving me money that I wouldn't take no matter how you presented it, isn't your point."

"No. It's not. Obviously, Frank has you focused on money being your salvation when it's not."

"You yourself wanted to know the financial status of the winery," I point out.

"Because if it's a sinking ship, there's no reason to save it. That isn't the case, so we move on to your primary problem: the absence of a will is the issue."

"I have my father's will that said my mother inherits on the stipulation that I inherit next."

"But we have no idea what documents came after that will that might say otherwise. There may be none. The bank may just hope they can pressure you into walking away. They may even have an investor who wants the property and wants you to sell cheap."

"Can they be a part of that? Can they do that?"

"There are a lot of things that shouldn't be done that get done. And I'm having someone on my research team look into the money trail and the mystery of your mother's barren bank accounts."

Guilt assails me again and it is not a feeling I enjoy. It's heavy and sharp, and mean. "Please don't spend money on my behalf."

"I have people I'm already paying," he says. "I promise you, the bank will know what we don't. And we won't, nor will I allow us to have, that disadvantage." He slides my plate in front of me. "I got this. Stop worrying."

"Faith."

At the sound of my name, I look up to find the restaurant manager, Sheila, standing beside us, and the distressed look on her face has my spine straightening. "What is it, Sheila?"

"There's a man at the door asking to see you who looks like…he looks like…"

My blood runs cold. "My father," I supply, without ever looking toward the door. "I'll be there in a moment."

She nods and leaves and Nick glances at the man by the

door that I know to be tall, fit, and with white hair that was once red. "Bill Winter," he says. "Your uncle, your father's twin, and the CEO of Pier 111, a social media platform that's giving Facebook a run for its money. He was also estranged from your father for eight years before his death."

"Reminding me that you studied me like you were picking a refrigerator out isn't a good thing right now, Nick."

"As I've said, I studied you like a woman who intrigued me," he reminds me. "And I'm not going to pretend naiveté I don't have and I know you well enough to know that's not what you want."

"No," I concede. "I wouldn't. I need to go deal with him. And it won't take long."

He considers me for several moments before releasing my knees, he's still holding. "I'm here if you need me."

Has anyone I wanted to say those words ever said them to me? "Thank you."

I stand and turn toward the door, and sure enough, there stands Bill Winter, and I swear seeing him, with his likeness to my father, turns my knees to rubber. But it also angers me and my spine straightens. I start walking, crossing the small space to meet him at the archway that is the entrance to the restaurant. "What are you doing here, Bill?" I ask, my voice sharp despite my low tone.

Towering over me by a good foot, he stares down at me, his blue eyes so like my father's it hurts to look at him. "How are you, Faith?"

"What are you doing here, Bill?" I repeat.

"I'm your only living family. I'm checking on my niece."

"You're my blood, but not my family. My father would not want you here."

"Your father and I made peace before he died."

"No you didn't," I say, rejecting what would add another irrational personal decision to my father's track record.

"We did, but regardless," he says. "I owe him. And that means protecting you. The bank called me. I understand there are financial issues. Let me help."

I am appalled and shocked that the bank went to Bill. "I don't want or need your help and if I did, my father would roll over in his grave if I took it."

"I told you. We came to terms before he died."

"I don't believe you, but it doesn't matter. I don't care."

Nick steps to my side, his hand settling possessively at my back, his presence drawing Bill's immediate attention. "Bill Winter." My uncle introduces himself. "And you are?"

"Faith's loyal servant," Nick assures him. "And everyone else's nightmare. The name is Nick Rogers." He doesn't extend his hand, nor does Bill extend his own.

Bill's eyes narrow at the name. "I've heard you're a real bastard."

"And here I thought I got rid of my nice guy reputation. I understand you're leaving. We'll walk you out."

Bill gives a smirk that almost borders on amused, and then looks at me. "I'm staying at the cottage. I'll be close if you need me." He turns and walks away.

Nick flags Sheila. "Make sure he leaves and if he doesn't, call Faith."

I nod my approval to Sheila and Nick turns to me. "Where can we talk?"

"This way," I say, motioning us into the hallway that leads nowhere but an exit door and the minute we're there, Nick's hands are on my hips.

"What cottage?"

"He owns a property up the road, but he's rarely here, and when he is, I don't see him. He says the bank called him about the default. Can they do that?"

"Context is everything and he holds the family name. Does he want the winery?"

"He's a billionaire, Nick. He doesn't want or need this place."

"Then why was he here?"

"To help, he said. Basically, to repent for his sins."

Nick's energy sharpens. "What sins, Faith?"

"He's the reason I stayed in L.A. after my graduation. He's also one of the reasons I don't believe in happily ever after and therefore make such a good fuck buddy. He slept with my mother. She got mad at him and to get back at him, told my father, who predictably forgave her, but not his brother. And that was it for me. I was out of here."

I blink and Nick's hands are on my face, his big body pinning me against the wall. "Don't do that," he says for the second time since we arrived. "Don't decide what we are or are not based on that man or anyone else. We decide otherwise, or they win and we're weak. We are not weak."

Emotions I swore I wanted to feel, but don't, well in my chest. "Nick, you—"

"I am not my father and you are not your mother. We decide who we are, Faith. Not them. Say it."

"We decide," I whisper.

"We decide," he repeats, stroking my cheek a moment before his lips brush mine. "I fucking hate that I have to leave you right now. Come with me."

"You know I can't. You have to see that."

He looks skyward, seeming to struggle not to push me, before he says, "Let's make sure uncle dearest has left before I leave."

A full hour later, I finally convince Nick he has to leave. My uncle is gone. His number is in my phone. He has a deposition he has to prep for. I walk him to his car, and despite the many people most likely watching, he pulls me to him and kisses me soundly on the lips. "I'm going to miss the hell out of you and I don't even know what to do with that." A moment later, he's in his car, as if he fears he won't leave. Another few moments, and I'm standing on the steps of the mansion, watching him drive away, a storm brewing inside me, while I replay his words: *I am not my father and you are not your mother.*

The problem is, I have a whole lot more of my mother in me than Nick Rogers knows.

Chapter Twenty-One

Tiger

WHAT THE HELL IS THIS WOMAN DOING TO ME?

That's one of many thoughts I have as I leave behind Reid Winter Winery, and Faith with it. Leaving her kills me, and I have never in all the many fucks I've shared with a woman, given two fucks about the morning after, or the second morning after as it may be, and what do I do? I choose Faith, a woman I went looking for to destroy. She's not the killer I thought she was, but she might be when she finds out who my father is, and why I sought her out. And she'll have to know there's no way around it. Really, this is poetic justice. I told Faith I'm not like my father, but running through women, and not giving two fucks, is something he did well, and I do better. How profound that the one I give a shit about is going to hate me like she's never hated before.

I pull onto the main highway and tail lights greet me. "Fuck," I growl, forced to halt behind a line of cars, while debating the pros and cons of turning around, throwing Faith over my shoulder, and taking her home with me. Something feels off with her uncle. Something feels wrong in general and it's not her.

Looking for answers and action, I fish my phone from my pocket and use Siri to find the shop that has Faith's car, making arrangements to pay for it and have it delivered to her over the weekend when I plan to be with her. By the time I end the call, the traffic still hasn't moved, and I dial Beck. "Nicholas," he greets.

"The uncle," I say.

"Filthy rich snake of a bastard," he says, clearly aware of who I'm talking about.

"He fucked Faith's mom."

"Who didn't?" He laughs. "That woman saw more action than ten Taco Bells on Friday night at two am."

"The uncle," I repeat.

"He had random contact with Meredith Winter over the years, but nothing notable after the obvious falling out between him and her husband. And I'm sure you know that he's married to one of the billionaire Warren Hotel heiresses now."

"I knew," I say, having done plenty of my own research. "That's how he got the money for his start-up. Any contact between him and Faith?"

"Aside from him attending both her mother's and father's funerals, none."

"Find out if he, or anyone for that matter, has an interest

in the property the winery is sitting on," I say, before moving on. "Josh—"

"The agent," he says. "What about him?"

"Could Macom have used him to connect to Faith's mother or my father?"

"Interesting premise when I thought of it as well," Beck says, "but I cross referenced phone numbers and emails. There's nothing."

Grimacing, and with plenty of tail lights and time in my future, I lead the conversation to the bank, and draw Beck into a debate over their motives, before my mind takes me to a place I don't want to go. Not with Faith in Sonoma and me in San Francisco. "What if Faith isn't a killer, but now she's the one in the way of whoever is?"

"Any time a million dollars plus is missing and two people are dead of the exact same cause two months apart, the possibility of someone else ending up dead exists. But unlike you apparently, I won't conclude a murder or murders were committed until you get me your father's, and Meredith Winter's autopsy reports. And for the record, I'm far from thinking Faith Winter is innocent. She and her mother could easily have been a scam team. Always remember that in the absence of evidence, there is someone making sure there's an absence of evidence. I'll warn you again. Watch your back. You have my excessively large bill to pay."

He hangs up on the warning I'd feel obligated to give me, too, but I'm not a fool. I read people with a lot less of a look into their lives than I have into Faith's. I dial Abel Baldwin, my closest friend, and one of the best damn criminal attorneys on the planet. "I was starting to think you might be dead, too," he says, when he picks up. "What happened with Faith Winter?"

I glance at the clock on my dash. "Can you meet me at my place at four?"

"Now I'm really curious. I'll be there."

I asked him to help me destroy her. Now I need to pull back the reins and have him help me save her. And I return to: *What the hell is this woman doing to me?*

Just after four, Abel and I sit in the living room of my house, him on the sectional that occupies most of the room, me on a chair across from him. One of his many Irish whiskey picks he brings by my place weekly is in our glasses, and while the sectional he occupies is a pale gray, my mood is decidedly darker. "Good stuff, right?" Abel asks, refilling his glass.

"One of your better picks," I say, but when he lifts the bottle in my direction I wave him off. "I need to stay sharp. I have work to do."

"I'll hang out and get boozed, and ask stupid questions to piss you off because what are friends for?"

"You're a hell of a friend, Abel. One hell of a friend."

He downs his whiskey. "I love watching North geek out and start reciting facts."

"The kid's an encyclopedia," I say, motioning to his severely buzzed blond hair. "You thinking about going back to the army or what?"

"Starting a trial next week," he says. "The judge is an ex-SEAL."

"And you plan on reminding him that you are, too."

His lips quirk. "Gotta work what you got." He narrows his eyes at me. "And you got me, Nick. Put me to work here.

What's the elephant in the room you want to talk about but haven't?"

"What's it going to cost me to get those autopsy results sooner than three weeks from now?"

"We just filed the order," he says. "You can't buy your way past a medical procedure. This isn't a crime TV show and you know it. Toxicology, which is what we're looking at, will take weeks and even months."

"Understood," I say, "but we both know we can move certain aspects of this to sooner, rather than later. Whatever it costs, make it happen."

He narrows his eyes on me, and after a decade of friendship, I'm not surprised at what comes next. "You fucked her."

"I've fucked a lot of women."

"This one got to you. Nick, damn it. You got me involved in this because of one word: Murder. Let's recap. You find a million dollars in checks written by your father to this woman's mother, who is now dead, by the same means as your father, thus making Faith Winter, the biggest suspect, and you choose to fuck her."

"I'm crystal clear on the details. And murder is still on the table. I just don't think she did it."

The doorbell rings and I curse. "Leave it to North to be early." I scrub my jaw and I'm about to get up when Abel says, "Nick. Man. Many a good man fell over a woman and I'm pretty fucking sure the same can be said in reverse. Watch where you stick your cock."

"Says the guy who can't stop banging his ex," I remind him, standing and heading for the door, my booted feet heavy on the pale wood of the living room floor, only to have him shout out, "She has magnificent breasts."

I laugh, and she must, because that's not the first time I've heard that. But his warning about fucking Faith has hit a nerve and my own warning replays in my mind, when I swore I wouldn't let it again. You never find guilt when you're looking for innocence.

I open the door to find North standing in front of me looking like Clark Kent if Clark Kent was skinny and geeky. But that's the thing about North. There's more to him than meets the eye. He will slay you with facts. Superman-slay you. And damn it, there is more to Faith than meets the eye. I know it. I feel it. And I need to find out what and now, before a surprise slays me.

It's eleven when I finally have my house to myself again, and I walk into my office and bypass the pine carpenter-style desk that is the centerpiece. Instead, I walk to the oversized brown leather chair in the corner, a floor-to-ceiling window beside it, and sit down. Beside it is a stack of paperwork from my father's office and another from his home, that led me to Meredith Winter in the first place. I've been through it all ten times, and there is nothing that gives me the answers I need. Who killed him? I've told myself that it is simply my need for closure, but the truth is, the idea that that man was thwarted by anyone but me in his death, claws at me. Bastard that it makes me, I wanted the man around just to show him his son would always be better. Someone took that from me. And my gift to myself is to find that person. That's my form of grief. There is no guilt to it.

Guilt.

That's what I keep sensing in Faith, but my mind goes back to lying in bed with her last night. When she'd asked if I had cried for my father. When she felt she should have for her mother.

Guilt.

Acceptable guilt that I can live with and help her live with. It's nothing more than that. I let that thought simmer for several minutes, with space between myself and Faith, and I still feel the same. She didn't kill my father or her mother.

I remove my phone from my pocket and dial her. She picks up on the second ring. "Nick," she says, and damn it, how is it that my name on this woman's lips, can make my cock hard and my heart soft.

"Hey, sweetheart."

"Did you finish your prep?" she asks, once again showing concern about my work that I've never given another woman a chance to express. Maybe they would have. Maybe they wouldn't have. I just didn't care to have them try.

"We're ready," I say. "We'll kill it at every turn."

"I'm glad," she says. "I was worried I'd distracted you."

"You do distract me, Faith, but in all the right ways. Where are you?"

"My house," she says.

"I thought you were staying at the winery?"

"I was inspired to paint."

I lean back in the chair, shutting my eyes, imagining her standing at her canvas, beautiful, gifted, focused. "Are you painting me, Faith?"

"Yes," she says. "Actually I am. I'm still trying to understand you. Now that you're gone…"

"Now that I'm gone, what?"

"I don't know. Something."

"Something," I repeat, opening my eyes and standing up, facing the window, the glow of the lights on the Golden Gate Bridge before me. "There is something, Faith," I add, wanting her to tell me what I sense. "What is it?"

She's silent for several beats. "Are we talking about you or me, now?"

"You," I say. "I'm your attorney and the man in your bed and life. What haven't you told me?"

"We're new, Nick. There's a lot I haven't told you."

I feel those words like another claw in my heart and every warning that's been thrown at me the past few hours digs in deeper. I have never been a fool who thinks with his dick. I'm not starting now. "I want you to tell me, but you know I'll find out."

"Of course you will. You enjoy a challenge. Goodnight, Nick."

She hangs up.

Chapter Twenty-Two

Tiger

THAT CONVERSATION WITH FAITH HAUNTS ME MOST OF the night, and by seven in the morning, I'm at work behind my desk on the fifth floor of the second tallest building in San Francisco. By eight, I've woken up three clients, and drafted a contract. All while wearing a black suit with a royal-fucking-blue tie that reminds me of Faith's dress. Her ripped dress, and that moment in the car when I'd leaned in and tasted her. The pencil in my hand snaps.

It's at that moment that North pops his head in the door. "Can we—"

"No," I say. "If you aren't ready now, you won't be. You have three hours before they arrive and you need a set of balls. Go find them."

He shoves his glasses up his nose. "I actually know the location of my balls. The use of said—"

"I'm not going to teach you how to hold your balls," I bite out. "Go play with them alone."

He has the good sense to leave. Unfortunately, my assistant appears in the spot he's just left. "I have coffee," she says.

"You never bring me coffee," I say, but nevertheless, in a rush of bouncing brown curls and sweet smelling perfume, a cup is in front of me. I glance at it and her. "When I ask for coffee, you say 'fuck you.' What the hell is going on?"

"It's my twentieth wedding anniversary," she says waving fingers at me. "I woke up to a sapphire this morning. I guess at fifty I've still got the goods."

And at fifty, she's beautiful and devoted to one man, where Meredith Winter was devoted to many. "Happy fucking anniversary. Use my card and go to a ridiculously expensive dinner, and I need two things from you."

"Item one," she prods.

"I need a dress."

She arches a brow. "Is there something you need to tell me, boss?"

"Royal blue. A slit in the front. Expensive."

"I need more than that, starting with size?"

"Petite."

She grimaces. "I'm good or I wouldn't be working for you, but that isn't good enough."

"Look up artist Faith Winter. It's for her. Make your best guess."

"Am I shipping it to her?"

"Reid Winter Winery in Sonoma," I say, and hand her a sealed note. "Include this and have it delivered by tomorrow.

And I need a gift to celebrate an artist's success that says art. A necklace. A paintbrush. Both. I need options. Lots of options. I'll know when I see it."

Her eyes go wide. "Do I dare believe a woman finally has your attention?"

"I hope like hell the one standing in front of me." I push to my feet. "I need to know where Montgomery Williams of SA National Bank is by the time I get to my car."

"You have a deposition here in three hours."

"Good thing this won't take three hours." I round the desk and head for the door, on a mission to see a man I despise and try not to think about the woman I can't stop thinking about.

Considering I work in the financial district a few blocks from SA National, Montgomery Williams isn't hard to find. He's at a coffee shop a block from my office, and considering he's short, fat, bald and has a twenty-something girl sitting next to him with her hand on his plump thigh, I have no issue interrupting.

I walk to their booth and sit down across from them. "How's the wife?" I ask. Montgomery turns red-faced. The girl straightens and looks awkward. I simply arch a brow.

She purses her ridiculously red lips. "I'll see you tonight, honey." She slides out of the booth.

"Was she talking to me or you?" I ask.

"What do you want, Rogers?"

"Faith Winter," I say, and while I mean it in the literal sense, he simply registers the name.

"Why do you care about Faith Winter?"

Aside from the best blow job of my life, she's as talented

and intelligent as she is good in bed, but I leave out the details. "I'm representing her."

"You work for some of the biggest companies on planet Earth. You don't do probate."

"I'll supply a cashier's check for a hundred and twenty thousand dollars, which covers her back payments and six additional months. In exchange, I want you to stop holding up the execution of the probate, and drop all claims aside from the promissory note to the winery."

"We want a re-evaluation of the property before we agree to anything."

"With what end game?"

"We'll decide when we have the re-evaluation."

"And you ask why I'm involved," I say. "I'm involved because we both know this isn't just probate." I lean closer. "And we both know you're shitting your pants that I not only know you're fucking around on your wife but that I'm now involved."

I stand up and head for the door, my gut telling me that the winery is connected to murder. And the murder is connected to Faith. I step outside and dial Beck, who answers on the first ring. "The bank wants the winery, which means someone powerful wants that winery. You need to find out who and now. And get someone watching Faith around the clock," I say, doing what I should have done before now. "Today."

"I assume we don't want Faith to know she's being watched?"

"No," I say. "We do not."

"Then you don't trust her."

I inhale deeply, cool air blasting me right along with

his words that he's using to bait me. He wants me to argue my reasoning, outside of her guilt. But I don't give people ammunition to analyze me, and his paycheck is all the justification he deserves. "Just do it," I say. "I'm headed into depositions. Text me when it's done." I end the call.

Chapter Twenty-Three

Faith

I WOKE ON THE HARD FLOOR OF MY STUDIO, A SMOCK OVER my clothes, and I have no idea how I let that happen. Or maybe I do. Nick was on my canvas and in my mind, but he wasn't in my bed downstairs, where I'd be alone again. And those words: *I'll find out.* They'd haunted me then and do now as I sit at my desk inside my tiny office at the winery. Those words made me ask again: Are we friends or enemies? I'm confused and irritated that I somehow ended up in a black skirt and royal blue blouse today, the color reminding me of that damn dress he'd ripped. Of that moment he'd leaned in and licked me and then promised—*I won't stop next time.*

"Why are you flushed?"

I look up to find Kasey in my doorway, his gray suit and

tie as perfect as the work he does here at the winery. "Too much caffeine. Can you shut the door when you come in?"

"Of course," he says, doing as I've asked, and glancing around my box of an office. "Why do you stay in this hole? There are three bigger choices, including mine."

"You get the corner office," I say, as he sits down. "You're the boss. I'm just your assistant."

"You never wanted to be here. It hurts my heart that you feel you have to be. I can handle this place, Faith."

For the first time in a long time, I take those words to heart, despite knowing they're true. "You can run this place. You *do* run this place. But there was my mother. No one but me could manage her."

"Yes, well," he says. "That's a conversation we should have, Faith. She's gone. I hate to say it, but that changes things. You are an artist. You have a budding career. You had a show again, which I still hate I couldn't get a ticket to, by the way. How was it?"

"Wonderful," I breathe out, because I just can't stop myself. "It was really wonderful."

"Good," he says, his eyes warm with a pride I never saw in my father's. Not in regard to my art. "There is no reason you can't get back on that path."

"Right now, we need to talk about the legal issues."

"And the bill collectors," he says. "We've been avoiding the white elephant in the room too long. Why wasn't your mother paying the bills? What don't I know?"

Nick's words echo once again in my mind: *What haven't you told me, Faith?* And I shove them aside. "I don't have the answer to that question. We're making money. Not what we were before we lost part of the vines, but we're making money.

And we never stopped making money. Right now, without a will, I'm locked out of her accounts and there are legal steps I have to take to protect us. Nick Rogers, who you met yesterday, is coming on board to help."

"I looked him up and I was hoping like hell you were going to say that."

I breathe out, thankful to Nick for the relief I see in Kasey's eyes right now. "He wants to call you. He's weeding through this mess and needs input."

"I'm not sure how I can help, but of course," he says. "Anything to get this mess behind us and get you out of this office." He narrows his gaze on me. "There are at least three people here on staff that could step up and take on more, so you can get back to being you."

"You know my father—"

"Was obsessed with you running this place. We all know that, but Faith, life is short. This place is my life. It's why I get up in the morning and do so with excitement. Have you said that for even one day of your life that you've spent here?"

Yes, I think. This past Friday when I knew I had a show and I was going to stay at my house.

"I didn't think so," he says, when I haven't answered quickly enough. "You pay me well, little one. I get incentives that made a difference before we lost the vines. This is not your dream. Go chase your dream."

"The bill collectors—"

"You must think I'm a delicate flower," he says. "I am not. You have Nick Rogers now. You'll get your mother's bank accounts unlocked and get everything up to date."

I pray he's right. And as confused by Nick as I am right now, I'm glad he's involved.

"Your mother threatened to fire me," he adds, "and I believed she'd do it. That's why you had to run interference. The bill collectors can't fire me. Only you can and frankly, getting you the hell out of here is job security."

His walkie-talkie buzzes. "I need you, Kasey," comes a female voice.

"I'll be right there, Shannon," he answers, speaking to our garden manager before refocusing on me. "Stay at your house, like you did this weekend. It's a start. And I'll talk to Nick and whoever else needs to help you get past this probate issue." His walkie-talkie goes off again. "Ah. I need to go." He's on his feet and at the door, gone before I can issue the words, "Thank you."

I let out a breath and turn my attention to my computer, doing what I haven't done up until now. I google Nick Rogers. The minute his picture fills my screen, my stomach flutters, and I know that I am in trouble with this man. He affects me. He peels back the layers that are safer left in place. And he doesn't trust me, which means he's going to keep peeling. And why do I want to be with a man that doesn't trust me?

My phone buzzes. "Faith, you have a call," the receptionist tells me. "Bill—"

"Winter," I supply, anger spiking through me. "I'm not available."

"Understood."

I inhale and let it out. My father did not forgive him. I don't believe that for a minute. I key up my email and my heart skips a beat at Nick's name, when I haven't even given him my email address. I hit the button to open it and read:

Faith:

What the fuck are you doing to me?

Nick

P.S. Don't stop.

I sit back in my chair and pant out a breath, feeling so much right now. Feeling too much. I am one big emotion and I can't even name it. Maybe because I stopped recognizing anything but guilt. Guilt over not wanting this place. Guilt over my answer to my father. Guilt over so many things with my mother, when she doesn't deserve to make me feel that. I know that. But I still feel it.

But these feelings Nick stirs in me…They aren't guilt. But I think there's some fear. Yes. Fear. I hate fear. It's a weakness. But I am afraid of Nick and yet, that fear is almost a high. Everything about that man is a high that I crave. Maybe I'm obsessed because he's on my computer screen right now and I want to feel him next to me again. I want to call him and hear his voice.

And yet I don't.

I can't.

Why am I being this stupid?

He will find out who I really am. He will.

I stare at the email and I wonder how his deposition is going. I imagine him sitting in some big conference room, his suit as perfect as his body, those keen eyes of his intimidating the hell out of one person after another. I imagine those eyes, which tell a story I have yet to understand.

My phone buzzes again. "Another call," the receptionist says. "This time it's a man named Chris Merit."

"What? Chris…Merit? The artist?"

"I don't know. Should I ask?"

"No. No, put him through." The line beeps and I answer. "This is Faith."

"Faith. Chris Merit."

"Chris. Hi. I…thank you so much for including me in the show this past weekend."

"Thank you for being a part of it, Faith. I understand we have offers on your work."

"We do?"

"Yes, but your agent underpriced you. I'm going to adjust your prices unless you have an issue with it."

I hesitate but I say what I have to say. "I need that sale."

"You'll get your sale, and then some, and for what you're worth. Trust me, Faith."

When Chris Merit tells you to trust him and it relates to art. You trust him. "Why are you doing this?"

"My wife has decided to showcase a mix of new artists and established artists in her gallery in San Francisco. She and I both took a liking to your work. In fact, we'd like to showcase you in the gallery for our grand opening."

"You…I…" Oh God. I'm never speechless. "Thank you."

"I'd like you to present at least four pieces. You pick, but I'll need them in the gallery in four weeks."

"Of course. Not a problem at all."

"Excellent. We're holding a little VIP party at the gallery this weekend, Saturday night, which just happens to be Sara's birthday. We'd love it if you'd come. And bring a guest, of course."

"I'd love that. Thank you."

"You have talent, Faith Winter. Believe in you. We do." He ends the call.

I set the phone down and I'm not a crier. Not at all, but my eyes pinch. My chest is tight. This is my dream. This is everything. I grab my cellphone to call Nick. That's my first instinct. To call Nick. but I don't dial his number. He's in a deposition. I can't believe he's the one person I wanted to call. But I still do. Instead, I dial Josh and he answers on the first ring. "He called you," he says.

"You know already," I say, and my voice cracks.

"I know. So, are you in on this or not?"

"I'm in," I say. "How can I not be in?"

"Pick up the paintbrush and get to work."

"Josh—"

"I was out of line. I fucked up, Faith. I'm protective. That's personal and there's no place for that in business. I'm your agent because you're good at what you do. The end."

"Thank you, Josh. I'm fortunate to have you in my corner."

"That said, on a professional note that has a personal influence. Macom is my best friend, but creative types are inherently insecure. He put down your work because of his insecurity. It affected you and I think it's why you've used everything else as an excuse to stay away from painting. Make sure Nick Rogers does what you said. He inspires you to paint. If he does, I'll back off. If he doesn't, I'm not going to lose another two years of our work. Fair enough?"

"Fair enough," I say, appreciating the fact that he doesn't expect me to respond about Macom. He's right. Macom affected me in all kinds of ways. He still does.

"News on those sales soon and the show. I'll be in touch." He hangs up.

I set my phone down and lower my lashes. I'm so confused right now. And angry. If my mother hadn't created this mess, I could just let Kasey run this place. Now, that man trusts me and lives for this place, and I might lose it. He might lose it. And Chris Merit called me. Chris Merit! And I am painting again and that is because of Nick.

I look at the email again.

Faith:

What the fuck are you doing to me?

Nick

P.S. Don't stop.

I have so much I want to say to him and I decide that in the sea of lies that is my life right now, honesty rules and so I type:

Nick:

I hate what you made me feel last night and yet when Chris Merit called me today to invite me to an event this weekend, I thought of only one person: You.

Faith

P.S. Stop being an asshole like you were last night.

I lean back in my chair, and glance around my office, pictures of the winery on my walls. Not a one that is personal. Nothing in this office is mine and yet, I guess if I inherit this place, everything is mine. My cellphone rings and I glance down to find Nick's number. Adrenaline surges through me with crazy fierceness and I look at the clock that reads noon.

"Nick," I answer. "Don't you have a deposition?"

"We're on our lunch break. How did I make you feel, Faith?"

"Like you're my enemy again."

"I'm not your enemy."

"Are you sure?"

"Why would I be your enemy?"

I inhale and let it out. "You're making me feel like the minute you discover any mistake I've made in my life, it's over. We're done. You're making me feel I can't ever let you see a flaw, of which I have many."

"That is not my intention, sweetheart. You're perfect to me. Too fucking perfect for my own good."

"See. I know you mean that as a compliment, but the underlying inference is that you want to find a flaw. Stop being an asshole, Nick Rogers."

"Right. Stop being an asshole. This is new territory for me, Faith."

"You said that. I get that. It is for me too, and I don't even know what this is, but I apparently need to know."

"That makes two of us, sweetheart. Tell me about Chris calling."

"You have work."

"Tell me."

"He wants to showcase my work. I'll fill you in later, but I apparently need a date for Saturday night in San Francisco. Will you be my date, Nick?"

"You damn sure aren't taking anyone else. Yes, Faith. I'll be your date. I'll arrange to have a charter plane pick you up and bring you to me."

"That's not necessary."

"Can you come up Thursday night?"

"Friday night."

"I'll call you tonight with details. Faith?"

"Yes?"

"You're an artist. My artist." He hangs up.

I smile. I think it's my first real smile since my mother died. And for the first time in years, I am filled with possibilities: for my art and for this man who's taken my life by storm. And the possibilities are amazing.

Chapter Twenty-Four

Faith

FRIDAY AFTERNOON COMES QUICKLY, BUT NOT QUICK enough, and brings me to my house to pack, since I've been staying here all week. And I stayed here despite the fact that the winery has been crazy busy, but none of it has been collection calls. Nick assures me he has things under control, and to trust him until he can give me a full update in person. And I do. I tell myself it's because he's an amazing attorney, and he is, but after spending hours on the phone with each other every night, it's the man I'm connecting with, not the attorney. And while our conversations have been more about our youth, his school and mine, it's groundwork. It's a path to more. It certainly brings more to my canvas. I start a new canvas. The gardens. My mother's gardens. It's somehow therapeutic.

But it's staying here and I'm heading to San Francisco where I hope maybe I'll get news of those sales that I still hear are pending, but I've had no confirmation. I'd really like to hear about the L.A. show too, but Josh swears I've not been ruled out yet. More so, I am going to the Chris Merit event, with Nick by my side. Nervous and excited, I pack my weekend bag and fret over what to wear tonight. Nick wants to stay in at his place and have quality time together, so jeans should work. But jeans feel so plain. I've finally decided on black dress pants and a pink silk blouse, when my doorbell rings. Dread fills me that the bill collectors are back, and I walk to the door to find a delivery driver standing there.

Frowning because I've ordered nothing, I open the door.

"Faith Winter?"

"Yes."

"For you."

He hands me a big box and my stomach flutters because I know this is from Nick. "Thank you." I sign for it and carry it to the kitchen where I set it on the counter. Feeling ridiculously nervous considering it's a package, I cut away the tape and paper and find a beautiful silver box inside. I open it to find a card on top with neat, masculine script that reads: *Faith*.

I open the card.

I was going to send this earlier in the week, but I decided that if it pisses you off, I'll see you in a few hours to fight that battle in person. But know this. I'm happy to rip this version up too, as long as it's on you at the time. And I owed you a pair of panties anyway.

I actually hope you want me to rip it off you again.

All of it.

Looking forward to it and you,
Nick

I set the card aside and pull back the paper to first find gorgeous royal blue lace panties that I do *not* want him to rip. They're too beautiful. Beneath them is a dress. I pull it from the box and while it's not an exact replica of the one that was destroyed, it's close. I inhale and let it out. I wait for that feeling of being bought, but even with this and Nick flying me to San Francisco, I don't feel that. Maybe because he's done these things just because. Not to make up for something. And the dress. He turned it into something we shared and will share again. He made it special.

I gather everything up and walk into the bedroom. And right before I pack the panties, I take a picture of them, and laughing, text it to Nick with the words: *New challenge. And I love the dress. Thank you, Nick.*

He calls me. "You're not mad."

"No. Because you made it…about us."

"There's a lot of us going on this weekend, sweetheart. The plane is waiting on you. Hurry the hell up. The pilot is going to call me when you take off."

"I'm leaving here in fifteen minutes."

"See you soon, Faith Winter."

There is a deep, raspy quality to his voice that I feel from head to toe. "See you soon, Nick Rogers."

He ends the call.

With a grin on my face, I finish up packing. I'm about to leave when I open the nightstand by my bed and find the card from my father. I still haven't read it. I stare at the script and I shake myself before stuffing it in my purse. I need to read it and I might just need that spanking I mentioned. I don't know that I want to be under Nick's hand to forget something this weekend, though. I think I'd rather be there just because. Still, I decide to leave the card in my purse.

My cellphone rings and I remove it from the spot under that card, and the minute I see Josh's number, my heart starts to race. With a shaky hand, I punch the answer button. "Josh?"

"You're in, baby! You made the show."

"What? No. Yes. No?"

"Yes. Yes. Yes. You're in. I'm walking into a meeting, but I'll send you details. They love you. They say you are the next 'it' artist. So, drink some wine and start fucking selling it. I have to go. Congrats, baby."

He hangs up and I dial Nick. "You can't be at the airport yet."

"I got in the show. I got in."

"The L.A. show?"

"The L.A. show. I got in."

"Then why the hell are you not here already so we can celebrate. Get your sweet, spankable ass to the airport."

"I'm leaving now."

"Faith."

"Yes?"

"Congrats, sweetheart."

"Thank you."

We disconnect and in a rush of adrenaline I hurry to the door, exit to the porch, and lock up the house, then move on to load up my car. No. My mother's car. I hate driving this thing. I climb inside and I swear I smell flowers. I can never escape the flowers, but I'm not trying anymore, I remind myself. I'm painting them. I'm facing them and every demon associated with my mother. I start the car and glance at the house. I love it. I always have. If I can live here and paint, and just be near the winery, maybe, just maybe that's the path to compromise with my father's wishes and my own.

I'm about to place the car in gear when the rapidly setting sun catches on something in the yard. Frowning, I decide I must have dropped something. I place the car in park and get out. Walking to the spot I'd spotted something, I bend down and pick up what appears to be a money clip engraved with an American flag. It must be Nick's, but I'm not sure I see that man with an empty money clip. Maybe it's the delivery driver's clip. I take it with me, slide back into the car, and stuff it in my purse. If it's not Nick's, I'll call the delivery company next week.

Fifteen minutes later, I pull into the private airport and another fifteen minutes later, I'm the only person on a small luxury jet, with leather seats and even a bottle of champagne on ice. I pour a glass to enjoy while the pilot finishes his checklist and promises to call Nick. I've just taken my first sip when my cellphone rings. Certain it's Nick, I dig it out of my purse and freeze with the number. Macom. He heard about the show. And probably not even from Josh. He's an insider. He's a name in the business that I am not yet. But at least, I can say, yet. Not never. And while it's inevitable that I'll see him at the L.A. show and otherwise, if I'm to reignite my art career, I don't have to welcome conversation. I hit decline.

And I hate that as the plane starts to taxi, he's in the cabin with me. Old times. Old demons. A past that I don't want to exist. Of a me that I don't want to exist. Of a person I never want Nick Rogers to know. I'm reminded that on some level, he knows that person exists. *What aren't you telling me, Faith?* he'd asked. *I will find out.*

And he will. I know he will. Maybe he's more forgiving than I am of myself. Then again, he's Tiger for a reason. He's vicious. He's cold. He's not forgiving at all. But my sins were not against Nick.

Chapter Twenty-Five

Tiger

I'VE JUST HEARD FROM THE PILOT THAT FAITH IS ON THE plane in Sonoma when Rita walks into my office and sets a stack of papers on my desk. "You were served. It's all a bunch of nonsense meant to slow probate. Boy, the bank really wants to keep that place, don't they?"

I thumb through the stack of, as she called it "nonsense," and it's exactly that.

"What do you want me to do?"

"I'll let you know."

"Did she get the dress?"

"Yes. She got the dress."

"And?"

"And it's good."

"And you're happy with the other gift?"

"Yes. I'm happy."

"But not about that stack of papers. Got it. Removing myself from the line of fire." She turns and leaves and I thrum my fingers on the desk. The bank wants her in default. I don't know why and I don't care. They're gambling on the fact that I'll advise her not to pay the money until I'm sure she won't lose it. And without all the hidden facts they seem to know and we don't, that's exactly what I'd do.

I stand up and walk to the window, the fifth floor of the building allowing me the feeling of looking down on a city of millions and it's here, doing just that, that I find answers. And now is no different. Faith can't pay that money, but I can. I dial my banker. "Charlie," I say. "I need a hundred and twenty thousand dollars delivered to SA National Bank by closing today in the name of Reid Winter Winery. I need you to personally talk to him and confirm it's done."

"You got it," he says. "What else?"

"Note that this is back payments, fees, and six months in advance. And email proof to Rita and text me when the transaction is complete."

I end the call and walk to my desk. "Rita."

She appears in my doorway. "Yes, boss?"

"You will be receiving proof that the Reid Winter note to the bank is paid to date and six months in advance. I'll be filing a slaughterhouse of documents Monday morning."

"In other words, be here at six."

"That will do it."

"Got it. What else?"

"Go home and do whatever people who have been married forever do."

She smiles. "We do the same things you do, Nick Rogers, but better, because we've been practicing. Have fun with Faith this weekend." She disappears, and I'm already back at the window and dialing Beck.

"I just paid Faith's past due bank note and six months in advance," I tell him. "I like to know my enemies when I make them. And I pay you a lot of money to tell me who they are."

"I found a secretary at the bank that was at a party your father attended three months before he died. That same secretary visited Reid Winter Winery a year before Meredith Winter died. The interesting part about this is that Faith's agent, and her ex, were at the gallery where she just had that show, that weekend."

"With Faith?"

"Faith was in L.A."

"That's odd."

"Yes. It is."

"It gets even stranger. Her uncle was in Sonoma that weekend staying at his cottage, without his wife."

"You think he was still fucking Meredith Winter?"

"I damn sure wouldn't rule it out."

Which will absolutely kill Faith. "How does the secretary connect to that bastard, Montgomery, I'm dealing with?"

"She's his boss's boss's secretary. I don't know what your father got himself into, but it's dirty. I'm gambling on that murder connection. And I'll figure it out, but you need every bit of evidence when I do to take this to the police. You still believe Faith Winter is innocent."

"I don't remember saying either way."

"Well, let her tell you if she's innocent or guilty. We need two bodies and two autopsies. If she's innocent, she'll request one on her mother. If she's not, she'll refuse."

"Just keep working this," I say, and end the call, leaning a hand on the window.

Faith *is* innocent. The problem is, I'm not. I've lied. I've deceived her. And eventually, I have to tell her. And when I do, I'm at the risk of losing her but I've never lost anything I wanted in my life. And I've never wanted anything as much as I want Faith Winter.

I'm standing in the private hangar when Faith's plane pulls to a halt and the minute the doors open and she steps into the opening, adrenaline surges through me. Her eyes meet mine, and I feel this woman like I've felt no other. I'm obsessed with her when I have never been obsessed with anything but success. With how she looks. With how she feels. With how she tastes. With the way she trusts me when I trust her. The way she doubts me when I doubt her. I have read people as well as I read Faith, but no one has ever read me the way she reads me. And out of nowhere, I think: I'm falling in love with her. Which is insane. I don't believe in love and neither does she and she's new to me. I'm new to her. But when does someone know they are in love? A day? A week? A year? It doesn't matter. It's not love. Whatever the hell this is though, Faith feels it too. I see it in her eyes. She lowers her lashes as if battling what I'm battling.

I watch her inhale and let it out before her lashes lift and she starts walking down the stairs, her eyes on mine, and in them I see an echo of what I am thinking. We need to fuck this out of our systems. Fucking makes everything better. I meet her at the bottom of the steps, and in the quiet of the private hangar I do exactly what I want to do. I mold her to me and I kiss her like the starving man I am. And she tastes like everything I have ever wanted and didn't even know I wanted.

"Let's get out of here," I say, tearing my mouth from hers.

"Yes," she whispers, and I swear this woman's voice gets me hard and hot. I want her mouth everywhere, most definitely on my damn cock, and that's her fault for being so damn good at putting it there.

I grab her bag from the flight attendant and waste no time guiding Faith to the parking lot. Once her bag is in my back seat, I walk her to the passenger side of the vehicle and when she's about to get inside, I pull her to me again and kiss her. "I'm really fucking glad you're here."

"Is this where you say 'too fucking glad'?"

"This is where I take you home and get you naked before I find a way to piss you off and it never happens."

She laughs, soft and sexy, and slides into the car. I'm inside with her in a few beats, and before I start the car, she says, "Can I get the bad stuff over with real quick?"

I angle toward her. "What bad stuff, Faith?"

"Anything with the bank?"

"I filed papers. They filed papers. I'm filing more papers. Bottom line. I made a big move and I'll know more on Monday how that plays out."

"What big move?"

"Legal stuff," I say, not about to tell her about the money. Not now. I'll swim in the shit I've created all at once and with a plan. "And I'm asking you to trust me enough to set it aside until Monday. Okay?"

"Yes. Okay."

"Good." I lean over and kiss her because, fuck. I have to. And then I get us on the road.

"How was your flight?" I ask.

"Short and bumpy," she says. "But it was great. I love flying."

"But you've never flown internationally," I say. "We need to fix that. Paris is all about art and wine. We should go."

"That would be incredible, but right now I can't leave."

"We're going to fix that and soon," I promise. "Tell me the details you know about the L.A. show."

"Josh just told me that I'm in," I say. "I'm sure I'll get more specifics by Monday."

"And you know which pieces were selected?"

"Nick. Don't be mad, but…."

I glance over at her and laugh. "You put me in it, didn't you?"

"I did. My first portrait and on a whim when I was filling out the forms and submitting photos, I included it. You're not mad, right?"

"I don't care if you put me in the show, as long as it's about you."

"Maybe you are a little sweet, Nick Rogers."

"I'll put that idea to rest before the weekend's over, I promise you. And that means you have to let me see it."

"I will. When it's done. I have two weeks to finish. I think this weekend might just let me finish your eyes."

And on that note, I silently vow to make sure that every time she looks at me this weekend, she sees all the right things, and none of the wrong.

Fifteen minutes later, we pull into the garage of my house, which is only a few minutes from my office. Faith is out of the car before I can round the BMW to help her, and gaping at the dark gray sports car beside us. She bites her lip and glances over at me. "You are such a rich guy, Nick Rogers. What is it?"

"Audi R8 5.2 V10," I say. "And thank you. I work my ass off to be such a rich guy, and owned that assessment long before I inherited my father's money."

"How did you make your first million?"

"A drug company whose best-of-the-best attorney wasn't as good as they thought." He was also my father, but I don't tell her that. Not now. One day when there are no more secrets. "Let's go inside, Faith."

"Yes. Let's go see what a man like you calls home."

"A man like me," I say. "You can explain that later. Naked."

She gives me one of her sexy, confident smiles. "I will."

I open the back door. "I'll get your bag. The door's unlocked. Make yourself at home."

She doesn't hesitate. She drags delicate fingers through her long blonde hair and walks to the door and up the short set of steps that leads to the foyer of my home. I take my time pursuing her, allowing her time to decide what to do and where to go. Curious as to where that takes us both. Intrigued by this woman all over again, I join her, leaving her bag by the door, to find her slowly walking the rectangular-shaped space, and I scan it, taking in what she sees. Pale wooden floors, a gray sectional. Parallel to the living area is a bar that is shiny white with four barstools, and opposite it, are two modern steel and glass stairwells that climb the walls in two different directions.

She turns to face me, the distance between us I don't

intend to remain. "Clean, artistic lines. A house for a man who likes control."

"I do like control," I say, closing a foot of space between us. "I think that I like control."

She replies as if I haven't spoken those words. "It's a beautiful house, Nick. It smells like you."

"And how do I smell, Faith?"

"Like control. Like sex. Woodsy and sexy."

"And you, sweetheart, smell like—"

"Amber and vanilla."

"Yes, you do. And I'm obsessed with your scent. I'm obsessed with *you*."

"Obsessed," she says. "That sounds dangerous."

"It is dangerous."

And her reply is everything any man could want. "Where is your bedroom, Nick?"

"Up the stairs directly behind you."

She turns and starts up the stairs, her pace slow, seductive, calculated. She knows every swing of her hips makes me burn. And I fucking love it. I wait until she's upstairs, out of sight, and then with my adrenaline pumping, I follow her. I find her sitting on the end of my king-sized mattress, the centerpiece of my room, the gray headboard behind her. That card from her father in her lap.

"I need to read this. And you know that means I need *you*."

I inhale on a realization. Faith is once again using sex as a wall. And I almost let her. I had the word "love" pop into my head and I just wanted to fuck. And she just wants to fuck. But I'm not letting her hide from me. Even if it means I can't escape whatever the fuck this unknown emotion is I feel for this woman. I walk to the bed, and stand above her. She doesn't touch me. I don't want her to, and she knows this. I like that she knows. I shrug out of my jacket and remove my tie, both of which I toss to the center of the bed. I then set the card aside, and do what I know she does not expect me to do.

I take her down on the mattress with me, rolling her to face me. "I'm not going to spank you, Faith," I say, sliding my leg between hers. "Not now. Maybe not even this weekend. I want you to see and feel me. I want you to remember me this weekend, not my hand."

"Nick," she whispers, and when I kiss her, she does that thing she does. She breathes out like she needed my kiss, like it's why she exists. And right now, this woman is why I exist. I kiss her. I touch her. I strip her naked and me too. I lick her nipples. I lick her clit. I lick every inch of her until she is begging for me inside her and I need to be there. And once I'm inside her, and we're staring at each other, swaying together, I don't make love to her. I don't do love, but I damn sure don't fuck her, either. And when it's over, I hold her for long minutes before I settle my shirt around her and help her roll up the sleeves.

We order Chinese and eat in my bed, me in my pants, and her in my shirt, and I like this woman in my clothes and my bed. It's only after we finish eating that I am ready to show her one of the gifts I have for her this weekend. I take her hand. "Come. I want to show you something."

"Now you have me curious."

"Good," I say, guiding her down the hallway. "That's the idea."

We stop at a room with the door shut and I open it and motion her forward. She smiles and walks inside and gasps.

"Nick. What did you do?"

I step inside the doorway to find her standing in the center of the massive triangle-shaped room, next to the canvas I have set up for her, a supply of brushes and paint nearby. "They tell me the floor cleans right up. I had it installed this week."

"Why would you do this?"

"I didn't want you to be away from your brush."

"This is incredible. It's such a cool, crazy-shaped space. What was this room before now?"

"Nothing. I had no idea what to do with it."

She inhales, her chest rising and falling. "What happens when I'm not around?"

I cross to stand in front of her, cupping her face. "That's where we're differing here, Faith. I'm thinking about every moment I have with you and you're thinking about goodbye." I kiss her then, and damn it, I am obsessed with her. So fucking obsessed. And like she said, obsession is dangerous.

Chapter Twenty-Six

Tiger

I WATCH FAITH PAINT FOR HOURS, A STACK OF WORK NEXT to me that I barely touch. I just watch her work while my mind chases the puzzle that is her mother and my father together. Murder brought us together. Lies could tear us apart. I don't know what time I take her to bed, or how long I keep her awake once I get her there. But I wake with Faith pressed to my side, and I have one thought. In the right and wrong of things, there is nothing wrong about this woman in my bed.

The day is lazy, rain falling outside, and we have coffee on my balcony, talking, laughing, both of us in sweats and t-shirts with no plans to go anywhere until tonight. "Are you wearing the blue dress tonight?" I ask, sipping my coffee while thinking of the blue panties.

"I'm not sure," she says. "I wish I would have asked about the dress code. I brought several choices."

I set my cup down and grab my phone from my pocket. "Let's find out. I'll call Chris." I punch in his number from my auto-dial.

"No," she says quickly, setting her cup down. "No, don't—"

"It's already ringing," I say, and Chris immediately picks up, while I get right to the point. "What's the dress code tonight?"

"Translation. You're Faith's date tonight and she doesn't know how to dress. Put her on with Sara."

"Good plan." I hand Faith the phone. "Sara."

She pales, glowers and takes the phone. "Sara. Yes. No. Great. Nice to meet you, too. Yes. I'll see you then." She hands me back the phone. "Chris."

"I'm here," I say, placing the receiver to my ear again. "And I need nothing else."

"Works for me," Chris says and we disconnect, and I focus on Faith. "Blue dress?"

"You shouldn't have called them, and actually the blue dress is too fancy, and I want to save that dress for the L.A. event. It was lucky the first time."

"Luck is good," I say. "But you do have a dress to wear, right?"

"Yes. It's pink and doesn't require you to spend money on me."

"You're going to have to get over this money thing, sweetheart. I have it. I spend it. If I want to spend it on you, I'm going to and that doesn't make me an asshole unless I use it against you in some way, which I won't." And those are words I'm going to have to repeat loudly when she finds out I paid the bank on her behalf. "Moving on," I say. "Your dress is pink. Do I get the royal blue panties underneath?"

"They're pink and I don't want you to spend money on me."

"I like spending money on you and I like pink."

"Don't rip them this time and you can like them twice."

"Twice is good. More is better."

"Do you know what you're wearing?"

"Why? Are you considering which knife you need to undress me?"

She grins. "I think that's a moment I need to capture on the canvas. That moment when you first saw the knife in my hand. It was priceless. I'm suddenly inspired to paint."

"Then go and paint a masterpiece. I've got work that I can dig into in my office. I'll come get you for lunch."

"Are you cooking?"

"If ordering take-out, counts, then yes. At your service, Ms. Winter."

She laughs and starts to get up, but sits back down. "I never asked what time the party is. Chris never said."

"I'll find out," I promise. "You go paint."

Her eyes light. "I actually can't wait to pick up a brush again."

"I prefer you with a brush than a knife in your hand."

She laughs and pops to her feet, rushing through the house, and I sit back and enjoy this moment. I could get used to having this woman around.

The day passes too quickly, when Faith will leave tomorrow unless I convince her otherwise.

It's nearly seven, and I'm standing on the balcony off my bedroom in a blue suit and blue tie, waiting on Faith to finish dressing, a glass of that whiskey Abel left behind in my hand. And while outside, the storms of earlier in the day have passed, stars dotting the skyline before me, while the storm that is the lies I've told Faith are clear and present, haunting me tonight in ways they haven't before now.

"Nick."

At the sound of Faith's voice, I down my drink, set the glass on a small table by the railing, and walk back inside. "Well?" she asks, holding out her hands to her sides. "How do I look? Is it too much? Too little?"

"Sweetheart, I don't let women in my house, let alone invite them to dress here. So no one has ever asked me if a dress was too much or too little." I close the space between us, my hands settling on her tiny waist. "But you look *beautiful*." And she does. The dress is pink lace and knee length, which offers me the benefit of easy access to her gorgeous legs. Her shoulders are bare, her blonde hair caressing the skin the way my mouth will later. And the neckline is high, reserved, but still somehow sexy, but how can it not be? It's on her.

Her hands go to my chest, her eyes searching my face. "You don't bring women here?" "Never," I say. "In the five years since I bought this place, not once. Just you."

"Why me, Nick?" she asks, her tone earnest.

"Because you're you, Faith. There is no other answer." And while it's the truth, it guts me to know that she'll see it as one of my lies, and do so sooner than later.

"Where did you go?" she asks. "To their place?"

"Anywhere but here," I say, when the truth is, I go to what is my club now, a place, that doesn't matter to me, but she does. "You're nervous about tonight. Why?"

"Chris Merit is a big deal in the art world. His support could change my life."

"You admire him."

"Yes. He's talented and successful. And even though he's really not from Sonoma, he just always felt like a local, and if one local could make it, another could, too."

"Did you admire Macom? Was that part of the draw to him?"

"I met Macom before he made it. We both loved art and the creative process. And yes, he's talented, but it was different. I don't admire him." Her hands settle on mine at her hips. "He called me yesterday and I just feel like I should tell you."

I go very still, that possessiveness I feel for Faith rising up inside me. "And?"

"I didn't take the call. I can guess what it was about. He heard, probably before me, that I was in the show."

"And he wanted to congratulate you?"

"More to gloat. He's been there done that, but of course, he'd mask it as a compliment. I don't need that in my life right now and just wanted to tell you, Nick." She pauses and then adds, "*Thank you*. I've known you such a short time and you've been more supportive of my art than anyone else in my life."

"It's self-serving," I say, leaning in to brush my lips over hers. "I want a beautiful artist in my bed and if we don't go right now, I might rip this dress, too." I turn her toward the door.

We arrive at the gallery at seven thirty, and it's not long before we're ushered into a room full of at least fifty people, shiny white floors beneath our feet, wave-like rows of displays in random places. Faith and I work our way through the crowd, and when we're offered champagne for a birthday toast, we both accept. "My preferred drink," she tells me, sipping her bubbly. "It's sweet and we don't make it. It's also low alcohol and I don't tolerate much."

"You really don't like the winery do you?"

"No," she says. "I really don't, but I've never said that to anyone but you. Just now."

My hand settles at her hip. "It's our secret."

She looks at me, shadows in her eyes. "That's trust, Nick. Just in case you didn't know."

Trust.

That I've already betrayed.

"Welcome everyone!"

At the shouted greeting, I look up to find Chris Merit at the front of the room, the only person here in jeans, but it's rather fitting. He's a rock star in this world, complete with longish blonde hair and a brightly inked dragon tattoo sleeve on one arm. "I just want to say happy birthday to my wife," he announces, "and to tell her how proud I am of her, and this gallery. Enjoy the art and chocolate cake, because it's her favorite."

Everyone applauds and there are shouts of 'happy birthday.' Chris catches my eye over the crowd right as soft music begins to play. He motions us forward and I lift a hand to acknowledge him. "Empty that glass," I tell Faith.

Her eyes go wide. "I can't just down it."

"Chris is waving you over."

She downs the champagne and I do the same with mine before handing our glasses to a waiter. I lace my fingers with Faith's and lead her through the crowd, while cake begins to circulate on trays. Chris, however, is cornered by fans and Sara appears in front of us. "Faith!" she greets her, hugging Faith, her brown hair a contrast to Faith's blonde, while waving at me over her shoulder.

I give her a nod, but she's fully focused on Faith, as it should be. "I love your work," Sara announces, leaning back to look at Faith. "Chris and I both love your work. Let's go talk." She motions us forward. "Come. Chris will catch up."

She starts walking and we follow her through the gallery where two glass doors lead us to a heated outdoor sitting area with at least a dozen seats, and rose bushes surrounding the exterior. "This space is our newest addition," Sara says, claiming one of four seats forming a square, while primly tugging down the skirt of her emerald green dress. "I want people to come here and talk art, then buy artists like yourself, Faith."

"I'm incredibly honored that you want to include me," Faith says, claiming the seat across from Sara while I sit next to Faith.

"We'd be honored to show your work," Sara says. "Just to be sure that you're aware. Everything we do has a charity component, but we're going to make that worth your while."

"Exposure is everything," Faith says. "I'm not worried about the money."

"Thus why I'm her attorney," I interject. "Because I am worried about her money."

Faith glowers at me and Sara laughs. "He's fine, Faith. He should be worried about you. Chris would be the same way." She refocuses on business. "I'm not sure what Chris told you, so I'll start from scratch. The gallery officially opens in six weeks, but we're basically letting people have VIP cards to enter a week sooner if they're here tonight. I'd like to get your work here a week prior to that."

"That would be incredible," Faith says. "And Chris said you need four pieces to make that happen?"

"Yes, please," she says. "But I need to know that you're a for-sure placement by next week. And I can talk to your agent if you wish." She laughs and glances at Nick. "Or your attorney."

Chris joins us at that moment, greeting everyone as he claims his seat, his hand instantly on Sara's. "Where are we on things?"

"I was just telling her the details on the gallery," Sara replies.

Chris flags down a waiter who is immediately by his side. "I know you know what I want."

The waiter reaches into his apron pocket, removes a beer, and hands it to Chris. "At your service."

"Thanks, David," Chris says, eyeing Sara, who shakes her head, but accepts his replying kiss more than a little willingly.

"Beer anyone?" Chris asks, as the waiter holds two more up.

"Don't mind if I do," I say, accepting it, while Faith and Sara wave off the offer.

"In explanation," Sara says, as the waiter leaves. "Chris hates wine and champagne."

"You hate wine?" Faith asks. "But your godparents own a winery."

"And I still ask for a beer when I'm there," Chris replies.

In other words, he's his own man, the way Faith wants to be her own woman, and I squeeze her hand, silently telling her there is no reason she is that winery, and not her art. She glances at our hands, the tiny gesture telling me that she hears me even before she squeezes back.

From there, the four of us start talking, and I take in this world of art that is Faith's now, listening to the ins and outs, interested in a way I wouldn't have been before meeting Faith. It's not long and we're eating cake, and Sara and Faith have hit it off so well that their heads are together, and Chris and I are left to our own devices.

"You care about her," he says, his voice low, and the women too absorbed in talk of art to hear us anyway.

"She matters," I say without hesitation. "Yes." And admitting that to someone else, saying it and meaning it, tells me just how deep I am in with Faith.

He leans forward, elbows on his knees and I do the same. "Does she know about the club?"

"No," I say, and while I have pushed this topic aside, with bigger problems to face, I can't ignore the topic forever. "Now is not the time."

"It's never the time," he says. "And telling Sara was hard on us but we had to go there to get here. And one small secret becomes bigger over time. The bigger the secret and the longer you keep it, the bigger the problem."

The bigger the secret.

He has no fucking clue how much bigger my secrets are than that fucking sex club. There's a hell of a lot that I have to come back from with Faith and at some point, I'll have to decide if I spill it all, fast and hard, or in pieces.

Chris has just leaned back in his seat, when the music changes and an old seventies song, "Sara Smile," begins to play, a soft, easy, sexy tune. Chris sets his beer on the small table in between us, and stands, walking to Sara and taking her hand. "I need to borrow my wife for a moment," he says, but he's not looking at us when he speaks. He's looking at her. And she's not looking at us, but at him.

Chris pulls her to her feet and leads her inside the gallery, the words to the song filling the air:

When I feel cold, you warm me
And when I feel I can't go on, you come and hold me
It's you and me forever
Sara, smile

Faith stands up and I catch her hand. "Where are you going?"

"Bathroom," she says, but she won't look at me.

"Faith."

"I need a minute, Nick."

She tugs against me and I release her but I don't want to. I watch her walk back into the gallery and I know this woman in ways I should not yet be able to know her. Chris and Sara have this way of radiating love. You feel it. You almost believe in happily ever after. And then she suddenly feels like we're nothing but sex and goodbye. I'm on my feet in an instant, pursuing her, following a sign to the bathroom. I spy Faith just before she is about to round a hallway and the minute she looks around that corner, she flattens on the wall, as if burned.

I'm in front of her in a few long strides, my hands on her waist. Her eyes pop open in shock and I lean around the corner to find Chris kissing Sara and it's one hell of a kiss. Intense. Passionate. I refocus on Faith, and I cup her face. "We're whatever we decide to be, Faith." And I kiss her, just as passionately as Chris is kissing Sara. I kiss her my way. I kiss her and let her taste my words: *We're whatever we decide to be.* And when I tear my lips from hers, I say, "Instead of a hard limit, we have a new hard rule: *Possibilities*, Faith. We have them. Say it."

"New hard rule," she whispers. "Possibilities."

"Let's go back and wait on them until we can say goodbye and get out of here."

She nods. "Yes. Please."

And with her hand in mine, I lead her toward the patio but footsteps sound behind us and Faith and I turn to find Chris and Sara returning. "You're leaving," Sara says, seeming to read our body language, her focus on Faith. "You have my email and phone number, right?"

"Yes," Faith says. "And I'm excited about being a part of the gallery. Oh and happy birthday."

"Thank you," she says. "I actually wanted you to come here tonight to give *you* a gift, Faith."

"Me?" Faith asks. "I don't understand."

Chris reaches into the pocket of his jeans and produces a check. "I negotiated your price for the showing last weekend, as promised, Faith. You now get twenty thousand a painting and accept no less, or I will personally come kick your ass." He looks at me. "Twenty thousand. Don't let her get screwed." He hands Faith the check. "Sixty thousand. You sold three paintings."

Faith starts to tremble and my arm goes to her waist, my hips pressed to hers. Her hand shakes as she accepts the check and looks at it. "I think…I…I'm going to cry and I don't cry."

"Don't cry," Chris says. "Celebrate."

Faith looks up at him. "I'm going to have to hug you," she says, taking a step toward him and then grabbing Sara instead.

Sara laughs and hugs her. "Best birthday gift ever," she says, and when Faith releases her, she adds, "You can hug

Chris, too."

Faith laughs through tears. "No. No I...thank you, Chris. And thank you, Sara."

Chris grabs her and hugs her, giving me a look over his shoulder that is filled with admiration I see but Faith would dismiss. "She's talented," Chris says. "Take care of her and her gift."

I nod and damn, I want to take care of this woman.

We say our goodbyes and cross the gallery to exit to the street. We're a few steps away from the door when Faith turns to me and holds up the check. "I can't believe this just happened."

"It didn't *just* happen," I say. "You started painting at age five."

"I know but, it feels...I don't know what I feel. But now the winery—"

I cup her face. "Do not make this about the winery. That is your money. That is your first big success."

"But Nick—"

I kiss her. "No buts. We'll deal with the winery. This is for you. Okay?"

"Yes. Okay."

"Good. Now. Let's go home."

"Your home."

"My home," I say. "That is far better with you in it." I turn her toward the car, and she's still trembling. And the depth of her emotional response affects me. Everything about Faith affects me.

Thirty minutes later, Faith and I are standing by my bed, her shoes kicked off, and she is finally coming down from her high, her body calming. "I'm completely wiped out," she says. "I think you are going to wish I was someone else tonight."

I cup her head and pull her to me. "What did you say?" I don't give her time to reply. "That came from someplace I'd most likely name as Macom. I'm not him. And we are more than the sum of how many times we manage to fuck each other. And for the record. To repeat what I've already said. I don't want anyone else."

Her lashes lower. "I think that was possibly the most perfect thing you could say to me right now."

In that moment, I remember her comment about Macom competing with her and I decide Faith thinks her success comes with punishment. A problem I need to fix. For now, I kiss her, a soft brush of lips over lips before I turn her around and unzip her dress, dragging it down her shoulders. Her bra is next. Then her hose, but I leave the panties and as much as it kills me, I hold up the blanket and urge her to climb under. She turns around and faces me, pressing herself against me. "You feel good, sweetheart, but you'll feel better when you're rested. Climb into bed. I'll be right there after I make sure I've locked up."

"You, Nick, are nothing I expected."

"*You*, Faith, are nothing I expected."

She kisses my cheek, a mere peck, which might be the best kiss this woman has given me and I don't fucking have a clue why. It's a peck, but it's sweet. It's emotional in some unnamed way and I like it. She climbs into bed. My bed. And damn, I like her there more now than I did this morning. She snuggles down in the blankets, and I walk to the door, where

I find myself just staring at her, watching as her breathing slows, and turns even. She's asleep. She trusts me. Damn it, I need to solve this mystery so I can tell her everything and deal with the aftermath.

I exit the bedroom and head down the stairs to my office, walking to a chair in the corner and removing a box I have shoved underneath it. Stacks of my father's papers. I shrug out of my jacket and pull away my tie, and start going through them again. Somewhere in here is my answer. I just have to find it. Time passes. Documents are read. My eyes are blurry. Finally, I decide I have to go to bed. I'm stuffing the papers back in the box when a small book on legal ethics falls to the ground and a piece of paper pokes out from the side. I grab it and open it to read: *Faith Winter is the problem. She's dangerous. Far more than her mother. She must be stopped.*

I stare at that piece of paper for long minutes, and I try to make sense of it. I return the box to its spot under the chair with that piece of paper inside it. I stand and walk upstairs, standing at that doorway again and at the naked woman in my bed, wondering which one of us is now exposed. Knowing it's time to find out.

The End... For now.

Don't miss the conclusion to Tiger and Faith's story in
SHAMELESS!
Book 2 in the WHITE LIES DUET is coming July 11, 2017!

Visit http://lisareneejones.com/duet to pre-order now!

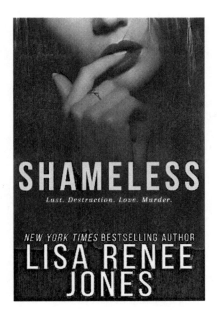

And now as promised a bonus novella—*Rebecca's Forgotten Journals*, the continuation of Rebecca's Lost Journals from the INSIDE OUT series!

For those of you who have not read THE INSIDE OUT series, with Chris and Sara, you can read their entire story now! Available in print and ebook everywhere.

Remember the painting of the funeral for Rebecca that Tiger bought? Rebecca had her own story to tell and I wanted to include part of it for you here...

Rebecca's Lost Journals are featured in the INSIDE OUT series.

A set of journals is found in a storage unit. A woman's is life revealed. Her insecurities, dreams, love, and life.

But now, I've written NEW journal entries and included them as a HUGE THANK YOU for ordering your copy of PROVOCATIVE!

How It All Started…Dark passion and sweet obsession… Her journal. My fantasies. A set of journals comes to Sara McMillan by chance, when she unexpectedly inherits the key to a storage locker belonging to a woman named Rebecca. Sara can't resist peeking at the entries inside, finding a scintillating account of Rebecca's life, and an affair with an unnamed lover, a relationship drenched in ecstasy and wrapped in dark secrets. But when the final entry ends ominously, Sara dares to seek out Rebecca, taking a job at the art gallery where Rebecca worked, only to be inexplicably drawn to two men. Both want to possess her but only one–the dark, mysteriously sexy artist, Chris Merit, will win her heart. But where is Rebecca? And is Sara trusting the wrong man?

CONTINUE READING FOR REBECCA'S FORGOTTEN
JOURNALS

Part One

June 2011

I am sitting in my apartment, in the living room on my couch, with twelve dozen roses surrounding me. I've written this before, you say. Why yes, I have, about five months ago, I think. And yes, *he* sent them again. This time they are white, not red, and this time rather than an apology, they feel like a promise. An invitation to be something other than what we have been in the past. Something more than master and submissive. Oh, I know that master and submissive is quite special to many, but to those many, it is right for them. It was never right for me. *He* was, though. But I'm getting ahead of myself. Maybe it's the heady scent of the flowers he's made me love. Maybe it's the heady sense of hope these flowers, delivered after a month of silence between us, have now created. Or maybe it's the fact that the card reads: Tonight. Eight o'clock. I'll send a car.

I admit that when I opened the card, my hand had been shaking. And I admit that when I read that card, my heart hurt. It hurt because that is the kind of note he sent me when I was his submissive.

He ordered.

I obeyed.

Now don't get me wrong. There is something about the power and sexuality of this man that makes an order hard to resist. And safe. I am not sure why I feel safe with him when the truth is that he's made me feel emotionally betrayed. I am sure if I go back now and read my prior entries there would be many examples of why that is the case. But the reality here is that he always, *always* felt safe. He felt like my protector. He felt like the other half of my soul and I was his. And I think he needed–still needs–me to heal that soul. It's crazy, I know, but I'm getting ahead of myself.

It's been weeks since I have written a word. Why did I go silent when this is my therapy and sanity? I visited my mother's grave, and it opened that barely sealed wound all over again. And the nightmares. They were there every single time I went to sleep. Honestly, I didn't want to remember what I was feeling during those weeks. I lost me for a while when I lost my mother, I think, and it was like it was happening again. It hurt. Imagine me laughing bitterly right now. I mean, does the word "hurt" even begin to define what losing a mother means? I think, even if you aren't close to a parent, it's like having part of your soul leave this earth. You are alone. Only I wasn't alone because I found *him*. He went with me to the grave, but he wasn't really there. It felt, like he wasn't with me. Like he'd shut down and cut me out. I think the visit hit some nerve in him, cut him, where he was already cut as well. But he wouldn't say that. He wouldn't let us evolve and heal together. My reaction was to shut him out the way he had me, and even though it was my choice, the result was: I lost him, too.

Him.

Funny how I never write his name.

I just call him Master.

But you see, that's where life has become complicated. When I revisited the loss of my mother, I was reminded that life is short. And I knew that I could no longer play this game of master and submissive with him. That isn't who I am. I'm so far from submissive, it's really comical that I ever decided to sign his contract and wear that rose-adorned ring he'd given me. I did things with him, for him, *because* of him, that I would never have done with, or for, anyone else. I often ask myself how I went down this path when I am not a natural submissive. I've actually thought a lot about this question.

I think step one was what I felt when I looked into his eyes and when I was in his presence. Like he owned the world around him. Like if he said I would feel pleasure, I'd feel it. If he said I was safe, I would be. Like he would be the escape I didn't dare myself in any other part of my life. I found that part of being his submissive addictive. There was no room for worry or fear because he was that consuming. And then there was what I saw in his eyes when he let down his guard and often, I'm not sure he even knew that he did. The pain. The need. The tenderness. The past that torments him and makes him protect himself even from me. But I've earned his trust. I deserve to have that wall fall. That's when I said, no more. Not until he gave all of himself to me.

And so, the flowers came. And the card that read like every other card. After fifteen minutes of debate, I called him. Oh God. I called him and hearing his voice again, when spoken just for me, not for anyone else, as silly as that sounds, slid through me like salve to a bleeding soul.

"Rebecca," he'd said softly, but with that familiar command radiating through his tone.

"Hello," I said, because I could not say master, and I could not say his name. Nothing felt right.

"The flowers-"

"Are beautiful. Why are they white?"

"Because we can color them, and us, any way we choose."

I sucked in air, and breathed out my reply. "What does this mean?"

"It means I don't know if I know how to be what you need me to be."

"I don't want you to be what I want you to be. I want you to be you. The real you."

"You've seen more of me than anyone else ever has."

"I know."

"And yet it's not enough."

"It is, as long as that isn't all I ever get."

"I'm not ready for more, Rebecca, but it's not about you."

My chest had tightened. "Then why even send me the flowers?"

"Because I miss you."

"You do?"

"Yes. I do. I haven't touched another woman since you shut me out."

I am stunned. "Not even at the club?"

"No other woman. I want you. Just you. I just need more

time to figure out what that means, but not without you. With you."

"Because of something in your past."

He is silent for heavy seconds. "Yes."

"Will you ever tell me about it?"

"I don't talk about it."

I don't push. This is more than he has ever given me. "I can't be your submissive again."

"Go to dinner with me tonight. On a date."

"A real date?"

"Yes. A real date, but I can't promise what that means. Say yes, Rebecca."

It's enough. It's a start and so I'd said what he'd ordered me to say, but not because he'd ordered it. Because I'd wanted to. I'd said yes.

And so, I'm going on a date with him tonight and I will be Rebecca. Just Rebecca. If he can't handle that, it will be our real goodbye. If he can, perhaps it will be our first real hello.

Part Two

June 2011
Friday, six am

I woke from another nightmare this morning. My mother was there. I wish I could say that was a dream, rather than a nightmare, and that I'd relived some fond memory with her. And I thought that was the case. But I always do. Everything was perfect at first. She was alive and not sick anymore. We were on the trolley with coffee in our hands and nibbling on pastries. It was sunny and warm even in the wind. We were laughing and smiling. I was telling her about my date tonight. She wanted to know all about the man romancing her daughter and I actually told her. I told someone about *him*. Not the Master he was to be, but the man he is to me. Suddenly though the sunny day became stormy. It was cold and rain pummeled us. My mother and I huddled together, and then what always happens in these nightmares, happens. The trolley starts to speed, the car bumping and jolting. The people around me fade, even my mother. I call out to her. She reaches for me. Of course, the inevitable happens, the trolley jumps the tracks and dives into the icy water of the bay. I feel the cold to my bones, and it hurts. The pain is so intense. I manage to push out of the trolley, but then I'm sinking. I start swimming and swimming but I can't reach the top. My mother appears, and I reach for her, but she doesn't offer me a hand. She just stares at me. *She lets me die.*

I woke up gasping for air and with tears streaming down my cheeks. My mother. I felt as if she'd betrayed me but that is kind of easy to understand. She kept on smoking and smoking, knowing it was killing her. She left me alone. I think it's strange though that I have this nightmare when tonight is my date night with *him*. It's almost as if my mind is telling me this isn't going to go anywhere. I'm headed for heartache. I'm not sure why I'm interpreting it like this, but I am. He's going to hurt me. I'm almost certain of this but I'm going into this experience with open eyes. He is a wounded man and the truth is, I am wounded in my own ways, too. I think we need each other and maybe it's not forever. But I believe, in my heart, that people cross our path for a reason. They help us grow or survive. That's it.

I think we are both helping each other survive.

Friday, seven pm

Almost date time!

Tonight is the night and while my nightmare this

morning had me concerned it was a sign it would go poorly, I've changed my mind. I sold a ridiculously expensive Ricco Alvarez painting at the gallery today and when I called to tell him, he was elated, and agreed to show more of his work with us. Ricco Alvarez. He's incredible and I am the reason he is showing with us. When I told my boss, he was pleased, too. It really set the tone for this night.

Tonight.

Tonight is the night.

Date night with a man I've called Master who is no longer my Master. A real date, where he will *not* be my Master. I might need to write that like ten more times to believe it's true. I'm not sure what to expect but my nerves are eased by the idea that he doesn't know either. This is new territory for me. This is new territory for him, and he told me that, which is big for him. He doesn't share pieces of himself and I don't know if he realizes he did by telling me this but he did. He shuts himself off. He uses sex and master and submissive to keep anyone from seeing the real him. But I have seen the real him. In those intimate moments, where I was his submissive, where he had full control and we were alone, there were times, when he looked at me, and let the walls down. He let me see the heartache, the fear, the pain. He let me see the brutality of a secret, I may not know by detail, but I know through him. I also know, as much as it gutted me when he invited others into our play, that it always happened after I'd seen a piece of him. It was his way of shutting me out before I saw too much.

I'm done with that. He's done with that. *We're* done with that.

No more hiding.

I get all of him or it's time to say goodbye.

I just hope this is a new hello.

Maybe I won't even have sex with him. That would truly be a fresh start.

Saturday, seven am

I haven't slept. I've been with him. And I have to work today so I can't write much now but I need to get at least some of my thoughts down. Remember when I said I wouldn't have sex with him? I did. Of course, I did. I mean that's how he hides his emotions so maybe I shouldn't have, but how could I completely remove his shield? How could I completely strip him bare? It's a decision I made almost the first moment our eyes locked last night.

He came to the door. Normally, he commands me to a car with a driver who delivers me to him. But no. He came to me. He knocked and I stood at the door, adjusting my little black dress, wondering if the shade of pink lipstick I'd chosen said "do me" or "love me." I think maybe it said both. I'd taken a deep breath and opened the door. He stood there, in a gray, custom suit, looking like every woman's fantasy, his eyes steel heat when they met mine.

"Rebecca," he said softly, his voice a rasp of emotion, and in that moment, I flashed back to intimate moments where I'd been naked and in his arms. When I'd given myself to him as I have no one before him and I doubt anyone after. I could taste him on my lips. Feel his hands. And yet he hadn't moved and neither had I.

I knew then, that we would be intimate that night, but I

knew, too, that it would be different. And it was. It was different. It was…so very different. I need to think about exactly what that means. I need to write out every moment and I will. Just not yet and not just because I have to go to work. I need to think. I need to process every touch, taste, and caress I experienced last night in my mind again before I put it on the page.

More soon.

Part Three

June 2011
Saturday, six pm

I'm supposed to write about my date last night but right now
I'm riding this high that I can't let go. Maybe I don't want to
write about that date. Maybe some part of me knows I handled the night wrong. Maybe I know I sealed the deal that
means THE END. Or maybe I really am just excited about today. I sold a hundred thousand dollar painting today. I almost
thought I saw Mark Compton smile, but Bossman, doesn't do
smiles. He does disapproval or approval. I pleased him today
but more than anything I pleased me. I'm good at this job. I
know art. I love art. This is my world. And that is the entire
point in taking control of my personal life. Since I lost my
mother, really since she got sick, I didn't own my life. I think

for a while I had a man at work and in my bed, that were such control freaks, I let myself lose touch with me. As I mentioned several entries ago, I've thought a lot about why such a strong independent person like myself dived into the role of submissive. What got me to a place with *him* that I had to say *no more.*

It hit me when I was with *him* last night, why I said yes, and it comes back to how it all started. What he'd promised me, what he'd made me feel. It came back to safety. I still remember the moment when things between us had changed. I'd been sitting at a little bakery coffee shop a few blocks from work. Not the one next door. That one is owned by Ava. She's in love with Mark Compton, Bossman himself, and from the moment I started working at the Gallery, she was snotty. I stay away from her. How I know she loves him is another story for another entry. Bottom line. I don't like visiting her coffee shop.

Anyway, this is about *him* and me. About the way things between us had changed from casual acquaintances to submissive and master. And actually maybe I have Ava to thank for that otherwise I might not have been avoiding her, thus being at the right place at the right time to run into him. So... I'd been at the bakery, sitting at a back, corner table when he'd walked in. I remember knowing the very moment he entered, the way the energy in the room had shifted and changed. The way I'd looked up, my gaze lifting to land on him to find his attention on me. Almost as if he'd come for me.

He'd crossed the bakery, and ignored the pastries and sweets, making a beeline in my direction, stopping at my table to stand above me, his attention landing first on the books I'd been studying and then at me. That man's good looks and intensity had overwhelmed me. Intensely consumed me. We'd known each other before that encounter, but when he'd sat down across from me, there had been this shift in the air, a shift between us. "There's a place I know that I'd like you to know," he'd said.

"What place?" I'd ask, and believe you me, my heart had been thundering in my ears.

"Say yes, and I'll take you there, and show you."

I remember knowing in the moments that followed, that if I did, everything would change for me. I don't know how or why. But I knew. I think that is why seconds ticked by without my reply but I remember that he sat there patiently, waiting, almost in need of my approval. He wouldn't pressure me. He didn't pressure me. And that's the thing. He never did. Every choice I made was mine. Every choice was absolutely mine. He said that was my control. He said I was always in control.

Needless to say, I said, "Yes."

He always insisted that I say "yes." He always insisted that I make the choices. That's part of why I was able to be submissive. But there was more. He promised me, that for those windows of time I was with him, none of the hell that was my life at that point in time, would exist. And that's what became addictive. I could go to him and for the time I was with him, there was room for nothing but him. No fear. No loss. No worry. Just him.

And yes, sometimes driving everything else away became my way of him pushing my limits, most of the time it did. But it worked. He worked for me. I trusted him. Would I have been able to be submissive with someone else? No. I do not believe it could have been someone else.

Just him.

But that relationship was not a whole relationship. We were not whole. And so the question remains, can he be the whole package, my dream man, or is he only capable of being my Master?

Monday, eight pm

I'd barely gotten to work today when our receptionist, Amanda, appears in my doorway, looking as excited as a school girl and holding a box with a red ribbon. She sets it on my desk and then stands there. "Who's it from?"

"I don't know," I'd told her.

"Open it and see."

"Later," I'd said, setting it aside, though it was killing me. I wanted to know what was inside. What I didn't want was for anyone else to know. I'm private that way. And so is he.

"What exactly are we doing?"

At the sound of the boss, or Bossman, as we call him, Amanda jolted and turned around, and while I couldn't see her face or his, I could hear the exchange.

"I was just passing a delivery on to Rebecca."

Bossman says nothing, which means he's giving her one of those steely gray-eyed stares of his that intimidate even the most confident a person, which Amanda is not. She's too young and sweet, as well as without experience, for the likes of that man.

"I'll just go watch the front desk."

"See that you do," he says.

She scrambles away and he appears in my doorway, and

what can I say. He's tall. He's blond. His gray eyes striking, hard. And he wears a custom suit better than any man who's ever graced the pages of GQ. The problem is that he knows it. He owns it. And he owns everyone around him. He's wanted to own me from the moment I came to work for the Gallery. A part of me wanted him too, as well. But after my recent submissive experience, I've learned that being owned, isn't right for me. Oddly though I can say that the more I was owned outside my work, the harder "Bossman" Mark Compton found it to intimidate me as he does everyone else in the office.

And he knows that, too. I thought this would displease him, but another oddity. It doesn't. He seems to in fact, be pleased by this new side of me. If that is even possible. Maybe I'm wrong. Whatever the case, Bossman stood there in my doorway, staring at me. Never once did he look at the package. Never once did he speak. He just stared at me and I stared at him, and tried, like I always try, to read his thoughts. To feel what he was feeling, but that isn't something that happens, unless he allows it to happen. And I suspect, that in his workplace, that would never, ever happen. But still I try. Still I want to peel away some layer of this powerful man's shell, to see inside his mind.

"What are we doing Ms. Mason?"

"Amanda brought me a package that I intend to open alone and at an appropriate time."

"As it should be," he approves, and with that, he'd disappeared back into the hallway.

I'd wanted that private moment to be then, right after he'd left, but when I'd stood to shut my door, to open the package, I'd changed my mind. I'd waited until I arrived home. And now it's sitting here, beside me and I can't seem to open it. For some reason, I just...can't. I haven't even written about what happened last night. But I know that this package is about just that. What happened. What I didn't think could happen. What he didn't think could happen and yet, it did.

And it changed us. I'm not sure he can handle that. Maybe I can't either. Maybe we don't know how to be anything but what we once were and I can't be that anymore. Maybe I've already lost him and he's lost me. That scares me. Outright terrifies me. So the package. I think I'll wait to open it.

Part Four

June 2011
Monday, eleven pm

The gift he gave me is still sitting on the kitchen table un-opened while I'm alone in my bed, writing this. I suppose most people would be going crazy, wanting to know what is inside the package. I suppose too that I'm really not differ-ent than most people. I do want to know what's inside it. I simply dread what it might be more. Besides, I've never been big on gifts, but then, I've never had anyone to give me gifts, at least, not before *him*. My mother wanted to give me gifts. She wanted a lot of things that she never found, and I think her cigarettes became her drug of choice and as we all know, drugs kill, and her drug killed her. But they were the one joy she had in life. He's my drug.

The problem though is that the first gift he ever gave me was a beautiful ring with a stunning rose on top of it. A ring I was to put on only if I signed the agreement to be his submissive. A ring I wore for two months and gave back to him when that role no longer suited me. Every gift he gave me since then was during that submissive period, and tied directly to something we'd shared when I was in that role. But I wasn't his submissive Friday night. And he wasn't the master he'd once been to me. Oh don't get me wrong. He was sin, sex, and powerful, as I always expect from him, but the man beneath the master, I'd seen glimpses of in the past was there with me. And as I wrote before, I'd sworn not to have sex with him, but that didn't work out.

Really though, considering how it happened. I don't regret it. I regret nothing about that night. I'd opened the door and I'd been overwhelmed by not just the force of his presence but the way he'd looked at me, emotion he doesn't allow anyone to see in his eyes. "Torment" is the word that had come to my mind. Wordless, I'd stepped into the hallway outside my apartment and before I could shut the door, he'd done the unthinkable. After he'd breathed out my name, he'd pulled me to him and kissed me, deeply, passionately, intensely. This is not a man who does such a thing. He builds tension. He makes you crave him and the kiss that might not ever come, even if his mouth finds its way to intimate parts of your body, which most assuredly it always did mine. But no. That night he just kissed me. And then there was this explosion of uncontrolled passion between us, that he has never allowed.

One minute we were in the hallway, and the next we are ripping off each others' clothes – yes, he let me help him undress, which he never allows. He lets me touch him. And then we're on my couch. I'm on top of him, and we are just crazy wild making love. Or having sex. I don't know what it was. It was nothing I'd ever experienced in my life. I just know that there was this moment, where he twined fingers in my hair, and said, "I missed you," that stole every breath I've ever owned. I know that sounds small, but it is not with him. Wild, crazy sex, and admissions of missing someone, missing *me*, does not fit the master I know. Nor does the desperation I'd tasted in his kisses.

And when it was over, he'd held me for long minutes, like he didn't want to let me go, until finally he'd rolled me to my back and declared, "Don't move," and he walked to my bathroom and returning with a towel before, in all his naked glory, and let me tell you, that man naked is all about glory, he brings me my clothes. "I owe you dinner," he said. "If you still want to go?"

"Of course I want to go," I'd replied.

Approval had lit his eyes and I cannot explain how that look affects me, and even arouses me. I shouldn't need a man's approval, of course, but it's really not about that. In that moment, I'd remembered how intensely erotic, and addictive being owned by this man can be. I'd almost changed my mind about dinner out of fear that this was headed right back where we'd once been: master and submissive. And I'd feared I couldn't say no.

But I just couldn't say goodbye right then. Not when he'd just told me he'd missed me but after we'd dressed, and headed to the car, I remember holding my breath, after asking, "Where are we going?" afraid it would be some familiar spot that would stir more of those old feelings.

He'd surprised me though, and opened my car door, to

announce, "Someplace new. Someplace you pick."

"Me?"

"Yes. You."

And since as my master he always chose, I knew this was him telling me, he was really trying to give us a new future. "There's this hole in the wall Italian place," I said. "I love it and I want to go there."

"Then we'll go there," he'd said.

And so we went to dinner, and while we didn't share deep, dark secrets, we'd talked about art, which we both love, for hours. While true, even as his submissive, I'd shared dinners and conversation, with him, and there was always a bond between us, it felt different. Maybe because we'd had that passionate explosion that started the night. Maybe because at the end of the night he'd taken me home and kissed me on my doorstep, before leaving with a promise I'll never forget. He'd held me close, his lips near my ear, as he'd said, "If I don't leave now, I'll do things a proper gentleman would not do to you." He'd turned then and left me tormented. Because you see, I do not want him to be a proper gentleman. I just don't want him to be my master.

And that brings me back to the package, that I fear is an invitation to be his submissive again.

<hr />

Tuesday, seven am

I woke up in a cold sweat, gasping for air. I'd had the nightmare again only this time I wasn't in the icy bay water. I was on that trolley, racing toward the plunge that never happened, dreading it. Fearing it. If dreams have meanings to me this one was about the package I haven't opened. It was telling me that dread and fear, feels as horrible as an unpleasant outcome we don't want to be real. And you see, fear is what kept me ever entering the art world, where pay tends to be low, and dreams high. But I've made it work. Because I got over the fear. I don't ever want to live my life in fear again.

So I opened the package, and inside was the ring he'd given me as his submissive, but the note inside, stunned me:

Rebecca,

It belongs to you, the way you once belonged to me.

That is all the note says. He does not even sign it. And I don't know what it means. I just know that as much as I love that ring, I'm not ready to put it back on my finger. Because you see, I fear losing him. I do. I'd admit that to no one but myself. But I fear losing me more than I do him and I was losing me as his submissive. So I put it on a chain around my neck. It's a message to him. He can have me but this time, it's on my terms.

Part Five

June 2011
Wednesday, twelve pm

Have you ever gone to bed dreading the next day then woke up and felt the same? Not because you just didn't want to get out of bed. More like something was wrong. Something was going to go wrong this day. That's how I felt this morning when I woke up, and it had nothing to do with a nightmare. For once, I didn't have one. I thought perhaps it was about my former Master discovering the necklace that would bind us together, on a chain at my neck, rather than on my finger. I mean, yes, I want more from him, but the truth is, I have enough self-worth that I do not need more at the cost of settling. And I don't think that is what he really needs or wants either. I think I fear finding out I'm not the person who can help him see that though. That I'm really not *the* woman for him. But if that's true, then parting ways is right for both of us. Painfully right. Anyway, maybe that was part of the dread I was feeling, but it felt more foreboding.

The day has officially started weird. This morning, I arrived at the gallery and parked in the back lot, only to find no other cars. Everyone but me seemed to be running late. I headed inside and the lights were out. I left them off because I didn't want to encourage people to come to the front door when no one else was there. But here's the weird part. I entered the back offices and *my* light was on. Bossman, as everyone calls our boss, left after me last night. He's methodical and anal. Even if I had forgotten to turn my light off, which I wouldn't do, he would never have left it on. A shiver of unease had slid down my spine and I'd pulled my phone from my purse and dialed "911" without punching the call button. Just to be safe. A girl who is single, and a girl who was raised by an absent single mother, learns to be cautious.

I walk to the door and peek around the corner, and to say that I was stunned is an understatement. Mary, my co-worker, who not only has an obvious crush on Bossman, but wants the opportunities he's allowed me with his family's auction house letting me place and sell through them, was sitting at my desk, reading one of my journals. I felt violated. Which is crazy considering the things I've done at the club with a master in control but that had been a choice and I'd always known, no matter how uncomfortable I felt, that he'd protect me. I'd also known I'd made the choice to do those things, no matter how reluctantly at times. But this. This I did not choose. This was, *is*, an invasion of my privacy. Thankfully, it was my work journal, which was at least a little less invasive but it still had my inner most personal thoughts on the staff and our clients. On her.

I rounded the corner. "What are you doing?" I'd demanded.

Shock had radiated across her pale face, and she shoved her bleached blonde hair behind her ears. "Oh I...I..." She'd shut the journal and shoved it in the drawer. "I was looking for sales records for last month. I can't find them and need to do a presentation for Bossman." She'd stood up. "You weren't in and I was desperate."

"How long did desperate make you read my journal?" I'd asked.

"Journal? That book? I'd just opened it. I need to get to my desk." She'd rushed toward me and I wanted to stand my ground and make her explain herself, but really, what would it have solved? She'd lie and it would get more awkward. But the interesting thing. She didn't ask me for those sales figures.

I'd rushed to my desk and opened my drawer, removing the journal to thumb through, wondering how bad the damage would be from my words. I'd barely opened it when I'd heard, "Ms. Mason."

My gaze had jerked up to find Bossman himself leaning on the archway of my doorway, his blue suit, fitted to perfection, his very presence an explosion of power. And my God. He's just so overwhelmingly male. So overwhelmingly good-looking. It's hard to work for a man like that.

"Mr. Compton," I'd said.

"Why was Mary in your office?" he'd asked, his stare hooded, his tone unreadable but somehow expectant.

I considered that answer with caution. He's a man who doesn't like any game he doesn't create, though he certainly excels, at those. And he wouldn't be asking me this question, staring at me right now, and waiting for a reply, if he didn't suspect trouble. In a matter of seconds, I decided that if I were to tell him what Mary had done, he'd fire her.

"We're co-workers," I'd said.

"You mean competitors."

"Because you pitted us against each other," I'd reminded him. "She wanted to work with Riptide."

He'd stared at me with those hard gray eyes, several intense beats before he'd said, "Yes. She did. But I don't trust her."

"And you do me?" I'd asked, taking the bait he'd lead me to, and waiting for what I was certain would be an answer I did not expect.

"You get trust when you give it," was his reply, and he'd watched me, expectation in the air again.

He'd wanted me to say that I trust him and I was, am, stunned by the fact that I don't want to give him the power that would offer him. I realize now that I don't want to play his games. I don't want to play games at all. I'm changing personally and professionally.

My silence had told him this. I'd seen it in the darkening of his gaze, the hard set of his jaw. Something had flickered in his eyes. I didn't like that. His lips had twitched, and I'd known in that instant I'd displeased him when I'd spent a year trying to please him. Too often, I did not.

He'd turned and left without a word. He does this often. It's his way of making you wonder what he is thinking. And as you do, he has control, but remarkably, I find, it also makes me self-reflect to the point, I know me better. Maybe that is why I work well with that man. His games, even when I do not, want to play them, make me grow. And this time was no different.

I sat there after his departure, my fingers on the ring where it hangs at my neck, and I'd asked myself why I couldn't give him my offer of trust. This is work. This is my career. And then, I'd realized many things, but one quite large thing I think. When I'd come to the gallery, to Mark Compton, I'd been an innocent girl, eager to earn this job. I'd come to him a young girl who had an open heart and I had trusted easily. I'm not that girl anymore, if I were the ring would be back on my finger.

Wednesday, six pm

I cannot write everything there is to write. Not now. I'm still at work. But this day has been crazy. I was at Ava's coffee shop grabbing coffee to get me through what will be a late night, and I found her and Mary huddled in a corner. It made me uncomfortable. I don't know why but I felt that it was about me. That is very self-centered, I know. I'm not that girl. I don't think everything is about me but it just felt off in some way. I'd left before they'd seen me and that's when I'd come face to face with *him*. I'd stepped outside and was halfway back to the gallery when he'd stepped in my path. Have I ever mentioned he smells like a wonderful spice? I don't know what kind of spice. Just spice. Really, yummy, delicious spice. Nutmeg and honey? No. No. That is a strange comparison. Just warm and wonderful. And he'd been so close I could reach out and touch him, but of course, you never touch a master without being told to touch him.

Which is why I touched him.

I put my hand on his chest, and I swear he sucked in a

breath. And I was holding mine. To my surprise, his hand had covered mine, and he'd held me to him. "Rebecca," he'd breathed out, and this new way he says my name, like I'm the reason he has a voice, set my heart to racing.

"Hello," I'd said, which was silly. *Hello?* I should have said his name. Why can't I ever say it? Why is he still Master to me?

"Did you get my gift?"

"Yes I-" My free hand goes to the ring on the chain. "I'm wearing it."

He'd gone still. So very still.

And I have to go back to work.

More soon...

Part Six

June 2011
Wednesday, eleven pm

Somehow, I made it through an evening at the gallery that included an open house with a wine tasting. Normally, having artists in the house like the famous, Chris Merit–a local that is famous worldwide–would enthrall me. Tonight, I couldn't stop thinking about that encounter on the street with my former Master. *Former.* There is the key word that we defined tonight. I think he really didn't believe I would stick to my word. I think he really believed I'd become his submissive again. I know he did. From the very instant his heavy stare had landed on the ring where it hung on a chain at my neck, I could feel the dark energy radiating off him. I could feel the iron will of that man, telling me without words, I'd broken the rules.

I knew then that sending me that package, with my ring in it again, had been his way of reclaiming me.

In all of sixty seconds, he'd taken my hands and led me to an alcove in front of an antique shop, the concrete wall hiding us from the public eye. I'd ended up against the wall, that big body of his, caging mine, against the stone at my back. But not touching me. See, that is what he does. He makes me feel him, even when he's not touching me. He makes me want him, when I swear, I'll never want him again. He smells good and it makes me remember how good he tastes and feels.

"This is how it is?" he'd demanded.

"What does that even mean?" I'd whispered, and God, my throat had been so dry. And my heart had been racing. It's racing now just typing this.

"You know who and what I am," he'd said, without directly answering my question.

"What I know," I'd said, "is who and what *I am*. And it's not your submissive. I am, however, the woman who loves you. I'm also the woman who says that to you, and never gets a reply. That's not enough anymore."

He gray eyes had sharpened, and he's stared at me for so many seconds, it had felt like a year. "You know you're special to me."

"I know every submissive you've ever had was special to you."

"You aren't them."

"I know," I'd said. "I'm not. And I will never pretend to be again."

His hand had come down on my hip, a branding that had scorched me from the inside out. "You belong to me."

When he says those things to me, I get wet, and hot, and

want him in so many ways. There is just something about that man saying you belong to him, that makes me want to be owned. In bed. That's the thing. I like how he owns me in bed. I don't, however, want to be owned the rest of the time. And damn it, I want to own him, too. I want him to belong to me, too.

"I belong to me," I'd replied, and I'd let the defiance I'd felt lace my words.

"I'll share."

"That's the problem," I'd said, those words cutting me with bad memories. I'd remembered him inviting another Master to our games. I remember him inviting *her* to our games. All to push me away. And I hate myself for letting him. For saying *yes*. "You will share," I'd added. "And that's not okay with me." I'd reached up and removed his hand from my hip. "When and if you ever want to be with me, not a submissive, call me. Until then, this is goodbye." I'd tried to step around him, but he'd tangled fingers into my hair, and stared down at me, "Rebecca," he'd breathed out, and even now, I can still taste the kiss that had followed, the power in its depths. The push and command. It had been his body claiming mine, where his words had failed. And my body had responded. Before I'd known it, his hand was under my skirt, under my panties, and I'd been panting and moaning. I'd shattered, in too few seconds. He'd owned me.

And yet, nothing had changed.

I still wanted more.

I still *want* more.

And I'd told him that. "This changes nothing," I'd said.

He'd tilted his head upward, torment he never allows me, or anyone, to see etched in his features, the hard lines of his body, telling the same story, as the edginess radiating off him. Seconds tick by, before he lowers his chin, and looks at me. "I'm me. I can't be anyone but who I am."

"And I can't be anyone but who I am."

Seconds ticked by, before he'd stepped back, giving me space to leave. Oh God. My heart had hurt in that moment. I'd taken a few steps and my back was to him when he'd said, "Rebecca."

I'd stopped but not turned, as he'd added, "You matter to me more than you will ever know."

I wasn't sure what to say to that. I wasn't sure of anything anymore than I am now. I just knew it wasn't enough and I'd started walking again. I'd left him there in the alcove and despite the orgasm he'd given me, nothing about the experience had been satisfying.

Anyway, back to the open house. There had been a man there. A good-looking, rich, charming man. He asked me out. I said no when the truth is, maybe I should have said yes. Did I mention he's good-looking, rich, and charming? He made me laugh, even tonight, after the alcove. He made me feel pretty and wanted. He was what most would call a Dream Man.

And yet…I said no.

Part Seven

June 2011
Thursday, eleven pm

It's been a week and one day since that encounter in the alcove. He hasn't called me. He hasn't sent me a note. I haven't contacted him either. But I've seen him several times. We've made eye contact. And I've felt him. Not literally, but in those looks, I've felt his torment, his desire, his need for me. But I've also felt his resistance to what I need from him. I think this means we're over.

That Dream Man I wrote about stopped by the Gallery today, and bought a very expensive Chris Merit painting from me. It was a big commission, and I should be pleased, but he asked me out right after, and it made me feel as if he were buying me. I just…I don't want to be owned in any way ever again. I declined the date, and when I left work tonight, he was waiting for me, leaning on a fancy sports car that I'm pretty sure cost more than that painting which was a cool hundred thousand dollars. His suit, a black pin striped number, had cost thousands too I assume. I still felt the same. Like he was trying to buy me. And so I decided to just be clear and direct. I marched right up to him.

He'd pushed off his car, and we'd stood toe to toe, closer than I'd meant to stand. "Rebecca," he'd said, giving my velvet coat, a gift from my mother, I'd paired with an emerald green scarf, a once over, his brown eyes both warm with a gentleness and hot with attraction, when they'd met mine. "You look beautiful," he'd added.

I'd gotten pretty warm then, too, which had stunned me. I'd really started to believe no one else but my former Master, could make me anything but cold. It had kind of scared me. It made me feel like I was losing the man I love. But then, I'd suddenly remembered a saying my grandmother used to tell, when she was alive: *If you have a bird and it flies away, if it comes back, it was yours. If it does not, it never was.*

"Thank you," I'd told him, in response to the compliment. "Is there a problem with the painting?"

"Yes," he'd said. "There is. It made you uncomfortable."

I was blown away that he was in tune enough with me to know this. "It didn't make me uncomfortable," I'd said, daring to say exactly what I'd felt. "You asking me out after buying it did."

He'd arched a dark brown. "Because you don't want to go out with me?"

"Because if felt like you bought the painting to buy me."

"It's my second Chris Merit painting," he'd said. "The first

I picked up in Paris. And at the risk of sounding arrogant, I don't buy women. I don't have to."

"Oh. No. I mean–your–of course you don't. I'm sorry. It's just…I'm coming off a strange relationship."

"And you felt like property?"

"Something like that. And at the risk of sounding like a jerk, you do flash your money around. How do you even know if you're buying a woman or not?"

"You can tell a lot about a person when you flash your money around. It certainly has told me a lot about you."

"What has it told you about me?"

"That you don't care about my money. Go to dinner with me."

"No."

"Go to dinner with me," he'd repeated.

"I don't even know you. I know nothing about you."

"That's what you learn over dinner. But if it makes you feel better, let's make it coffee. Now. Next door."

I'd found myself wanting to say yes, but still I said, "No."

He'd given me one of his warm brown stares, seconds ticking by before he'd said, "I'll walk you to your car. Where are you parked?"

"At a meter around the corner but you don't have to do that."

"If I had to do it, I wouldn't want to do it."

I have no idea why but that comment charmed me. Really. He'd charmed me from the moment I met him. "All right. Thank you."

We'd started walking and I remember thinking that he was so very big and powerful, beside me. By big, I mean, his presence. I felt him there. I think everyone and anyone would.

And really, it's perhaps because he has that force about him, that he could even get my attention right now. I mean, my Master–ugh–no, no, no–*former* Master–consumed me.

"How long have you been interested in art?" he'd asked.

"Since I was a teenager," I confess. "I wanted to be an artist, but I wasn't gifted enough."

"Perhaps you're hard on yourself. Do you have any of your own work?"

"Oh no. I'm not hard on myself, just realistic, but that's okay. I appreciate art. I love it. I get to work around it every single day." We round the corner. "When did you decide you loved art?"

"My father's an art collector and has been since I was a small child. Museums and art exhibits have been a part of my life for as long as I can remember."

I'd stopped walking and pointed to my car. "This is me," and then feeling curious about him and his family, I don't know what really happened then but I'd blurted out, "How do you, and your father, make all this money you make?"

He'd laughed, this low, sexy laugh. "My family is in real estate, and I write novels, for a living."

Enthralled, at this creative side of him, that is in itself, a form of art, I'd quickly asked, "Novels? What kind of novels?"

"Thrillers."

"Do you have pen name?"

"I do and you'll have to go to dinner with me to find out what it is."

"No," I'd said again, when I really wanted to say "yes," but a date with this would-be, could-be, dream man, means deciding the man I love is not my dream man. And I just couldn't do that.

He hadn't looked surprised. Instead, he'd reached in his pocket, then taken my hand, to press a card into my palm, and his touch–it had been surprisingly electric. "Change your mind and call me." It had been an order, but then, he'd shocked me with this low, raspy. "*Please.*"

It's the "please" that had gotten to me. The way he'd managed to command me but still ask me. It was sexy and right, in ways that I needed it to be right. But he hadn't pushed. He'd turned and walked away. And now I sit here, staring at the card, that simply reads, "Alex Marque" and wondering if I should call. Of course, I googled him, and there is no writer, that has this name. There is a mega real estate empire though. I find myself wanting to know his pen name. I find myself wanting to call. But even more so, I want my former Master to call.

I'm very confused.

Maybe I should go to dinner. Maybe that will help me know if the past is the past or the present. I'm going to do it. I'm going to call Alex, and just say "yes."

Part Eight

June 2011
Friday, ten pm

I know I said I was going to call Alex and accept that date, but I didn't. I felt guilty, like I was betraying the Master, who is no longer my Master. But the thing is, I feel like I'm betraying my heart, too. I love him and I know the pain he's hiding from. I've seen it in his eyes over and over and over again. I feel like I am hurting him by leaving him even though he's hurting me by keeping me at a distance. And it's not about being his submissive. Being a submissive, though not natural to me, is not a bad thing. In fact, I found it to be an incredible bond, shared with someone you trust completely. It can be freedom and a connection shared with someone else, that I don't think I could explain if asked. It's something you just have to experience. But my master used the role of submissive as his way of keeping me at a distance. It was a tool to protect himself from the emotional bond growing between us. The problem for him though, was it became a way that we grew closer, and each time I felt that happening, he'd push me to do something he knew I wouldn't like. He'd bring in the second master, to share me. He'd bring in *her*. God. I can't believe I let myself be shared. I can't believe I don't hate him for doing it. But I have no one to blame but myself. The power is always with the submissive. The submissive says "yes" or "no." Until recently, I never wanted to say no to him.

So, I didn't call Alex last night when I'd planned to do so. I told myself it was too late since it was nearly midnight when I put my journals aside. I went to work this morning trying to convince myself to call him today, but I just kept finding work to do and yet, I managed to find time to call down to the bakery and find out if they had my favorite chocolate cookies. That tells you, I didn't want to call. And yet...I did. I'm very confused about why I felt that way. How could I have wanted to call Alex, and still be in love with another man? And almost as if Alex knew my conflict, he showed up. Not literally, but he might as well have.

I'd just sat down at my desk for a late lunch which included a bag of those chocolate cookies and a cup of coffee, because my diet couldn't afford for me to eat a sandwich and the bag of cookies. And considering my tormented mood, I knew I was going to eat the cookies no matter what. I was three delicious cookies in when Amanda had appeared at my door.

"Flowers for you!" she'd exclaimed.

I'd nearly choked on crumbs, and had to wash them down with a hot swig of coffee, and not because of the flowers, but rather, the certainty they were not from the man I love. How did I know this? They did not match the ring on the chain at my neck. They weren't roses but rather some sort of orange blossom flowers.

I'd recovered from the attack of the cookie crumbs by the time Amanda set the flowers on my desk. "Are they from the same man who sent you the gift last week?"

I'd felt that question like a punch in the chest because, no. They were not from the master I love. "Let's hope," I'd said, with the hope she'd leave, because as much as I love Amanda, she's young and she pushes and pushes and in that moment, I just didn't have it in me to deal with that part of her.

I'd grabbed the card though, and read it:

Marigold's represent a desire for riches, but I find all I desire is you. I can't stop thinking about you. – Alex

"Well?" Amanda had pressed.

"Ricco Alvarez," I'd lied. Despite hating lies. "Marigold's mean desire for riches, and he's thanking me for selling so many of his paintings the past few weeks."

"Oh." She'd looked disappointed. "Well that's nice. And he is a good-looking, rich and famous artist. I think he likes you."

"I think he likes the money I'm making him," I'd told her and motioned for her to leave. "Scram, you. I have to eat my lunch before my next appointment."

She'd pursed her lips and headed away, and suddenly, Bossman, Mark Compton himself, had been standing in my doorway, looking better than any chocolate cookie could ever taste, in a blue suit and silver tie. And being that he's blond, he makes tall, blond, and hot mean way more than tall, dark, and good-looking. "Ricco sent you flowers?"

Lying to Amanda had been one thing. Lying to him, well,

you don't lie to Mark Compton. Those gray eyes of his just see right to the soul. "No. He did not."

I'd just admitted lying to Amanda, and he'd stood there, staring at me, assessing me in that way he assesses me, and really everyone. And then, he'd just pushed off the door and left. And this is the thing. When Mark Compton comes in the room, he charges the air, and consumes it. When he leaves, it's like a bubble being deflated. He takes all that energy with him. My shoulders had slumped and I'd sucked in air. That's when the sweet, and almost spicy scent of the marigolds had teased my nostrils. I'd sat up and stared at them and it had hit me that while Bossman has been assessing me, maybe judging me, I'd been judging me, too. I've been doing a lot of judging myself, and maybe, just maybe I need to be with someone who isn't judging me.

I'd opened my drawer and pulled out Alex's card, before punching his number in. I'd then stood up, and walked to the door where I'd shut it, and then before I could stop myself, I'd hit the call button. He'd answered on the first ring. "Rebecca."

"How did you know it was me?"

"I just knew. You got the flowers?"

"Yes," I'd said, my gaze landing on the orange blossoms where they'd sat on my desk. "They're lovely."

"You're lovely," he'd said. "Listen. Rebecca. I'm in Aspen on business."

"Oh I'm sorry," I'd said. "I didn't mean to interrupt."

"You didn't. Have you ever been here?"

"No. I hear it's beautiful."

"It is. I want you to come here. I'll fly you here to me. I'll get you your own room. No pressure at all for more than just dinner and a chance to get to know you."

I was stunned. I stumbled over my words when I never stumble over my words. "I…This is… I have to work."

"It's Friday. Aren't you off for the weekend?

"I work Saturday."

"Then I'll have a private jet waiting on you when you get off."

"I have to work Monday."

"And I'll have you back there. I'll send you a list of character references. I need to be here. And I need you to be here, too."

Need. He needs me. "This is crazy."

"Life is short, sweetheart. You have to live it. Live this part of it with me."

Life is short. Those words had resonated with me. They have even before he spoke them. They'd become my motto after my mother had died. They are why I dared a job in the competitive, often low paying art world, and I'd made it work.

"Say yes, Rebecca," he'd pressed.

I'd dared the art world. I'd dared to be submissive. And I'd decided right then, to dare do take an adventure. "Yes," I'd said, and I could almost hear Alex smiling through the phone.

"Excellent," he'd replied. "What time do you want the plane to be ready?"

"Five."

"Five it is. I'll text you the arrangements when I've made them. See you soon."

"See you soon."

We'd ended that call, and I'd had butterflies in my belly. I still do. I'm going to Aspen.

With Alex.

Part Nine

June 2011
Saturday, six pm

I'm on a private jet on my way to Aspen. I'm excited and nervous, in good ways, which I didn't think was possible earlier today, but I attribute that to the encounter I just had with him right before I left for the airport. Yes. Him. My ex-master. I'd just finished work, and my taxi had no showed. There's a convention in town, and it was nearly impossible to get a cab apparently. While a plane waited for me on a runway. I had to cancel so Alex could stop paying whatever fee that must be costing him. Aspen, I'd decided, just wasn't meant to be.

    Decision made, I'd walked, with my bag, to the coffee shop to grab a coffee, only because I'd been by for the gallery staff earlier and knew the owner of the shop wasn't in today.

Which mattered, because I really hadn't been in the mood to have her look me up and down and judge me, but then is anyone ever in the mood to be judged? I really don't understand why Ava behaves that way. She's stunningly gorgeous. Owns a coffee shop so clearly has courage to take risks and be her own person. I'd admire her if she treated people kindly, but it's not just me that she's nasty to. But that is another story.

Bottom line. Ava was gone so I went in to the coffee shop for a White Mocha. Once I'd had it in hand, I'd settled down at a table in a corner and dialed Alex, who'd answered right away. "Rebecca," he'd said in this warm, smoky kind of voice. And he'd said my name like it brought him pleasure and it made me think about the ways he might bring me pleasure. Romantic ways. Sexy ways. Not handcuffs, blindfolds, and spankings. It just feels like it will be different with him.

"Where are you now?" he'd asked. "The plane is waiting on you."

"I can't get a taxi," I'd said. "There's a convention in town. I should just-"

"I'll send a car. Where are you?"

"Maybe I shouldn't go," I say. "It's so late and-"

"I really want to see you," he'd said. "Come see me, Rebecca."

I'd had this warm feeling in my chest when he'd said my name again. "Okay," I'd said and I'd given him my location.

"The car will be there in fifteen minutes. I'll call you when it pulls up."

He'd hung up and I'd started, finally, to let myself look forward to seeing him, but my hand had gone to the ring dangling on the chain at my neck, but not intentionally. Almost like my subconscious knew it was there, and knew it was a problem. It ties me to another man, after all. It took me a full five minutes to convince myself to do it, but I'd taken the necklace, the ring, off. Once I'd tucked it into my purse pocket and zipped it up, I'd gotten anxious to get to the airport, and headed to the door to watch for the car.

That's when he had walked in. He was wearing my favorite suit that he owns. A blue suit with a blue tie, that softens those hard, calculating eyes of his. But it's also the suit he'd been wearing the day I'd met him.

"Rebecca," he'd said, and when he'd said my name, his tone had been impossible to read. There wasn't seduction there. There wasn't even torment or loss. Because you see, that's his way. He doesn't show emotion. That's why, in intimate moments, when he'd allowed me to see the pain and torment in his eyes I'd felt he trusted me.

"Hi," I'd said, because nothing more brilliant came to me.

"Let me buy you a coffee," he'd said.

"I have a coffee," I'd said, showing him the cup in my hand, and now, looking back, since I'd been exiting the coffee shop, he had to have known that, even without seeing my drink.

"Stay with me while I order mine."

It wasn't a question but a command. And one I declined to follow. "I can't," I'd said.

"Can't?" His eyes had sharpened. Why?"

My phone had rung then and I'd scooped it out of my pocket and answered. "Hi," I'd said, because why wouldn't I greet two men the same way in five minutes?

"The car is there," Alex had said.

"I'm about to walk outside now," I'd replied.

"See you soon, beautiful," he'd said, the charming endearment, warming my cheeks.

I'd ended the call and found my former master staring at me. "You have a date."

"Yes. I have a date."

He glances at my neck. "And you took off the ring."

"Yes," I'd confirmed. "I took it off."

He stared at me several beats and then to my disappointment, said simply, "Have a good night, Rebecca."

It had hurt. It does hurt. He essentially was letting me go. I'd stepped around him and exited to the then quiet San Francisco street, and the driver was holding the rear door of a limo open for me. I'd reached the door, and hesitated before I got into the car. I'd thought about being fair to Alex. If I got into that car, I needed to really be present with him this weekend. I needed to forget the man who'd just let me go, and really, enjoy a man, who called me beautiful and said my name like it was sex and seduction. I had to choose between the Master and the Dream Man.

I'd handed my bag to the man and gotten in the limo, obviously, since I'm writing this from a plane, but I'd felt my ex-master watching as I did. And when the door had shut, it had felt like me letting him go. And so, here I am and the truth is, I'm ready for this. I didn't think I was, but it's amazing how one encounter actually did what I didn't think was possible. Set me free.

Part Ten

June 2011
Sunday, midnight

I don't even know where to begin. I'm just home from my weekend with Alex and he treated me like a princess. And the thing about being treated like a princess that none of us wants to admit, is that it only matters if you're being treated like a princess by someone you *want* to treat you like a princess. If it's the wrong guy we try to convince ourselves he should be the right guy, but the outcome is the same. No matter how well intended, the princess treatment fails.

Alex did not fail.

From the moment I arrived in Aspen, he seduced me and not just my body. He listened to me. He made me laugh. I'd landed at the small airport to a private car waiting on me the moment I got out of the plane. A driver had held the door for me. At that moment, I thought I wasn't going to enjoy myself. It had just felt like all the times my master sent a car to pick me up. But then I'd climbed in the back of the car and found Alex was there waiting. I remember being struck by his dark good looks, a polar opposite of the man I've called Master.

His dark good looks were accentuated by his gray suit with a blue pinstripe and a matching navy blue tie. And those brown eyes of his burned with amber heat, the way he looked at me with such piercing intensity had stirred a physical reaction in me. My skin had warmed and my nipples pebbled, an ache forming in my sex. He hadn't even spoken and I wanted him. At that point, I hadn't wanted to have that reaction. I didn't want to crave him or want him. I absolutely didn't want to feel desire so intense that it became a need. I rejected that possibility despite my body telling me it was possible. Some part of me still felt it betrayed my master. But then I'd flashed back to another limo and another night.

My master had sent me sexy, black heels, and a skimpy black dress with a note that had read: *No bra and no panties.* It was not a dress I'd wear without a bra and panties. The bodice was fitted, my breasts barely concealed. The bottom half sheer in the light. But I would be wearing it for him, not me, or anyone else. I'd dressed, and walked outside to the limo waiting on me, and after the emotional connection we'd shared during sex the night before I'd hoped we were going to his house. I'd feared we'd go to his sex club where he'd put distance between us. It was worse. Master Two, as I've come to call him, was there. This man who my master trusts enough to share me. Who he always calls to join us when he feels we're getting too close.

I'd slipped into the car and they sat side by side in front of me. My master's eyes had met mine, and I'd seen hardness in them. He'd shut me out and this was all about him showing me that fact. Proving it to him and me. "Show us how to please you," he'd ordered.

"Show me," Master Two had commanded. "Move her in front of me."

My master had given me a slight incline of his head. My lips had firmed and I'd considered saying "no" but this is a part of being submissive. He commands. I obey. I'd scooted in front of Master Two and at his command slid my dress up my legs.

"Show me," he'd ordered, and I'd then touched myself. And he'd touched me. I didn't want to like it. I didn't want to feel pleasure. But I had. And that was the wall my master wanted between us.

Some might think that I am crazy for allowing Master Two to be a part of our play but it's in the contract. And that contact protects you physically by setting boundaries but it also protects you emotionally by setting boundaries. As it did with my master that night.

I'd blinked back to the present, to Alex sitting in front of me in that limo, and before either of us had even spoken, I'd had that memory create a realization. No matter what my master's intentions, no matter what his reasons for his actions, he'd created a wall that night and on many other occasions, but each time, he'd cut me just a little deeper. And I'm not sure you ever heal from that many wounds.

That's why when Alex had finally spoken and said, "I'm glad you're here, beautiful," it had hit me, that we are fresh and new, without any walls, without any pain. And this was a premise I found as alluring as the man.

Alex had offered me a glass of champagne then and I'd nervously gulped it down when I have learned never to gulp alcohol. I don't handle it well, so I've learned at wine tastings at the gallery, to make a glass last. But I didn't. I'd been nervous for the first time in a long time. I wasn't sure if that was good or bad. Alex had refilled my glass then and when our hands had touched the charge that sparked would have made me weak-kneed had I been standing. He knew. I'd seen it in his eyes. They'd darkened, sharpened. He wanted me and I wanted him.

I'd been certain we'd go to the hotel then and I'd probably do something I might, or might not, regret. And we did go to the fancy five-star property. Only, when we exited the car and he'd turned to me and offered me his arm it was clear he had no intention of taking me to bed.

"It's a warm summer night," he said. "How about we walk the town?"

He'd wanted to walk the town and spend time with me. I'd been charmed. And so we had walked and I'd been enamored by the quaint little town. Surprised that Aspen isn't glitz and glam like you'd think when you hear about Hollywood types visiting. It's just a cute town with stores, craft booths, and of course, food. And during off season, it's a ghost town at night. So we just walked and talked. He'd asked me about my mother, and I'd dared to share her death by cigarettes, which is how I think of her lung cancer. He'd listened and offered insightful thoughts. He'd then ask about my father. I'd laughed, bitterly.

"I have never met him but I hear he's a mobster in Vegas. That's why we moved away."

He shared with me that his father was not much better

and we'd talked for hours. He'd told me he'd learned from his father to be cautious who you trust. It's why he doesn't do serious relationships. Maybe that was my warning, his way of telling me this was just an escape for us both. But I was hit by the difference between him and the man I've come to know as my ex-master. Alex leaves himself open to be surprised, to fall in love. My ex-master uses a contract to ensure he can never make that mistake. And to him, it is a mistake. I was a mistake. It's another thought that gives me freedom to just enjoy this time with Alex.

At some point we'd stopped to sit on bench where we'd talked art and I'd become animated when I'd realized how intensely he was once again staring at me. The next moment he'd been brushing his lips over mine, his hand sliding to my neck, under my hair. His tongue this gentle, seductive caress, before he'd murmured, "I've wanted to do that since the moment I met you."

I couldn't say the same to him. I'd certainly had found him overwhelmingly male and good-looking when I'd first met him at a gallery event. I'd even thought of him as someone most women would want to kiss. Just not me at the time, because I had yet to open myself up to the possibility of life after my attempt at being submissive. But it didn't matter that I couldn't say the same to him. He'd then asked a question that had taken me off guard.

"Who is he?"

I'd pulled back to look at him. "What?"

"Who's the man I'm competing with?"

I didn't ask how he knows there's someone else. I imagine I still taste like him. "The past. He's the past."

"Is he?"

"Yes. He is."

"And I'm what?"

"Possibility," I say.

"I can live with that."

He'd brushed his lips across mine again and stood, offering me his hand. And once again he'd surprised me. We hadn't rushed back to the hotel. We'd walked and talked more only now each word and step, each touch of our hands and even brush of our hips, seemed to seduce us, or at least me, with those possibilities.

When we'd finally gone to the hotel, I'd discovered we were in a suite that had two bedrooms as promised. "I can get you your own room, if you'd prefer."

"No," I'd said quickly. "I want to be close to you."

Approval had lit his eyes, and he'd opened the door. My eyes met his, and there was a silent understanding between us. My choice in this moment opens the doors to those possibilities. I'd walk into the room, decisively making my choice to find out what this is between us. Again though, he hadn't rushed things. We'd ordered room service and ate in the living room, more champagne-filled glasses with our meal. The room had been warm or maybe it had been just me. And somehow a brush of a hand, a touch of legs, and I'd ended up on his lap, straddling him. He'd stroked hair from my face. "This doesn't have to happen now," he'd declared. "We don't have to do this."

"I know," I'd whispered, and amazingly, I had known. And knowing I had a choice had been the absolute most erotic part of that moment. There was no contract. There was no command. There had just been the chemistry I felt with an amazing man and the way he and I had lingered there, mouths close, just breathing together. As if we were both savoring the possibilities of all that might happen that night, and even beyond, expanding between us. It reminded me that daring to open myself to possibilities is how I found the art world again. It's how I started to live again.

I remember the very instant our lips had touched. I remember the freedom in our kiss that had started slow and sultry and I didn't hold back, the freedom of contract, or obligation between myself and Alex empowering. There were no expectations. No rules. I could go on and write details but I will leave it at this. He was tender at moments and wild at others. I am no longer someone with inhibitions and yet at times I felt shy in a really sexy way, that I can't explain. I'd melted for him.

Where does that leave us? He wants to see me again. I want to see him again. That doesn't mean I've forgotten my ex-master. That doesn't mean I don't love him. It just means that it's time to love me, too. As for Alex. We'll I'm not going to call him my dream man. I'm not sure either man gets that title. I just know that whatever choice I make will be about the possibilities that I allow myself to discover. And the rules, that only I make.

THE END… For now.

Also by
LISA RENEE JONES

THE INSIDE OUT SERIES
If I Were You
Being Me
Revealing Us
*His Secrets**
Rebecca's Lost Journals
*The Master Undone**
*My Hunger**
No In Between
*My Control**
I Belong to You
*All of Me**

THE SECRET LIFE OF AMY BENSEN
Escaping Reality
Infinite Possibilities
Forsaken
*Unbroken**

CARELESS WHISPERS
Denial
Demand
Surrender

DIRTY MONEY
Hard Rules
Damage Control
Bad Deeds (coming August 2017)
End Game (coming January 2018)

WHITE LIES
Provocative
Shameless (coming July 2017)

*eBook only

About the Author

New York Times and *USA Today* bestselling author Lisa Renee Jones is the author of the highly acclaimed INSIDE OUT series. Suzanne Todd (producer of *Alice in Wonderland*) on the INSIDE OUT series: *Lisa has created a beautiful, complicated, and sensual world that is filled with intrigue and suspense. Sara's character is strong, flawed, complex, and sexy—a modern girl we all can identify with.*

In addition to the success of Lisa's INSIDE OUT series, she has published many successful titles. The TALL, DARK AND DEADLY series and THE SECRET LIFE OF AMY BENSEN series, both spent several months on a combination of the *New York Times* and *USA Today* bestselling lists. Lisa is also the author of the bestselling DIRTY MONEY series, and is presently working on her new WHITE LIES series.

Prior to publishing Lisa owned multi-state staffing agency that was recognized many times by The Austin Business Journal and also praised by the Dallas Women's Magazine. In 1998 Lisa was listed as the #7 growing women owned business in Entrepreneur Magazine.

Lisa loves to hear from her readers. You can reach her at www.lisareneejones.com and she is active on Twitter and Facebook daily.